Copyright © 2017 by Charlotte A. DeVries

Library of Congress Control Number
ISBN: 978-1546437093 Softcover

Cover and interior design: Parvin Keller
Cover art: Karen Oiseth, Waiting, acrylic paint on canvas, 2017

This book was printed in the United States of America.

Lament
of a
Gettysburg
Widow

A novel based on the life of
Henrietta Shriver

To Henrietta,
who invited me to weave a story around
her loves, her losses, her life.

He hath made every thing beautiful in his time
and hath set the world in their heart.

Ecclesiastes 3:11 ~ King James Bible

Chapter 1

I believed George Shriver would come home to me. That he would walk in our front door and set right my world. This is what it all boils down to, my struggle, even after forty-some years—a fierce belief that became my undoing.

And on what crumbling foundation was this misplaced trust built? Some ancient holy words? A delusion? Or a blinded faith in mankind that a war would be swift to end? That loved ones would come home, and everything would be returned and restored, to carry on as it was before? That we could start where we left off, and all would be well?

I think it is my longing to know what to believe that has ushered me through a doorway of madness, with all manner of unwelcome questions clambering at my side until they make sure I am fully undone.

"The Lord watch between me and thee, when we are absent one from another"—a verse Pa spouted often enough during my growing up. How he loved his Bible, especially the very beginning part where the "absent" words come from.

"*Anfang*—in the Beginning!" He should have been a preacher.

Such *Muzik* to his ears, he would say, reciting that verse about parting more than any others I remember, all of his lofty sayings seared into my brain. Some days when he was heading out to his fields for the afternoon, he would kiss Ma and say it as a secret joke between them. "The LORD watch between me and thee, when we are absent one from another"—as if he would miss so much as one supper at her table, no matter where his work took him. There was no absence to speak of between the two of them.

But "absent one from another"—a simple phrase ever present in me while I waited for two, almost three years with the sort of magical longing that my husband and I would no more be apart from one another, cut off by that great war of separation. I clutched a fading belief that the Lord would watch between George and me.

As it turned out, the Bible and its comforting words of wisdom did not work in our favor. Ma used to say that time works wonders. I can hear her mumbling from the kitchen stove, turned away from us in her work: "*Zeit wirkt Wunder.*" But I cannot think how anyone could find a stitch of wonder or wisdom left in all my years, one great river of time without him.

To you who have found my testimony and the contents of this box: I, Henrietta Weikert Shriver Pittenturf, leave my writings and the paltry remains of my worldly possessions. Herein lie the secrets of an old woman who fears her story will soon fade into the wallpaper of this cramped room that has become my cage and, at the same time, my refuge.

I am in a rush to empty my days onto these pages. My dizzied mind cannot tame its thoughts, as though memories have become the flashing minnows we tried to snag with our young hands along the banks of Marsh Creek. The sun may have been baking hot on our backs those sultry Sundays. But we stood intently by the hour, shrieking and laughing, teetering on mossy stones, our legs iced by the summer waters lapping against them. Did we catch any minnows? My brother most surely did, but I cannot remember ever having such luck.

As I write, I fear there are hours when my very names are as slippery as those tiny fish, for I cannot seem to keep them in straight order. Of late it grows stranger and stranger for my hand to write them down. How do I make sense of what is left of me if even my name grows foreign to my eyes?

My thoughts may be all of what remains, a few cents worth of joy, a bottomless, troubled pond of sorrows and regrets and unanswered questions that I have sat beside and stared into for far too long. Any slippery shards of peace I could have grabbed slipped through my fingers long ago. Oh, to catch hold of that "peace that passeth understanding" Pa used to speak of, just enough *Frieden*, blessed peace, to let me reach my final rest alongside my girls inside the waiting gates of Ever Green.

I cannot, will not speak of these things to the strangers

waiting out there to bellow at me as though my ears were sewn shut. I try my best to sort out their names and faces, and I am weary of the whole lot of them. They have hidden my things (or stolen them away from me), something they deny every time as though it is a game. Better I stay in this safe *Korb*, my cage of thoughts. Dark as it grows, only here can I still recognize the Hettie I used to be, the tiny bits of me that remain.

May you show mercy, dear reader, on my unsteady hand and dimming eyes that make for script I sometimes have trouble deciphering myself. And for heaven's sake, do your best to be patient with my story. It rambles and wanders like a town drunk who locks his rough hands on my shoulders and nags me into taking up the pen, every time without warning.

It hardly matters, I know, but I was a fair young woman. Everyone said so. He said so. You would not know that now, would you? But I remember standing at the looking glass as a girl and thinking as much.

Know this, *mein Freund*: Every one of us sits in the same fragile boat, paddling together through a lifetime that has shaped and misshaped us, through all the drenching, all the battering and scraping etched into our skin, with us to our dying breath, whenever that fleeting air is drawn into our bodies for the last time. Each of us moves along day by day without a notion of what storm might lie around the bend. I can tell you this: No one escapes troubled waters. No one.

Despite my dimming memory and my long-departed

beauty, what sits with me is a clear and certain knowledge that I have lived too long. I am prisoner to this decrepit body and clouded mind, witness to the passing of too many souls I have loved. Oh, the many hours I have been made to remain tethered to this world! There is no remedy for the sorrow of my situation.

It is a confounding thing: I cannot remember if I have just eaten supper or where I am in the dark of night when my eyes open to the stillness. But I know the rhymes of the songs he used to sing to us. Sometimes I conjure up a fancy theater stage in my mind's eye, and I can picture how those dear girls would sit silently enraptured by the stories and poems their Papa acted out for them. Even with my failing memory, I remember the beauty that his voice, his music, his way held for me. I remember.

Listen, already there is a lifting of the burden from my shoulders, from my mind, as the stories rise up, demanding to be recorded onto these scraps of paper I have been known to steal from off the floor or the table out there or, more than once, from the trash barrel. You might look at my remembrances as an answer to the riddle of one woman's life, and along the way you may find some light to shed on your own riddles.

If you were a curious child you might ask, "What was it like when you were a girl?" And who can know what you would make of the stories you would absorb from my writings? Will your own journey through this sad world be inched one way or the other by reading about the olden times? Could the tales of an invisible old woman make any difference to you or anyone else?

I sometimes sit at the table with that bunch out there and listen to them tell their colorful yarns. You would think they were performers, the way they laugh and tease, and then, with voices rising, disagree and laugh some more, and go on and on. You see? Every family has its own legends, and usually there is more than one version of how things unfolded. You have your own story. This is mine.

Here is my desire: I want you to know that I matter, or should I say, I mattered. Is that too much to ask? The story of my life begins in your hands, and it may well end there. But at this very moment you are reading what you hold, and that, to me, is sufficient unto my day.

For how can I know what you will take to heart from these remembrances? Who can say where these pages will find their final rest? I know the sum of my days is no more than a thin thread. But whoever you are, your story is a thread as well, and together we are a part of a great garment, a cloak, something that we and all who went before us and all to come after us share in the wearing, most of the time not giving it so much as a thought.

Ach, if only the generals in that Great Civil War—in all the wars, for that matter, stretching all the way back to those dreadful Bible battles—if they could have seen the enemy across the way for what they were: brothers in the family of man, every one of them a thread in the weave.

No matter where we hail from, Pennsylvania or Texas, Africa or the Orient, our lives, their lives, are part of the weaving as well: the ones that fell on the fields of Gettysburg, the one who ended Abraham Lincoln's life, the ones who watched my George die, the ones who were chained and kept to work the fields, the rich and privileged and the filthy poor, the ones who shut the door on those who called to be let in, and the ones who even today welcome the stranger to the supper table.

Our threads, yours and mine and the rest of the world's, are as many-colored as that boy Joseph's in the Bible, with his fancy cloak that led to so much misery. My thread, too, is colored in hues of sadness.

I came to know this too soon, that life is strife. It can pierce, it can strangle, it can knock you down over and over until one day you cannot struggle to your feet anymore. Happiness is precious and frail as a newborn, fleeting as a garden bird. It is nothing that can be counted on. We never know while we are standing in the sunny part of our days when that one cloud will suddenly drift in over us and stop stone still, leaving us stunned and alone in the dark, chilled to the bone with not a penny in our pocket.

You and I may go to our graves never knowing what our *Zweck,* our purpose on this earth was, or if there was such a thing as *Zweck* to begin with. What was the meaning of all the death, the sorrow, the crying and pain, all the goodbyes? Why were we put onto the loom of this life to begin with?

What kind of journey have I had? In a thousand ways, mine has been the most ordinary of lives, all these years of being me, from sunrise to sunset, doing the mundane things that keep a soul breathing and moving for yet another day. Were it not for that *verdammt* war coming to the streets of Gettysburg, were it not for all of the out-of-order dying—for even though a child's death is as common as rain, a mother should never have to watch her babies go before her, nor should a wife be widowed in her youth—were it not for the years of separation that threw us all off our tracks, I would probably not be writing this right now, in this strange house, with a mind mired in a thick gravy of confusion.

You should know I waited for a good stretch. I kept watch on Baltimore Street long after the town was shuttered in sleep, even long after I knew the truth of his whereabouts. The habit of waiting was so set that, way past a logical time, the lantern and I sat silent witness to my hope, as though all my yearning might be enough of a pull to bring him home. Now, these many miles and endless days down the road, I am still waiting, still longing for George's return.

So. Here you hold my box of puzzle pieces, the bits of me that remain after these endless years. I knew people who had it worse than me. I did. And I cannot figure how it was that the likes of us carried on. But we did. ❧

Chapter 2

MA TOLD US THE BOX MADE ITS WAY from Germany, across the ocean with her grandmother long before Pennsylvania became a state. Eventually it would pass into my hands from the farm, from Ma's trunk.

When I was a wee girl and accomplished some small task she had set for me, my reward would be a peek at the mysteries under its lid. She would set me down on the floor and nest the thing into my waiting lap to sort through its treasures.

Each time I would line up the pieces like soldiers on dress parade—bits of jewelry and fancy old buttons, tiny glass vials (empty and all pearly green and blue but still conjuring the memory of some fine exotic fragrance), lengths of lace, and the two copper miniatures, their images painted in fine brush lines of long-past ancestors who were at once foreign and familiar to my eyes. She told me more than once what the names were that went with the solemn faces, and I never could remember them.

And if she found the time, Ma would gather her skirts and plop down alongside me to repeat a tale or two about one piece or another. At story's end, she would tuck all the contents back into their resting places in the box to fit it back into its waiting spot in her trunk with such tenderness, as though she were handling a spider web.

The grand day that George and I hosted a proper celebration to welcome our families into our ordered house on Baltimore Street, Ma arrived with the empty box that made the bumpy ride into town in her arms, swaddled in her good shawl, much as she would have carried my newborns. Without a word, she set it on the parlor table, as dear a sacrifice as I could imagine her making for me. It has been with me ever since.

See the lining? Ma added that after I married and left her, cut from the very bolt of fabric that became my wedding dress, still all cloud soft. You can tell what a fine wool it is. The first time my fingers touched that weave was such beauty to me.

I have come to understand that neither the box nor the things in it matter so much as the stories that the things hold, every last piece cradling my history. I am more than ready to surrender these few bits of my life with no need to know of their final fate. In the end, all will be forgotten. If I cared to know, what would it matter?

He and I were so the same, and yet so different. We came into this world only months apart, George Washington Shriver and me, to two clans that might have appeared to be cut from the same *Deutsche* cloth. But we were not all that alike when you held us up to the light.

The Shrivers boasted a dearer wealth than that of my folks. They had settled in Adams County a generation before our family and planted the Lutheran church over in Emmitsburg, down the road a piece from their farm. They had influence. George's father worked business dealings my Pa never dreamed of, most of them around the distillery he operated in his barns. He lost his first wife early on and raised their two sons on his own for ten years or so, that is, until he married again. A long time to be without a woman at the helm, but long enough to throw his weight even more into the increase of his bounty.

His new wife Mary (they called her Polly but I never knew why) gave him three babies right away. The youngest he named for himself—George, the one who grew to be the love of my life. The Shrivers were the religious, wealthy Germans across the way who enjoyed too much drink and too little humility, Ma would say.

And then there were Jacob and Sarah Weikert, who shared fifty years in the same bed and issued a tribe of children. There would have been thirteen of us had the two baby girls who came after me survived. That was a fair share of mouths to feed and fevers to sit through and feet to shod. I was too young to remember when we moved onto our Gettysburg land, into what we all thought of as our very fine house on Taneytown Road.

Ours was a prosperous farm, to be sure, but the Weikerts

were not as highly regarded in their holdings as the whole kin of Shrivers were in those parts. There was more afoot on their acres. The corn in their fields went into the profitable spirits business and their barns were stacked with barrels of ambered whiskey and rye brought over from the two busy coppered distilleries behind the grain barns. From the surrounding buildings came the sounds of the blacksmith's hammer and the weavers' shuttles and heddles that added to what George called "the sweet music of success" his father was so fond of hearing.

George's family home was outfitted in finery a cut above the Weikerts'. Back then, there was endless talk of "refinement"—from dress and furnishings to books and music—and I think George's mother put much more effort into that sort of betterment than mine did in her tableware and linens and library. It seemed all of Adams County regarded the Shrivers to be of a higher standing, as though the family's success put them a notch above us on the respectability scale.

A crow could fly in short order between the two farms, so there was never a time I did not know who the family was. The grownups may have seldom sat at the same table, but children have a way of finding each other in the draw of summer fields and snow-drifted hills, and in the waning days of autumn, when a circle of us would be in the mix of the crows trying to finish off what was left in the orchards that stretched between us. The meadows that spread around Gettysburg were the finest of playgrounds.

George and I were born in the same year and grew up surrounded by the same lush meadows, under the same stars, eating the same fruit from the same trees.

With five before and five after me, I was in the middle of my parents' nestlings, of lesser standing than my brothers before and after me. While the boys were pressed into the important work of running the farm, I was the one Ma put to work in the house, especially after my big sister married and left. I learned to stitch and stir and sweep and scrub and set a garden as well as the best of them by the time I was ten. It was the same with all the daughters.

Every child must feel *vernachlässigt*—neglected or taken for granted as I did at times. But George would often tell me I was the pick of the litter, the one he would choose every time. When he was near, even when we were *junger*, I knew I counted with him.

Who can understand the way of a girl's heart? Or of an old woman's, for that matter! I have spoken his name to no one for so very long. But this George—his voice, his smile, his hands, his dark eyes—my George was my all and always will be the dearest love to my heart.

You must know this, the mighty power of a girl's affections, how there is not much she can do about where it leads her. My heart raced when he paused next to me in a cloud of playmates. I was a blusher, and though I tried not to meet his eye, my cheeks would rush with color all the same. And when

George was not near, oh, my wandering thoughts, away from chores, away from learning, away from evening prayers, to rest my mind once again on my heart's desire.

There were other boys, you know. Pete Hildebrandt came to our door more than once. And the Michelson boy—who would drown in the river before his eighteenth birthday—he fancied me. I was polite to all of them, but my mind had long been made up. I was set on staying beside young Master Shriver.

George was a fair boy, smart, a keen reader, much quicker with numbers than the rest of us, and a singer with a honeyed voice. He could memorize a poem faster than anyone I knew. His father took pride in his namesake's bright and inquiring spirit and ordered in *Knickerbocker* magazines for his son, the ones that we packed up for the move to Baltimore Street, its pages chock full of writing and poetry and all manner of lofty ideas.

I can feel the spring breeze on my skin when I think of how a group of us children would gather to play Red Rover, and out of the blue George would stop the action to sing or recite some silly rhyme at top volume with his finger jabbing at the sky:

Here-here! The raccoon has a ring-ed tail, the possum's tail is bare,
The rabbit has no tail at all, but a little tuft of hair!

Or one he would someday sing to his adoring daughters:

Did you ever go fishin' on a warm summer day
When all the fishies were a-swimmin' in the bay
With their hands in their pockets and their pockets in their pants
Did you ever see the fishies do a Pennsylvaney dance?

Of course, we would all start up a laugh with his antics. Each time he would suddenly break into a run, right through the barrier of linked arms on the other team, leading to protests and cheers and propelling the game forward.

When we were twelve, he carved our names in a tree that to this day may still be rooted in a patch near the Sugar Loaf. If you went to see it now, you could tell from its scars that it took a captain's share of punishment from artillery, enough to split it in two, right down through the middle of its trunk. Still, the thing lived to sprout leaves the next spring and drop them in the fall.

I walked out to that elm alone one still evening, the first spring after the battle and before I knew of what the war would end up doing to George. I traced my fingers deep into his carving, facing downward on its underside.

Back then, folks could see we were sweet on each other, even as young as eight-year-olds. If not in the fields and orchards, we would find each other in town on market days. I was forever on the hopeful lookout for him.

We were fifteen when he made his first proper call one autumn morning. He had come to escort us—a cousin and me—to the St. James harvest fair. He was his father's favorite, such that he trusted George with the good Shriver carriage at such a young age. That was a much fancier buggy than my Pa's. It was a crisp, sun-drenched October day, you know the kind, perfect for a drive into town.

When my mother met George at the door, he stood there waiting soldier-straight and serious, hair brushed and slicked down except for that one strand that refused to stay put, his best shirt fresh-starched and gleaming white, peeking out above his jacket like a priest's collar.

My father was at work in the barn, and George was required to go out there and announce himself and his intentions for our time together. I peered down from our upstairs window perch to see him step back out into the sun, as solemn as he was when he headed in.

That summer, Ma had pulled my sister Mary Ann's old blue dress from her trunk to rework for me. I was shorter and my waist smaller, and Ma tailored it to me and added some ribbon and buttons from one of her own gowns. She was good with the needle and had an eye for detail to work miracles on an old piece. For all I know, my cousin may have looked prettier than I that day when we came down the stairs, but George was smiling at me, not her.

When he offered his hand to help me into the carriage, there on the bench lay a tiny red rosebud, barely parting open. He slipped it into my hand without a word. I cannot know how he found one so perfect that late in the year. Surely we must have had a frost by then. But there it was, and this was beauty to me.

It was then, for the very first time, that he called me "Hettie Rose"—an endearment he used only when no one else was close enough to overhear him. I always figured my blushing was part of the nickname.

Look inside the envelope here. Do you know I pressed that flower in Pa's great German Bible that very night? For twelve years I kept it wrapped in between the folds of a handkerchief in my bureau drawer. Twelve years! The girls somehow spotted its stripped stem on our bedroom floor in the mattress stuffing I swept up after the rebels ransacked the house. It always was such a mystery to me that their young eyes could spy such a thing.

The handkerchief never did show up during all those weeks of sorting through the ruin. I believe if I had been smart enough to hide it before we fled, that flower would be whole and swaddled in the box here right now for you to unwrap, instead of a lonely stem rattling in a tattered old envelope.

Once upon a time, with Hettie Rose in mind, he had tugged on that little bud still secured to his mother's rosebush, to cut it and lay it on the carriage bench that day.

Since then, I have let it be known that I have no love for roses. All these years I have insisted that none be planted under my windows or set on the table or even arranged beside me at my wake. But, you see, I was lying all along, *Gott* forgive me.

The thing is, I have never stopped regarding the rose as the dearest of flowers, of George's shy gift to me that day, or of that endearing name, the one he whispered the morning he left us to join his company. I have always loved the red rose.

He told me I was the pretty one, you know. Mine was a neat and tidy waistline, especially when I was cinched in and corseted tight as a whipstitch. My cheeks were velvet smooth and held color even when I was not blushing, and my eyes could be as blue as a summer sky.

But *ach,* all of my youth has somehow been snatched from me by Father Time. And here, left in its stead, sits a toothless crone, my chin spiked with whiskers, my fingers swollen and useless. I am set apart like a leper from the rest of them on the other side of my door. I am a lifetime removed from the young Hettie Rose I was those years. ❧

Chapter 3

It was almost a year after that fair autumn day that George found his father's body limp and sprawled face down in the stable. He was out there alone at the end of his work day, tending his beloved horses as he did every evening—the work he trusted no one else to do as well as he expected. When he failed to come in to wash up for supper, George was sent out to gather him.

Imagine the shock experienced by the boy at the sight of his namesake stretched out on the barn floor in the stark coldness of death. He had been a picture of health to be so suddenly taken. There was a closeness between those two, and the father's death set up a sadness in the son that I believe never left George.

I can hear my Pa's voice to this day, the Bible words he spoke to George at his father's burial: "Your father was a good man. 'He has entered into *Gott's* peace'"—the very verse from the book of Isaiah Pa read earlier that week in the growing dim of our supper table. God's peace, a "peace that passeth understanding." Peace in the name of the father, perhaps, but not so for the son.

At the time of his father's passing, George's brothers were already working their own land. The farm and all its thriving activities had been left lock, stock and barrel to the youngest son, the one with his own name, with instructions for George to continue to make the businesses prosper, to be an honest man of sound business dealings, and to hold his mother's welfare in high regard.

The Shriver land fairly shouted with abundance, fields to barns. And such a beautiful house, the layout George would reproduce almost room for room for our home to come on Baltimore Street, right down to the spare room upstairs where all the tallying, the purpose to prosper, would be managed.

But here he was only sixteen and now a sudden landowner and manager. All peace aside, he was forced to step up to the front line and manage the sprawling enterprise, all in a day's time. His brothers would lend a hand, of course, but the farm was clearly left to George. He was always a boy of purpose, very much in his father's footsteps. And in the end, I believe it was that purposefulness that was part of his, no, *our* undoing.

It was something like what Pa had pronounced more than once in my growing up, usually pointing upwards as if he were a man of the cloth perched high in a pulpit: " 'The Lord knoweth the days of the upright: and their inheritance shall be for ever.' It says so in the *Buch* of the Psalms!" And then for emphasis, he would add his German—*Erbe*—inheritance. "*Erbe!* What we do with what we have been given by *Gott*, what we pass on to our children for their children!" Pa could get himself mightily worked up over inheritance and the responsibility it leveled on households like ours.

All my life, Ma and I never ceased speaking German to each other. It was our way. But it was another story with Pa. He was proud to be a Pennsylvania landowner, and while Gettysburg might have thought of him as one of a tribe of rough-hewn German farmers, he worked hard at being a good American who spoke decent English. The unspoken rule was that when gathered at the supper table, English was to be spoken, no matter how broken or accented it might be coming from his or Ma's mouth.

Between the two of them, I learned to read and write and be a young woman who knew her rightful position in the world and the duties that came with that. Ma may have struggled with speaking the American tongue, but she taught me in the best English she could manage. A smart one, had she not married and had so many babies, she would surely have made a grand teacher. She was demanding with her pupils, all of whom happened to be her children.

For a time, I attended the Gettysburg Female Academy—almost two years, I think. But the walk into town and the hours inside its stuffy quarters did not suit me. It was agreed that I would finish my schooling with Ma. Miss Darling was too stern a taskmaster in my estimation, although there certainly were enough parents who found her and the academy to their liking for their daughters. In the end, with Ma's teaching, I never felt I was any less *gebildet*, any less educated than the town girls.

But the funny thing is, not long after Sadie was born, I decided that my own girls would get a proper schooling in town. I think that decision was more about me than anything else. I knew I never could measure up to Ma's skill with teaching or with her high standards. I did not inherit her hunger for book learning.

The shelf by their hearth held two heavy Bibles, an English and a German one, the latter being the very one handed over to Pa by his mother, given to her by the mother before her who lived by its precepts in Germany a century earlier. Nine times out of ten his hands reached for the English one.

Who can know why he insisted on these supper table readings? Maybe it was the practice he grew up with. That unwieldy book was his trusted English primer. But it was something more to us. His Bible was a sort of guidebook for how he believed we could best live in the world, from the Ten Commandments to the parables of Jesus.

Half the time I was unsure of the lesson he wanted us to learn, and yet those readings were a comfort, a sort of blessing to our day's end. He used those verses at other times, especially when he wanted us to better take in a valued lesson. His sermonizing was something we never questioned, or poked fun at, or forgot.

So now the *Erbe* Pa spoke of was in George's hands—the upright's inheritance forever. Young George inherited a great deal of land buzzing with industry, and along with that, a weighty responsibility, namely, the mandate to continue to make it prosper and to bring honor to his father's legacy. ❧

Chapter 4

How DOES A YOUNG MAN sort out his future when dealt the cards George was? Formal book learning was set aside. The farm, his mother, his scheme for what lay ahead were front and center. It was a lonely stretch of time for me to not get a sight of him, and when we first met weeks after the funeral, it was a *Katastrophe*—a near disaster for me.

The only real *Streit* George and I had was a thunderstorm of an argument that brewed up around the weeks that followed his father's passing and his mother's desires around her son's eventual marriage. It was my brother Emmanuel who made the grand announcement at the supper table that she had invited a cousin and her daughter from Baltimore. "She has her mind set on that girl for her son," he said, passing the potatoes to me knowing full well how this bit of gossip would slam into me at that moment. Brothers can be cruel.

I learned in short order of the guests' arrival, from carriage to trunks. She was George's fair second cousin, Catherine Mary, the girl he spoke of when we were children and the families would visit back and forth for a holiday or a death. The cousin and I even played together one autumn afternoon at Rock Creek. We must have been eight or nine years old then. I cannot quite remember.

When George's father suddenly passed, Mother Shriver flew into action with letters to the Baltimore relatives, opening the discussion of an arrangement between her son and her niece. Much of her scheme had to do with the *Erbe*—the land, the businesses it carried, George's and her standing in the extended family. Or perhaps before he died, George's father and mother had set these plans in motion. I never asked and was never told. What good would it have done for me to know?

I stood off at a distance and watched them at market that Saturday, the four of them, coming out of Hoffman's over on Chambersburg. C. W. Hoffman and George's father were good friends, with moneyed dealings between them—that much I knew—and it was likely that Mother Shriver was including him in the news of her marriage designs for her son.

The proud mothers strolling ahead of the young couple, Catherine's arm was linked through George's, her head canted in his direction. I could see that she was doing the talking and that his gaze was not quite fixed on her—a small comfort to my heart about to pound out of its cage. I tell you, I was dizzy with despair at seeing them side-by-side and knowing why they walked on display that morning.

Catherine's features were not at all comparable to mine.

Her hair like corn-silk in the sunlight, she had a narrower face and a more delicate nose and was almost as tall as George. That morning she was decked out in a lavender silk, likely from a Baltimore dressmaker, trimmed out in piping that you would be hard-pressed to find sitting in any Gettysburg shop.

It was a sport in town to regard visitors like her, from bonnet to boots, and she was surely gathering her share of approving stares as the couple promenaded through the streets. To be honest, Catherine cut a finer figure than I, and it made sense to me that he would most likely choose her. I will admit that. But seeing them that morning was a knife to my heart.

I stole far enough behind them, out of their view, until they turned onto Franklin, when I called a halt to my pursuit. The only thing I can remember taking from the market back to the farm that day was a heavy heart and a bundle of worry.

An endless week dragged by before George appeared at the farm gate. From the garden I could see him tie his horse and stop to talk with Pa who pointed him in my direction. I know I did not look my best right then, pulling beets and wielding a hoe in the afternoon sun. But I stood with my chin held up as he walked towards me. I was not about to let him see my anguish at the announcement he was about to make. I remember my face feeling as though it was on fire. I could not help but blush in George's presence those days, but the color at that moment was ignited more by anger and fear. That, and two hours of gardening in the autumn heat.

We spoke more like distant cousins, without smiles, without warmth, without looking into each other's faces. But when I had enough of it, I blurted out, "I understand, George. I do. It is how it will be." He replied that I did not understand, but I went on until the tears sprang up. It was the first time George Shriver made me cry in his presence.

Pa watched from across the way, squinting to get a better look at my cheeks already streaked with garden dirt from my hands trying to dam up the tears. But he left us to it. Now George waited in silence until I settled down enough to listen.

He told me that he had indeed seen me in town near Hoffman's the week before, and when I heard that, I wanted to crawl under a rock, I felt so embarrassed. He guessed what I must have been thinking, and he said he felt low about how it looked, to me and to everyone else that morning.

It was true that his mother was hard at work behind the scenes fashioning arrangements for Catherine and him to marry. His cousin had that very morning headed back to Baltimore, and this moment was the first time he was able to talk to me about it all. My stomach sank into my shoes as he went on.

"She is a fine girl," he said. "There is not a time we have not known each other."

I could not let him go on, and I cut him short, my anger flashing out of me fast as lightening. "And you and I? Are we new to each other!? We grew up on these fields together, and I mean so little to you?"

"Let me finish, Hettie. Listen to me"—words he would echo in the years to come whenever my temper flared. And after a long pause, he spoke: "My mother expected I would fall in line with her marriage plans for me. But I said no to her."

I remember repeating in my head what he had just said to better take it all in as we stood there facing off in the afternoon breeze, as though we were about to turn our backs on each other to pace out a dual. He said no to her.

"I love Catherine, but as a sister, not a wife. She is not the one I would choose to be beside me. Could you see me growing old, living between Baltimore and here? This is where I want to make my own way in my own life, run my business, raise my family. I told her no."

There would be no more talk of a wedding with his Baltimore cousin, no more talk of joining households and inheritances, he assured me. Mother Shriver was, of course, not pleased. But her youngest son had stood his ground and would not budge from his decision.

"Let things settle," he assured me. "She will move past her anger. She has to." His mother had held that the brother-sister affection the cousins shared in time would blossom into a loyal love between husband and wife. But George told her no.

When he rode off that day, I could have hoisted up my skirts and danced a jig right there in the garden. My whole countenance suddenly changed. I was a different girl by the time I washed up and sat down to the supper table that evening. Believing my future suddenly restored, the burdens of the long week seemingly lifted in four words, all the hopes returned to their proper pockets of my heart, the possibilities of a lifetime beside him back on track. He told her no.

But I did not see a hair of him in the following weeks. The gardens died back and welcomed their first blanket of snow to tuck them in for the season of darkness, of shorter days and longer nights, of rest. Still, I clung to our autumn encounter out there and held my longings and my fears close.

George did finally appear briefly at our door once in December, all solemn and formal, with a gift for me. See the book of poems here? Growing up, we all knew that George was fond of poetry, and now he was handing me a collection of Lord Byron writings.

That visit was a brief one as he stood before me, my mother never moving from her perch at the hearth. He handed me the book, wished us a good holiday, and spoke of the trip he was about to take—to Baltimore! Ill at ease and with no more of an explanation, he turned and was gone, all in an instant.

You might guess how I felt at that moment, standing there with a book of poetry in my hand and George already on his horse, headed down Taneytown. And at that moment, I was taken prisoner again by the great warden of worry.

That Christmas, dinner was not a happy one for me, in spite of the table buzzing with laughter and chatter. I remember not having much of an appetite for food or conversation that day. My mind was in as sour a turn as my stomach, and all thoughts wandered to images of George dressed in his finest and seated next to a glowing Catherine at a fancy Baltimore table.

But not two weeks passed after the New Year when he stood at our door yet again. I was cautiously excited to see his face that afternoon from the upstairs window, my heart racing, my cheeks burning, always the same. Right off I noticed some change in him—I could see it even before he knocked at the door. Alongside the solemnness he had taken on with his inheritance in the fall, he now strode up our walkway with a new steadiness, as though he had grown into manhood over his weeks away. With nothing else but his absence on my mind that holiday, I feared the worst with his sudden arrival.

As much as I dreaded what the visit might mean, I gathered my wits, smoothed my skirts, and traipsed down the stairs as slowly and gracefully as I could manage. I opened the door and stood there for a moment and, without speaking a word, took in the sight of him, his boots fresh polished, hair brushed and neat, vest buttoned over a snow-white shirt.

I suppose, too, that I had grown up some over those days since I had last seen George, with such an investment in hours of worry over him and my place at his side. I missed the lightness of our time together only months before, in the warmth of summer before his father passed. I stood there with a whole litany of unspoken questions—about his intentions for Catherine, for me, for his farm, for his destiny, and dare I even hope, for *our* destiny.

Ma, bless her, eventually bustled in from the kitchen with cider and slabs of the gingerbread we had minutes before pulled from the oven, the smell of cinnamon wafting behind her as if to warm the house in her wake. She had convinced Pa to stay with her at the kitchen table to give us some moments alone, the first time George and I shared that privilege, I think.

The gulf of silence gaped between us with our nervous glances at the treats on the table. Conversation came slowly at first as we settled onto the bench, and both of us kept shifting our glances downward the way new acquaintants might. But eventually the tone shifted, the tension in our faces eased, and we traded snippets of news from friends and town.

Then, out of the blue, George's face grew solemn again, and after what seemed an eternity of silence, he spoke of his travels, of his mother's reluctance to accept last fall's decision, of his weariness with the drama of it all.

And then, as though he were asking about the weather, George suddenly wrangled up the courage to speak the words I was not prepared for at that moment: He asked me if I could see myself becoming his wife.

Well, it would be a *Lüge*, a flat-out lie, if I told you that I had thought of anything else since October, even in the midst of the unending cousin drama. Henrietta Weikert becoming Mrs. George Shriver, a proper wife of a prosperous farmer, the helpmate of the winsome young landowner who sat beside me waiting for my answer that afternoon. Our children will have his likeness, I remember thinking, which, of course, is how it eventually came to be.

Have you any doubts as to how quickly I replied? He certainly did not need to go down on his knee to plead with me. But the task that lay before him like a boulder was to go through the paces of facing my father waiting in the next room. George stayed put while I stepped away to fetch Pa, who instructed me to wait behind with Ma "while the men talk." Ma and I stood in the silence of the kitchen's warmth holding our breath, trying to hear their muffled voices on the other side of the door.

My Pa was a good man, good to Ma, as good as he could be to a house full of children and a farm to oversee. But he also could be very stubborn and mired in his ways, and especially concerning how folks surveyed his family. "No sixteen-year-old daughter of mine is going to marry..." I could hear that much of Pa's low voice. I had warned George that this might be the case, that if he consented, we still might have to wait.

Ma and I remained still as statues, her eyes locked on mine, her eyebrow arched, the look she used with her children when she called us to task. After an eternity, we heard Pa clear his throat, and then more silence, with the tick of the hearth clock thundering in my ears.

When Pa finally summoned us in to join them by the fire,

no one was smiling. But after a moment, Pa cleared his throat again and announced that George had asked for my hand and he had granted it, that is, once I reached my eighteenth year.

"*Heiret*…Marriage!" he corrected himself. "Marriage is hard enough," he said, with a long glance toward Ma. "And more so for a girl. Henrietta, you need to finish up your learning and sit two more Christmases at the Weikert table. Your Ma needs your help, and there are enough things you do not yet know."

And he was, of course, right about that.

"And as for you, George," he added solemnly. "You have a thing or two to get in order before you become a husband and start a family." And with that, the discussion was ended, and George and I stood betrothed by the hearthstone where we would someday pledge our lives to each other in marriage.

What we did not know that afternoon was that less than a year would pass before over in the Emmitsburg church my brother Emmanuel would take George's older sister, Maria, to be his wife. The two of them had been discreet, you could say secretive, about what people saw, and news of their engagement was more of a surprise than George's and mine, I think. Their wedding would smooth out most of any wrinkles between the two families concerning our engagement.

What did Ma and Pa think of George? For years they spoke of him as a *reicher Junge*—a rich boy. That kind of talk stopped once I was promised to him. They had watched him grow up maybe a bit spoiled, a bit privileged. But my folks were smart. They never uttered an unkind word about the Shrivers once the betrothal was agreed on.

And never did they hint at any misgivings they may have harbored about his long months of absence once he went off to serve. I think, as I was the middle child, there were plenty other concerns to keep them too occupied to worry over me or how my life was unfolding. I would marry a wealthy heir, and I would be cared for, and they let things stand.

That day when Pa said yes to us, George asked if I might ride along with him to share the news with his mother, and he consented. Mother Shriver still wore her widow blacks, still carried the solemn air of a woman in mourning. When our carriage arrived at the house, she sat watching us from the parlor window as George helped me out of the carriage. He brought me straight into where she waited, and with little in the way of lead-in, told his mother that he had asked for my hand and that my Pa had given his blessing.

She managed a wan smile in her pinched congratulations as she took my hand, but not much more than that. I was too young to understand why she clung to her role of the long-suffering widow as though it was her "pearl of great price" like in the parable. To me, it seemed she wore her sadness proudly, like it was a military honor. I knew that her rejected ideas around Catherine and George marrying took their toll and would always leave me out of her best graces.

As a young wife I had *wenig Toleranz*, meager tolerance for her dour bahavior. But looking back, despite our cold history, I would come to allow that it takes a widow to know a widow.

Later, George asked me on our way back to my house if I liked his poetry book, and I said yes, but that I struggled with some of the meanings. And that is the truth. If I were to read these pages today, it would be the same, and George would not be here to help me make sense out of it.

But that evening as he bid me adieu at my door, he told me to read again the one titled "She Walks in Beauty." See how that page is earmarked?

"The last two lines are for you," he said smiling as he turned toward the gate. Once back inside, I grabbed the book and plopped near the fire straightway to read and memorize the lines before I went upstairs to bed:

> *A mind at peace with all below,*
> *A heart whose love is innocent!*

These lines I understood, and I rested better that night than I had in weeks. With my doubts scrubbed away, the most peaceful of sleeps came over me. I now knew with every breath in me that I would become George's wife.

In our years together, I think his hands held this book much more than mine ever did. Poetry was so dear to him, and he could repeat so much of it by heart, something I never could do. It was a beauty of a thing to hear him recite those lilting verses.

From the day our marriage was first spoken of, I would have almost two years to grow up, to go from short skirts to long ones, to pick up whatever more remained from Ma's teaching, to prepare a new wardrobe and lay my whole marriage trousseau in order.

It was how we did it back then, you know, clothing ourselves in a few good things that were made to last. Today I hear of these closets, they call them, and I think who would ever have so many dresses that you would need a whole set-apart space with hanging contraptions to store your clothes on. Oh this modern, vain world.

Once we were promised, George and I were of one mind, and it was an easy thing for me to pass those many months knowing we would marry in due time. He came to our house often, sometimes two or even three times in a week. Ma and Pa were long-suffering about his presence, and I was, of course, delighted. With my mind set on my happy destiny as his bride, I was relieved of my dreaded fear of the Baltimore cousin.

One sunny Sunday afternoon in October, the geese honking their flight across the skies overhead, we laid out a leaf house in the field that skirted Pa's woods across the way, as though we were children playing grown-up, laughing and pushing long rows of piled leaves into rooms and hallways, already dreaming of a future with family and fortune and a fine house of our own, from parlor to kitchen, stable to garden.

That poet Tennyson came to his mind, and as we stood inside our leafy creation George said something about "handsome houses where wealthy nobles dwell." By then I would gladly have settled with him in a shack by the side of the road, but his was a nobler dream than mine.

The autumn before Jacob was born we laid out leaves into just such a house with the girls, who were too small to understand or remember that afternoon but took great delight in it all the same.

Once we were promised, at the end of every visit, without fail, I walked George out to his horse, no matter the weather. And every time he sang and kissed me before taking his leave. My favorite then was "A Rose Tree," in his soft voice, for my ears only.

A rose tree in full bearing had sweet flowers fair to see
One rose beyond comparing for beauty attracted me.

That time of waiting was beauty to me. I sometimes think that the world has forgotten how to wait.

If I had begun writing this account of my life when I was sixteen and newly promised to George, you would read an entirely different story, a playful one, maybe even a silly one, because I had no idea what lay ahead in my young life. All that I knew back then was my love for him. That, and being a daughter at a farmer's table, cared for, fed, taught, shaped, loved. Those were perhaps my happiest years, so uncomplicated and sun-drenched, so clean of what haplessly lay ahead for me.

Here is what I grew to realize in those two years of waiting: That George did not choose me to be his wife because I was special. Quite the other way around. I would come to believe, I still believe, that I was special *because* George chose me above all others. Such were the ways of love back then. I have not known it to be that way in the years since. ❧

Chapter 5

My sister Mary Ann was eleven years older than I, the first-born. Her wedding was *wichtig*, an important affair to Ma. For mine, she was not so worked up. But she ordered the best quality deep blue wool she could find from Fahnestock's, and it arrived from Philadelphia with her approval.

With its fine, soft weave, her creation for my day would measure up to the beauty of the cloth. She also ordered two new heavy petticoats that made such a whispered rustle when I moved. Talk about feeling grown up! It was a time when so much was beauty to me, from stockings to poetry.

I thought that dress was finer than anything you could order in town, and I wore it for many years afterward, as long as I could still fit into it, reworking it time and again. Ma and Pa gifted me with the soft Kashmiri shawl that I failed to hide away or to grab and take along with me that hot July morning before the Southern army boys helped themselves to it. I held three babies at their baptisms in that shawl, and it was too precious a possession for me to have been so foolish as to leave behind.

There was not much of a need for me to collect linens or curtains or kitchen things into a trousseau. The Shriver farm was well-stocked with whatever I might need as a new wife. Still, the gifts came to our door, one after another, and I was grateful for every last one of them. One day all of them would be moved to Baltimore Street with us. But for then, they were packed up and sent to George's house where they would be waiting for me to arrive as the new Mrs. Shriver.

My Mason soup tureen somehow survived the war, and I think I brought it to this house. No, I am *sure* I packed it on High Street to bring along with me. My folks had ordered it in from England at great expense, and I was very proud of that piece with all its rosy hues. When any occasion special enough brought it out onto the table, Sadie and Mollie would sit before it and conjure up story after story from the fancy garden scene that encircled it.

I have not beheld that pot for so very long, and I think those people out there must have stolen it away from me or sold it, or worse yet, dropped it and shattered it to pieces.

George's sister Marie sewed us pillow covers and bed sheets from a bolt of quality linen she ordered in from Germany. The cloth was broad enough that there was no need to seam pieces together. One day all of our beautiful linens, stripped from the beds in our absence, would disappear, likely to be ripped apart and torn into bandages. But George and I got to enjoy the soft luxury of them for our year together in the new house.

She may have complained, but I believe Ma took great delight in the outfitting that would carry me from girlhood to grown-up wife in short order. I recognized her quiet pride in overseeing my new trunk as its contents grew—from drawers and undervests, to shoes, a new nainsook night dress, those petticoats, chemises, a dressing sack, two house dresses, and a trim paletot jacket for Sundays. I cannot remember exactly what else, but it was a great pile to fold and pack away.

Oh, yes, and she convinced Pa of the absolute necessity to order in a new quality corset that fit me just so, and a supply of the nicest stockings I had ever owned. The corset seemed to take on a life of its own as it waited on my bed to be cinched and squeezed around me on the morning of my wedding.

I felt like royalty when that trunk was finally locked up and sent off the afternoon before our celebration. Levi needed a farmhand to help him hoist the thing out of the house and onto the wagon so he could deliver it to the Shriver house. It was a bride's treasure chest of new beginnings.

There is not another time in a girl's life like her wedding day. Mine began as a frosty, sunny Tuesday morning—as the old rhyme says "a day of wealth" to be wedded on. Ma and Becky spent a good hour with me upstairs, plaiting and pinning up my hair and fitting me into my dress, and once they crowned me with silk flowers and baptized my wrists and neck with lavender water, I was a bride any man would be proud to take as his own.

I descended my family's stairs for the last time as a Weikert, feeling like Queen Victoria herself in all my finery, finally coming to a halt beside George at the hearthstone. He looked as fine as ever, straight-backed and dignified in his morning coat with that sly smile in his eyes that I grew up loving for as far back as I could remember.

Our gathered families watched expectantly with Reverend Myers standing before us. "In the fear of the Lord," and before our solemn assembly, George and I promised to be loving and faithful husband and wife, "until it shall please the Lord by death to separate us." One moment we were two single eighteen-year-olds—he in his gentleman's frock, me in my good wool. And the next, we were married, pledged to each other before the great cloud of witnesses that encircled us that winter morning.

We were a confident couple, with lofty intentions to take our position alongside the best Gettysburg had to offer. Our children, our farm, our accounts would prosper, and folks would respect the young Shriver family.

Ma had laid out a fine wedding breakfast waiting for us in the dining room: sliced ham, ginger and pound cakes, spiced peaches and cherries, their best cider, and quantities of spiced tea. Pa gathered us together, cleared his throat to make one of his short speeches, and raised a glass to congratulate us.

And, as was his way in his Germaned English, he blessed his daughter with a proverb from the Bible that he had practiced for the occasion: "Whoso findeth a wife findeth a good thing, and obtaineth favour of the Lord."

Our glasses were raised. Mother Shriver dabbed her eyes. My brother Levi was unusually full of the devil that day, and I remember Ma shushing him with her one eyebrow arched in his direction. He was only thirteen, I think, and he joked long afterwards about being reprimanded for having a bit of innocent fun at his sister's expense on her special day.

It had begun, my life as Mrs. Shriver, and it pleasured me to sense George's presence beside me that brisk, sunny day, and then to glance down at his ring on my finger on the bracing ride home to the Shriver farm. His mother sat silent in the buggy with us, bundled up against the cold as the afternoon skies began to drain of light.

When we pulled into the circle at the Shriver house, George helped his mother out of the carriage first. Then he turned to me with a smile and said, "Mrs. Shriver?" I took his hand, and for the first time as his wife, began our practice of saying, "*Danke, mein Schatz.*" Thank you, my love.

After my young lifetime of growing a love for George, he finally stood before me as my husband, and at that moment I understood the *Verlangen*—the desire Pa spoke of from the Bible: "Thy desire shall be to thy husband." This was a new kind of desire, and it was beauty to me, *wunderbar*—a wonderful mystery to be standing there before him as his wife. *Danke, mein Schatz.*

We stepped into the warmth of what was now *our* home, with my heavy trunk of fine new clothing, a crate of my keepsakes, and our wedding gifts waiting stacked and huddled in the parlor like so many servants gathered to welcome me. There would be hours of unpacking and sorting and assigning proper spots, and all of that would wait 'til the morrow. Mother Shriver already had climbed the stairs to her room, so there we stood by the fire, alone for the first time as husband and wife.

George loved the work of his English poets—Byron and Wordsworth and Tennyson—and as he did when he was a boy, he found the right lines to fit the moment.

That night, before we made our way upstairs, he spoke the Tennyson phrase I had asked him to write down for me on birch bark the day he spoke it as we created our leaf house: "All of this is mine and thine." All of this: the Shriver estate, this wedding night, a lifetime together. All of this was now ours from this day forward.

Dusk could not come soon enough that evening, when we could at last climb the stairs together. It was not that we were strangers. But that night we were clumsy, timid children learning to be husband and wife in the bedroom down the hallway from his mother's.

George smiled as he slowly pulled the flowers, and then the pins from my hair. He fumbled to undo all the lacings and layers my mother and sister had wrapped and threaded and tied me into that morning. It was one of the few times he was shy with me. Still, he had a way about him.

True to form, he sang to me in the blessed darkness before we drifted off.

> *Her voice is low and sweet, and she's all the world to me;*
> *And for bonnie Hettie Rosie I would lay me down and die.*

I thought my joy might light up the night skies, his voice was such beauty to me.

*   *   *

The next morning, *älter und weiser*—at least a touch older and wiser—after I finished dressing, he lifted the hair tumbling down my back and went on to braid it into one long strand. We may have laughed at how it turned out, but he had done an admirable job of it with not much in the way of practice. I wound and pinned it all up with him silently watching, and I remember closing my eyes with the pleasure of it all.

Hand in hand we trundled down the stairs to sit down together at the table where my mother-in-law sat finishing her coffee, a quiet witness to our first breakfast as husband and wife. Listen, I knew she had been the woman of the house for a good twenty years. Here she sat with her son before her, smiling beside the one he had chosen to be his wife, a girl who surely would not, could not measure up to her niece. I was the young woman who would come to depose her.

While Mother Shriver sat solemn as a deacon, we newly-weds were bubbling with *Spielen*, playful and giggling with the good fortune of having shared a bed for the first time and were now sitting down with hearty appetites, ready to make short work of our wedding breakfast.

I could not care that morning about her stern face. I was bursting with joy and the prospects of this new chapter. It was almost two years to the day that George showed up at Pa's door to ask for my hand. I sometimes wonder if back then had he stopped to ask for his mother's permission, or even for her blessing, before he knocked on our door. I never asked how his intentions came to win out over hers.

But I clearly remember thinking over that first breakfast, "Never mind. None of that matters to me." And really, could any girl be happier than I was that morning with George's ring shining new on my finger?

See the small tin box here? I took his ring from my hand the day I got the nurse's letter. For many years, even after I took the name Pittenturf, I carried my first wedding band, hidden out of sight, but never apart from me. For a long time it was sewn into the seam of my undervest, closest to my heart, or so I reasoned. Can you imagine that! I was never again to wear it on my finger.

Why I stopped carrying it with me, I cannot say. There

simply came a moment when I tucked it away to rest in this tin. But that ring has never been far from me since the cold winter morning he first slipped it onto my finger.

The year of unknowing, when George's whereabouts were unclear and my questioning letters went unanswered, I grew so thin, my wedding band could have flown off of my finger on its own. But now, you can see that it would not fit over even half of my smallest finger. So much has changed.

Do you know, before Easter that first year, I was carrying Sadie inside me. She would be born before Christmas. So much changed, indeed. ❧

Chapter 6

WHERE WILL WE AND THIS ALMIGHTY Union of ours end up with this suffrage nonsense? Lucretia Mott, Susan Anthony, Elizabeth Stanton, and the other one? What was her name? Lucy Stone!

Had they nothing better to do with their time? And what far-flung notions do they have in mind? How far will these ladies drive their suffrage wagon down the road with this madness? Do they want a woman in the pulpit on Sunday mornings? A woman in the White House? A woman pouring glasses of whiskey for the men lounging in her tavern?

I remember reading about the Women's Rights convention they called together soon after the smoke cleared from the war and wondering where they found the time and energy for that folly. Equal pay, equal rights for men and women and White and Negro, as if equality was a thing that could even be brought about and accepted by the likes of us flawed beings.

And a woman voting? I think I might not even choose to cast a vote, if it came down to it. Better to leave the mess in the hands of them that wage the wars. Better to keep the woman's hands clean of gunpowder to tend to the toddlers and the table.

And yet. And yet, what if back then I had the "right" to run a tavern? What if I had been given the blessing of the good citizens of Gettysburg, the menfolk I would take money from, the women who might think better of chirping their gossip about me and painting me with scandal? What if I had the courage after George mustered to open the doors of the Shriver Tavern and tenpin alley out back on my own? Would people have eventually stopped whispering about Henrietta and her daughters? Could I have somehow become a respected businesswoman?

Oh, it was all well and good to host Union soldiers that December before the war came to our doorstop. It was fine for my home to be taken over as a hospital afterwards for as long as they needed it. It was expected of me and part of what it meant to be a good patriotic citizen of Gettysburg!

But woe unto me if I should have swept the ruins away and opened the tavern on my own back then. No doubt I would have been shunned by every woman in town, maybe even by my own folks. The time would come soon enough that I would be the dirty linen to some of them for selling the properties as quickly as I did in the end, for taking up with D. and then for that *verdammt* story around his boy's death. I think those that I considered friends may have been the quickest to wag their tongues.

But women's rights? Even with the help women like me and my mother before me had with laundering and cooking and cleaning, our lives in Gettysburg back then could be back-breaking. There were too few hours in my world to think of carrying a banner and protesting a woman's plight in a man's world.

* * *

After George had finally decided we had enough of farm life and moved us into town, there was less time spent in the carriage, to be sure. And it was a luxury I never took for granted, being able to stroll over to the Diamond and have shops and merchants at our bidding. They stocked nearly everything a woman could ever desire for her home. And just a skip away lay all manner of sweets lined up in jars and barrels for my girls. I had neighbors within feet of me to chat and laugh and trade news with. I had all the sounds of town life. I had my own girl, Nonie, at my beck and call most every day.

But still, it was a far cry from a life of leisure. The demands never lightened on me, especially as our new house was being built. With Nonie working alongside me, I cooked and laundered while I sorted through choices for wall coverings and furnishings I would need to order in. And there were those two dear children underfoot.

The workplace George was building was his turf, and I

would not meddle in his designs, or his ledgers. This would not be woman's work or a woman's world—serving liquor to men while they played cards and traded stories in language likely not fit for fairer ears. George had designed my life into the walls above his cellar tavern, and that was as it should be.

Packing up our life on the farm, moving into town, watching our house take shape across the way: all of this went on while the demanding hours of my day churned away without a pause. I have no regrets about those years, except perhaps for the coolness between Mother Shriver and me. That, and, of course, baby Jacob's passing. Back then, we did not count on our babies making it out of nappies. Sickness stole so many of the young ones that mothers were seldom surprised when they laid them to rest in the ground. But that does not mean we were without hopes. Oh the prayers that went up when we held our babies to us, silent pleas for our darlings to thrive against all odds.

A woman may not remember years later how the pangs of giving birth felt, but she does not forget the rush of love she feels when she swaddles her newborn for the first time. She remembers the peace of cradling him to her breast in the hush of night, alone in the darkness with her suckling baby and the cricket's song, while the rest of the household slumbers on.

So it was with the births of our girls. Both of them came into the world in a flash.

With firstborn Sarah Louise, who took her name from my

Ma—our Sadie—George was off to town on some matter, and Mother Shriver's girl Flora ended up catching the baby, something she had done enough times for her own people. What did I know about the pangs of labor? My back had been aching something awful that morning, and I had gone upstairs to rest. Almost as soon as I lay down, the pain swelled up in me, with the power of what a volcano surely must be like. Flora and Mother Shriver came charging upstairs when I cried out for them, and within the hour, our first baby had come into the world and into my arms.

With the second one, I was standing in the garden when my waters broke and soaked my stockings and shoes. Like the first birth, the pains came right on top of each other straight away. An hour later, George caught our baby Mollie, who took her name from George's mother—Mary Margaret—in what was called the borning room off the Shriver kitchen. It was where Mollie's papa had come into the world himself.

They were fine girls from the get-go, and I was grateful that they were of sturdy stock, to grow hardy and well and mold me into a mother without my even knowing it. It was a chapter with equal parts of work and learning and delight for George and me. I have forgotten much of it. But seeing their first steps, hearing them babble their first words, watching them run to their Papa and cast their chubby arms around his legs—these moments were such beauty to me and have never left my mind.

George sang and sang to our daughters, and bedtime was much more to their liking if it was their papa who sat with them for a good-night crooning.

Sadie, Sadie, won't you come out tonight
Sadie, Sadie, the moon is shining bright
Put your cap and jacket on
Tell your mama you won't be long
And I'll be waiting for you 'round the corner.

Bedtimes with Sadie and Mollie are written in my heart, a fleeting time when *Kinder* are at their most innocent and sweet. It was a new kind of love for both of us, and we were happy prisoners of it.

Yet despite our pride and pleasure with our girls, there was an even greater delight with the birth of our boy. With this one, things went slower, and the midwife arrived in good time to catch him.

George stood proud as a peacock with his swaddled new-born son in his arms. It was his idea to name the boy Jacob after my Pa. "Too many Georges!" he crowed. "There is no need for royalty around here!" Our brothers' name (both of them Emmanuels) was added, and we had an heir with a proper sound to him: Jacob Emmanuel Shriver. My folks were as pleased with the name as Mother Shriver was not.

Oh, he was the loveliest of boys, a smaller baby than his sis-

ters, but with his father's mouth and long fingers. On a sweltering June morning, we dressed him in the gown his Papa
had been baptized in and a new *Mutze*—the lace cap I tatted
for him. With the St. James holy water trickling over his head,
Jacob wailed in the reverend's arms for a blessing to be recited
over him: "For this child I prayed; and the Lord hath given me
my petition which I asked of him."

Our proud families were a smiling circle of witnesses that
morning. I often longed to have preserved the moment in a
little tintype, but it was not something we did then like people do now. Mother Shriver stood proudest herself gazing at
her young son's son, the new heir of the *Erbe*. It is one of the
pleasanter memories I carry of her face.

Our joy was not to last long, for we were not able to protect dear Jacob from the angel who would swoop down and
take him in her grasp. Was my milk not good? I confess that
this was a fear I had nurtured through tears even before his
passing and for a very long time afterward. Or did the heavy,
dank July air bear a sickness that wormed its way into his
tender body?

He grew weak in the days following our sunny moment at
the baptismal font, sleeping more and more, eating less and
less. And then one still, warm evening, he simply drifted away
in my arms.

A mother's prayers that her son will grow up to take on his
inheritance are laced up with fears. Fear that we cannot protect

our baby or do right by him, fears I cannot begin to name that our hearts harbor in silence.

I was young when my mother lost two baby girls, and I remember as though it was yesterday, her weeping for weeks on end. I could not know how deeply she must have felt those losses until I grew up and paddled across that river of grief myself.

Babies are born, babies die—it is the way it is. But it is never an easy pill to swallow. As for George and me, we were brought to our knees by Jacob's passing, our innocent lamb, the heir we had already draped a happy future around, like a prince's robe.

It still is painful to my heart to remember that time. There was a steady drizzle of rain well into the next morning after he passed, as though the skies were weeping with us. I sat rocking in our bedroom chair all that long night with my quiet bundle in my arms that in short order went from fever-hot to clay-cold. I held him as though he would wake hungry and eager to go back onto my breast.

There would be no first tooth, no first step, no first word from our dear boy. Tell me, where did his sweet being, his dear soul—where did all of him go in that moment of passing?

George slipped out of the house to secret himself away in the barn long before dawn, without so much as a crust of bread for fuel. Hours later, he stepped out into the mist with a plain box to hold his boy, fashioned from the oak slats that would otherwise become a barrel to hold the whiskey his father had been so proud of.

Together we swaddled our darling in his snow-white blanket one last time for the bumpy ride to the graveyard. One of George's brothers harkened the minister to meet us there. We stood in the light rain as my girls tucked wildflowers alongside their baby brother's cheeks, and we said our last goodbyes. George gently tucked our boy into the box, the lid was tacked on, and a small hole in the rain-softened grounds of Mt. Joy received another angel.

In the name of *des Vaters und des Sohnes und des Heiligen Geistes,* our boy was gone from us. But I tell you, any trace of the Father, Son or Holy Ghost was distant from me that rainy afternoon. On the solemn ride back home, Sadie and Mollie, in that mysterious knowing way of children, somehow held their tongues and sat silently beside us. They were brave little soldiers that day.

Ever the dutiful woman, I rose numbly for many mornings following that dreary day, as though nothing had happened to our family. I plaited my hair, dressed and fed the girls, made the beds, instructed Flora, and all the while choked down my bitter grief. Oh how my breasts ached at the sight of one more of Jacob's things lying here or there. That boy's absence was as strong as any living creature's presence.

George's sadness steered him in another direction entirely. Faster than a flash, after we left our son at Mt. Joy, my husband had made up his mind that we would move to town now, not later. I heard his arguments with his mother from behind the parlor door.

To be clear, our dream of a life in town began long before our wedding day, out there in the autumn sunlight the day we fashioned our make-believe leaf house. We had talked a long while about all of this, but now our baby's passing had pressed my husband into action.

I wonder now if the fields around us had become cursed, too quiet, too lonely for George's grief, for *our* grief. As though he could not tolerate being a gentleman farmer a moment longer, he sprang to action with a new urgency to put his *Erbe*—whisky and all—to its new use.

I had tucked in the girls while there was still some light in the western skies. George found me standing in the garden again, as I had every night since we kissed our Jacob goodbye. The tears may have lessened by then, but the brick of sorrow in my chest had not lifted a hair's weight.

The two of us had hardly touched each other all that warm, sorrowful July. But now he slipped quietly to my side and put his arm around my shoulder. After feeling such a numbing loneliness those weeks, it was a relief to rest against him and take in the smell of his shirt, his skin beneath the cloth.

"We will start over," he said, with his hand reaching up to stroke my hair, which he had not done for so long a time. Yes, I thought, we need to wrestle out some joy between us again, make our own home away from his mother, from the walls that held the loss of our baby and the memory of George's father.

I was more than ready for a new start, to take on running my own house, to make my own blunders, away from Mother Shriver's interfering eye. My girls should be able to set a toy on the table without being corrected. I wanted to hear the sounds of life, of neighbors' voices and church bells. I longed to walk my own floors when and how I pleased.

By autumn, we would sell off part of the farm. Mother Shriver would stay behind in the home she loved, and her other son, who continued to work the fields and factories on both this farm and his own, would take on management of its businesses and be at her beckon. It would change the shape of the inheritance, but I was not concerned. I trusted George to make the right decisions in that arena.

George and I would become city dwellers. He was right about one thing. As long as we stayed behind on the farm, I would end up in that garden, alone in the stillness of too many twilights, turning my thoughts toward Mt. Joy, where our boy slept.

How had I been alert enough to have tucked his little baptism *Mutze* so deeply into our trunk? Somehow it survived all the madness. The lace has yellowed, but see? See how small he was? See how I would have loved holding his precious head to my breast? The cap, the ribbons and all, used to smell of that boy's sweetness, but no more.

The last thing on my mind back then was a woman's right to vote or having a hand in changing laws or joining some parade that would end up being shouted down by a red-faced crowd. With a house to tend and a pantry to manage and children's needs to be met, it was hard enough just to steal a moment of peace from the clutches of the day.

What woman would have the strength left to heft a banner and a batch of lofty ideals alongside a band of shrieking banties who should have been tending to their God-given duties back home anyway? ❧

Chapter 7

IN SHORT ORDER HE SOLD OFF a portion of the farm to begin our new chapter in town. The morning we left, George
and a farmhand made three trips with our household goods
packed into the wagon to load into the house we rented across
the street from the plot where our new home would be built.
He said it was the perfect perch to keep a careful eye on the
Fortschritt—the workers' daily progress. My husband's impressive house design had been completed and resting patiently on
his father's desk for at least a year before Jacob's birth.

George was so often bent over those drawings with such
concentration, changing a window or doorway, Downing's
architecture book spread open beside him. His creation was
unfolding before he even spoke to his mother of our intentions. Now we were poised to watch his careful sketchings and
measurements become our home of stone and brick, mortar
and timber.

The skies were cloudless when we carried our winter over-
coats swaddled into a coverlet down the stairs and out to the

wagon for the final load, alongside the rest of the horse's tack already piled in. Mother Shriver stood in the hallway for our final departure from her house. Although she would never have admitted it, I was certain she would long for the sound of our girls' footsteps and laughter in her rooms.

That morning her goodbye was an impersonal one, always the same. If not one thing, it was another that she disapproved of when it came to George's young family. Sadie and Mollie stood across the way, my giggle boxes, not sad in the least to leave their grandmother's house as they waited impatiently in the sun for whatever adventure their Papa was taking them on. George's departure that day must have peeved Mother Shriver to no end.

He remained an attentive son and never failed to make his way out to the farm for regular visits with his mother. But the January day we moved into the new house on Baltimore Street was the first she had beheld her son's finished product. She arrived with a flourish in her Sunday best, a chest of drawers and two Windsor chairs carried in behind her. They were gifts from her house that she made sure my folks saw hefted into the parlor.

They were good pieces, and despite the show she was making out of the presentation, I think it was her way of sending up some sort of truce flag. Ma never mentioned it, but she and Pa must have felt a bit outdone by Mother Shriver's gifts. My mother-in-law never reached out to us beyond that moment.

Perhaps if she had known George would be mustering out in the months that lay ahead, she would have made more of an effort to draw near. But it was not her way.

Once Solomon Powers' team had cut and haft and locked the stone foundation into place (and believe me, that was no small undertaking), it was almost like watching yeast do its work to leaven bread dough. You could watch and watch and nothing seemed to happen, but turn your back for a few moments, and the loaf has risen well over the rim of the bread pan.

Daily we observed our house reach higher and higher from across the way. By December, the structure stood strong and straight, roof and windows locked in to shut out the winter snows and shelter the workers inside. In and out they would parade, toiling away at endless horsehair plaster and trim work under our watchful stares from the windows across the way. I toiled over the paints and papers I would order in for the men to take up and finish the fresh walls. We would move in with spare furnishings, but in time we would be fully outfitted.

By then we had hired Flora's niece Nonie to help with laundry and cleaning. She was quiet and on the young side, but she was sturdy and earnest, and I was confident I could shape her work into the quality help I desired. It was when I had more patience, more tolerance for what it would take to bring her up to standard. I will say that Nonie was good with our girls, and perhaps this was her strongest suit.

There were some pleasant hours for me in those weeks, sitting near the stove, the girls playing behind me, glancing at the house across the way as I pored through the pages of my *Godey's* and *American Architecture* for ideas on the latest in home design. I did not want a copy of my mother's or my mother-in-law's rooms. Our home was to be one-of-a-kind, up-to-fashion, from ceiling to floor. George was generous with the money I would need to carry out the designs, and he seldom disagreed with what I chose to spread out before him after dinner. The next morning I would traipse over to the Diamond to order what we had agreed on.

The same year the house took shape, the Gettysburg Gas Company opened its doors for customers, and George was determined that our new home get piped for the lighting that passersby would admire as darkness set in, not something many homes could boast of in town. I watched the pipes get slotted into their holes on the front walls, never asking how the system worked or how the gas was made. I entrusted all of that to him.

I do remember it was part of the magic of our year together on Baltimore Street, the girls and I watching George start up the steady, clear lighting right before sunset and knowing that the glow was drawing attention. But once George went off to fight, I never once used the gaslights, relying on the lanterns I had grown up trimming and cleaning.

Did you know that Baltimore nearly burned down a year or two ago? And no one can say for sure, but it could well have been the gas piping that caused the fire to start up in the first place.

It was an almighty sight to see the red skies at midnight, to hear the thunder of buildings collapsing in the distance, the never-ending shouting of men wrangling their equipment. That fire could have made its way over to us, but they finally got ahead of it. You could go over there today and see the cleanup and rebuilding going on. In my thoughts, the whole spectacle harkened back to the chaos of those dark days of fighting and the aftermath in Gettysburg.

I remember reading about fires like that in Chicago and Boston, and there was so much lost between the two cities that the whole country slipped into what they called a "panic," the economy sliding down into a slump for a long stretch in the '70s. Who would know that the banking empire could be at the mercy of a spark of fire?

A catastrophe like that was something I was afraid of on Baltimore Street, an explosion from the gas feeding right through our walls. I tell you, none of it can be trusted. The people that brought me here seem to have no such fear of the pipes, even after what has happened, and George had no fear of them either. Lighting them up those evenings gave him too much pleasure.

Many an afternoon after the workmen packed up and hiked away from their work, the four of us would scurry across the street to do a walk-through and discover what new bits were accomplished. The girls made a sport out of spotting spiders for us to rescue them from, especially before the windows were built in. We even had picnic suppers, rainy ones on a quilt spread on the floor of what would soon become the parlor, sunny ones out back where our gardens were already taking shape.

Over the months of building, we ordered in the newest iron bedstead for our bedroom, clean and light, with brass finials and a fine wool and horsehair mattress. That room took shape as pretty as any parlor and was a point of great pride with me, although I could hardly parade people up there for tea to show it off.

If we were to walk into the front door together right this minute, I could point out the smallest detail of my house as it once was, from roof to cellar floor. I remember every nook, every choice I fussed over, right down to the pattern in the parlor paper.

See the piece of it here in the box? That regal marine blue is still as vibrant as the morning the delivery boy brought it to our door. I was so captured by the fine curling scrollwork pattern. I still am. Some artist must have fussed over the designs in a distant studio, the lines all braided and clean—just as I fancied them when I chose the pattern from the catalog.

Every room carried its own color: roses, greens, the blues and golds of the parlor. Looking back, I wonder if the workmen carried tales home to their wives about the demanding Mrs. Shriver's fancy tastes and critical eye.

I chose from three different bolts of lace for the downstairs window coverings and for our bedroom. The brocades for the flounces that were draped across the tops of the window casings harmonized with my wall colors. We had the wool carpets cut and stitched to size for each room.

From room to room, this was our palace, our pride, our dream taking perfect shape, all of it aimed toward our family's future. ❧

Chapter 8

OUR UNRAVELING BEGAN WITH that first call to arms on the front page of *The Sentinel*. By then, we were fully moved into our new home, and George had set his sights on an autumn opening of the tavern and tenpin alley.

But Gettysburg was abuzz with meetings in churches around town, and the seeds of war planted by months of speculation and a national election were sprouting and greening up fast in the heat of a grand patriotic show. It was the same in towns like ours all around the North and South.

I had just come downstairs from putting the girls to bed one night when George turned to me as I stepped into the room and said, "Well, I suppose sooner or later that will mean me," with the newspaper spread before him.

I knew what he meant, and, really, his announcement was not a surprise. But his words made my stomach twist just the same. I imagine it was much like this for countless women like me when they heard their sons or husbands utter similar intentions. We knew that those of us who would be left behind would have to fend for ourselves for a month or two, and even thinking of being alone for a week felt like a grievous threat to me.

We had a year to dissect the meaning of John Brown's raid on Harper's Ferry down in Virginia before the Wide Awakes came to life in the streets of Gettysburg to sow some fertile seeds of patriotism with their torchlight processions. They were not a bunch to be ignored, and their enthusiasm nudged folks into voting for a new man to take the reins in Washington.

Abraham Lincoln was the outsider from Illinois who won his party's nomination in Chicago, and we read that he was not one to back away from what was brewing in the South. Folks had their own ideas about Lincoln's tenets on slavery and what his election would mean to the country, and any direction you took on the subject led you to a confrontation between North and South. By the time the man won the election that November, you could smell danger simmering in the winter air.

Spring 1861 began like a row of domino tiles stood up on end. The first one had already been tapped—Harper's Ferry—and it fell into the next tile—Lincoln's election—then the next—a military island called Fort Sumter—until the whole row took up speed in its tumble.

It was in December when South Carolina was the first to make a show of pulling out of the Union. If you do not think that set off a firestorm of war talk around town, you would be mistaken.

The Lincolns could not enjoy their inauguration ceremonies or relax into the finery of the elevated Washington lives they were stepping into that chilly March. The South was mad as a stirred-up nest of hornets over the new president's abolition talk, and a Union army fort on Southern soil surrendering after being fired on was enough to ignite the whole powder keg that the war became.

Right off, the new president called for troops. That well may have been the very first order he put his signature to when he walked into his fancy office that month. And with that call, Gettysburg boys were raring to go off with other Pennsylvanians to protect the capital city. Before they even boarded the train, they were calling themselves the First Defenders. The dominoes were picking up speed as they knocked into the next one, then the next, then the next...

Prayer meetings and rallies all around town encouraged sign-ups, as though the coming bloodshed was God's Holy Will for the men to sign their names to. George, like so many others, could not resist those gatherings. Some women made it their business to be present as well, but I stayed at home with the girls. None of it sat right with me.

When the first batch of boys boarded the train for Baltimore, each one was sent off with a Bible, a pair of wool socks, and the cheers of what seemed the whole town at the station. Everyone's spirits were soaring that morning, and you would have thought we were sending these clueless volunteers off on holiday. Despite all the talk of victory and glory and preserving the Union, I can tell you no one really understood what they, what we all, were stepping into.

Well, right away our boys and the Massachusetts troops coming down to make their way together to the capital on a train out of the Baltimore station sparked awful riots in the streets all over this town, which you probably know about. Maryland leaned more toward the South than it did toward its new president. Either you were an anti-war Democrat or you were a Confederate sympathizer, and neither side liked what Lincoln had in mind. The rioters were ready to strike the troops coming through their territory to make their way to Washington. I think folks were surprised with the riots that exploded on the streets of Baltimore and became a bad omen for what lay ahead.

By now the kindling of a war was stacked sky-high, the country bent on being split and burned into two separate governments. It was like kerosene was being dumped on smoking embers. One state after another in the South caught fire with the passion to pull away from a Union growing fragile as an eggshell. The Secessionists fancied forming a separate country, a republic where they could do what they pleased with their slaves and their land and their laws.

That very first call Lincoln made for volunteers was built on the premise that ninety days was how long it would take to put down the rebellion. Ninety days! What a deluded bunch we were to drink in all that heady God-and-country talk and pronto! The boys were fit to take up the guns of glory. *Verrückt*—crazy, blinded thinking that led straight to hell.

Not many of us had even heard of Fort Sumter until that spring, some six hundred miles south of us and another world away, really. No one I knew had ever even been to the Carolinas. The Southerners surprised pretty much every Northerner when they bombarded the fort for—what? twenty-four hours?—and choked it into surrendering.

Then lickety-split, Lincoln sent out a second call for volunteers, another forty thousand or so to prepare for what would be the one battle that would put the Secessionists in their place, the one in Manassas. It was no more than a big empty field with a railroad crossing that was too close for comfort to the Capitol.

Now that the Union boys were trained and ready, surely they would put a lid on the Southern threat. To be safe, Lincoln made this second call for a three-year commitment, as though he knew something we did not.

We read of Washington's relaxed gentility making a holiday of it, hopping into their carriages, dressed in their finest, and heading west to enjoy a picnic outing while they chatted and watched the battle. All fun and games, high entertainment for the highly placed!

It came to be called the Battle of Bull Run, and it turned out the Union troops were the ones who ended up doing the greater share of the running, on the heels of the rich folks who scrambled off, scared for their lives, like an anthill emptying in a cloud of confusion. We Union folks had all assumed too much. The Seceshes were not the ones to be set straight. Our polished Union army was, generals and all.

The very next day, after the shock of Bull Run that we could hardly wrap our minds around, Lincoln was asking for five hundred thousand more volunteers, and for that same three-year commitment. It was towards the end of July, and George figured his time was up.

As stirred as he felt about the first, then the second call, George did not rush into joining up. Instead he focused his energies on getting the tavern and alley in finished order, the first establishment of its kind in town. He stood before the satin-smooth heavy oak bar Garlach built for customers to be served across and looked over his sturdy new tables and benches. Ample seating for a dozen or more men was tucked into the cellar.

Off to the side, my summer kitchen was fully outfitted with a grand new stove that would meet the family's needs upstairs in the warmer months but would serve the appetites of the tavern customers year round. It was a pleasant thing to step down into that space on a hot August afternoon and have the cool air waft over my skin. That lovely chill helped slow the ice melting in the new corner icebox. Our butter would never go rancid, our eggs would stay fresh even in the warmest summer months.

With its brick floor and higher ceilings, mine was a much finer cellar kitchen than Ma's, although I do not think she would have ever admitted it, and I certainly would not venture to suggest it so.

Behind our house and only a few steps away, the tenpin alley stood ready, its windows drawing the sun in to dance off the oiled floors George was so proud of. I can still smell the spice of the fresh timbers and lemon seed oil and turpentine he helped the men work into the alleys till they glowed a soft amber.

We could have had customers with the turn of a key. But his mind was made up. We would not open shop until he returned and the fighting was finished. With the July call and the fear in the air that Bull Run set up, George was ready. He would leave us and be back home by Christmas to open the business, and that was that.

Those nights after the girls were tucked in, our talk of the war, the strength of the Union machine, his safety, our safety, was quiet and unsettling. It might be a three-year sign-up, but surely it would not be as such. As long as we focused on that December goal being in reach, we could weather the time apart and get through. The Washington politicians spoke with confidence, hell-bent on wrapping up the fighting and yanking the South back in line in short order.

The army needed people like George for their cavalry units, and all the better if a man came with his own horse. These were men who knew how to ride and shoot and make their way through the familiar lay of the land they would be defending.

George's mare Valentine was a black beauty, glossy sleek, a smart creature he brought into our marriage. His father had established a good line of horses and taught his sons well how to breed and train and groom a stable full.

That horse was sharp, her ears always perked and alert to George's voice and at the ready for his commands. He liked to brag that she had the patience of Job and the strength of Samson. I imagine Mosby's men were glad to take the reins of the likes of her that January night. I dreamed plenty of times of Valentine standing loyally at our back garden gate, waiting to do her master's bidding, and I wonder still where George's ready horse ended up.

By the time August came into view, the daily papers were all of war talk, of what we were up against and the threats inching close enough around us to smell.

George and I had never traveled. I hoped to see the Atlantic and some of the big cities someday. Except for his boyhood jaunts with his family to Baltimore, he never had an interest in leaving Gettysburg for other parts. Even with his aim to invest his profits from the tavern—he seemed most drawn toward railroad stocks—his desire was to stay put on Baltimore Street and maybe step into town politics. He and I never had to pack up a travel bag.

Aside from basic military gear, we had no real idea of what

the army would issue him. I knit extra socks and sewed a sturdy shirt, stitched the edges of a broad cut of soft flannel to help keep his brogans and jacket clean, and gathered up a stack of hard soaps from the larder.

For a few evenings, after supper we stayed at the table for me to give him some quick lessons on how to turn a simple hem and sew on a button and patch a hole in a spot like the knee. I sewed up a cloth wallet with needle and thread for him and wrapped it into his socks. A "housewife" is what the army would call those kits.

That last night, he added his hairbrush and razor, his father's special writing set in the worn wooden box the girls begged to play with, the little notebook he was never without, a couple of hard apples from the bushel we had brought in from Pa's trees already heavy for harvest, a good chunk of dried beef from his own receipt, a new cup and fry pan, a good sharp paring knife, a few more things I cannot recall right now, all piled into what I had already gathered. I cinched his new life into the boot cloth, the bundle snug enough to fit into his saddlebag.

It was a warm, sleepless night for both of us, lying beside each other there in the silent darkness, my hand clasped into his. We could hear Valentine stirring out behind the house, as though she had a notion of some adventure lying ahead. Eventually George's breathing settled into a light sleep beside me. But I could not convince my eyes to stay closed or my mind to stop racing and lunging.

When would we next share the bed together? When would I again rest my head against his chest and hear the rhythm of his heart or take in the smell of his skin—things I knew as well as I knew the back of my hands.

The pink air of early morning pried through the lace of our windows too soon, and birdsong started up like nothing out of the ordinary was afoot. We could hear the girls whispering across the hallway. Our morning of goodbyes had come.

We had no appetite, he and I, as I busied myself through the motions of morning chores. He slipped out to finish readying the horse and bring her around to the front. Dressed in their Sunday best, Sadie and Mollie soon were sitting, chatting on the stoop, unaware of the weight of the moment.

I waited inside the open front door. There was nothing else I could ready for his journey. I watched him tie Valentine and come up the steps to gather me. And then he paused, as he often did, in the doorway, his back to the girls, to glance into the bones of his house.

Down the hallway flooded with morning light. To his left with our clock ticking in the peaceful embrace of the sitting room where we spent the richest of our family times and where he and I parked ourselves once the girls were asleep overhead. To his right, into the parlor where, come December, he would light the Christmas candles, and we would sing together and set our minds on a Holy Family's night of wonder. Up the climbing stairway that led to his ledgers, to Sadie and Mollie's treasures, to our welcoming bed.

"It is a fine place," he said, and with my arm linked through his, I nodded in agreement. We were well on our way, already realizing a good chunk of our dream in the months since we left the farm. And now his businesses and my peace of mind were to be temporarily laid aside.

For weeks, this morning of goodbyes had been at the front of my thoughts, and now there we stood, fresh out of words. Something like forty years have passed as I write this, and my husband's voice at that very moment is burned into my mind. I remember the feeling of some strange, heavy braided rope of pride and fear falling over my shoulders as we stood there. Since the morning we wed, George and I had never slept apart.

We stepped out into the bright sunlight, and with the girls skipping beside us, headed for the Diamond. Valentine sauntered obediently behind us in our sad parade. We passed Catherine Garlach's window where she sat at her table, and she sang out her good luck. There were others along the way who greeted George with their best regards.

I cannot rightly say how many men were gathered at the town center that bright morning, Gettysburg boys ready to sign up in the third wave to save the Union. It was not a small gang, to be sure. Things seemed less spirited to me than earlier that spring when the first batch of volunteers was sent off, before the surprise and embarrassment of Bull Run.

Shopkeepers came out to wish the men well, and women—

mothers and sisters and wives like me—were dabbing at tears while the men folk held their stoic stance. Sadie was gape-mouthed as she watched two girls hand flowers to the men about to set out, tugging at them to bend down for a kiss on the cheek.

A trumpeter and drummer (boys whose names I cannot recall) were perched on a wagon and started up "Columbia, the Gem of the Ocean," with a few folks adding their voices. The musicians glistened with sweat in the full sun while the rest of us took shade as best we could. I was glad George did not sing along with the throng at that moment. Normally music like that would lift our spirits, but it was not so for me. I can say now that it came to my ears almost like it might be a funeral march. I cannot bear to hear that tune, even as I write the lyrics here.

> *"Thy mandates make heroes assemble,*
> *when Liberty's form stands in view;*
> *thy banners make tyranny tremble,*
> *when borne by the red, white, and blue!"*

Assembled heroes and banners and tyranny, all empty glory to me and certainly of no use to an unthinkable number of dead by the war's end.

The moment I had dreaded all that anxious summer came, and my throat tightened into a knot. George knelt down in front of Sadie and Mollie and grasped their hands, looking them straight in their questioning eyes with marching orders to be good girls for their mama until his return. Oh their *klein* solemn faces! What could they understand of it all?

I choked my goodbye, and he put his arms around my neck and whispered that name dear to my ears before he stepped away. The men scrambled into the waiting wagons to set off, with a few like George among the riders going to war with their own horses, as though it were an ordinary Tuesday.

At the Emmitsburg church, they were to join up with recruits from Maryland and their young Captain Horner to make their way to the old military barracks waiting in Frederick. We heard later that the air was charged in that circle of men, spirits were high, and intentions were steady. Surely they were part and parcel of what was needed: a new influx of Union boys to get properly trained and help set things straight in short time.

The girls and I stood with the gaggle of Gettysburg stalwarts, straining our eyes to glimpse the men moving toward the horizon until we could no longer tease out the sight of them. I was nothing short of paralyzed at that moment, with grief at our parting and with fear of the worst. Pa's words had been in my head all that month: "The Lord watch between me and thee, when we are absent one from another." At times that verse seemed a hopeful promise to me, at other times a cruel joke.

The girls chattered away as we turned to make our way home, finally stepping into the house with only the sound of the clock's pendulum to greet us. Like baby Jacob's passing two years earlier, George's absence filled the rooms almost more than his presence had hours earlier. It is as though it were yesterday as I write this, my throat clenched, my chest aching with the rock of grief that our separation had rolled onto it in that beautiful tomb of a house. ❧

Chapter 9

THE SIMPLE RITUALS OF HOUSEWORK and caring for the girls were a balm to my soul. Routines I so often took for granted became soothing distractions, diverting my worried mind away from the tumult the what-ifs were pummeling into me.

Beginning our first night without him, the girls and I added "prayers for Papa" to every meal at table, every bedtime. Our chores passed the time, always undertaken "to be ready for Papa's return." I spoke of him as often as I could, and I overheard their sweet voices building his name into their play.

I often wondered what George's true thinking was at the start, whether he considered his first weeks as a "Union soldier of the Potomac Home Brigade" an honor or an adventure or a bitter pill. He could have complained more than he did in his letters, for we heard stories of the foul conditions in those camps, of sickness burning through the men, of death taking even the healthy, young ones.

In the beginning, apart from the hearsay on everyone's tongues, nearly all of what I would learn of the dirt that was a soldier's life came from George and my conversations, our silent jottings on the pages of our letters.

A week had not passed when the girls and I were handed his first post, written on brown paper he had picked up from behind a suttler's tent. He was so fond of the fine paper he used at his home desk, and I laughed as I read to the girls from that package wrapping.

We heard about the sorry meals the boys were fed (quantities of salted pork and dry bread, a far cry from the home cooking he longed for), the snoring and coughing of the men around him at night and his trouble sleeping on a military cot, the mosquitoes—"big as cats," he wrote, and the girls had quite a laugh over this—that filtered into the old barracks on steamy September evenings and lingered till dawn, and already, the growing menace of lice that no soldier would escape.

His uniform came out of a massive bundle shipped in from a Northern factory. The men had to choose from three sizes and make do. George's pants needed hemming, and he thanked me for my sewing lessons but was glad to report that he got help from the group's new bugler! It turns out Max Coble landed that job.

Six years prior, Max was the young apprentice who helped tailor George's new suit for our wedding, and I admired his work. My husband cared about his appearance, and I was glad to know that apart and away from my sewing skills, my man's uniform had been properly fitted and finished.

George bragged on and on about Valentine performing like a queen in the endless military exercises that weighed down their hours. He wrote that the talk at every meal was charged with grumbling from men bored and fed up with drill after drill, anxious to get down to the business of facing the enemy that at times camped only miles away.

The army was not nearly as organized as he expected, but there was sure agreement in his company that their captain had to be among the best a bunch could hope for. George seldom wrote about anyone in particular, except for those he rode closest to, and his captain. His letters never held an unkind word about Captain Horner. I think Company C was fortunate in this instance, for I later learned of more than a few in charge who were bad apples, as it is in so much of life.

He missed us, he dreamed of his bed and my breakfasts, he would soon be home.

We wrote back to George every Sunday, even though there was nothing much new in town to talk of beyond the fear continuing to take root and spread with every report of a battle or some new military threat coming from the South. I did not want him to know I was worried about money matters. The first of the checks from his army service came much later than promised, and I fretted that surely in time they would stop arriving at all.

The girls drew and scribbled in the margins of the paper, "writing" to their Papa that they were waiting for him to come back for piggy-backs and Saturday baths when he could sing *"O Susanny"* to them. I tried to keep his face fresh in their innocent minds any way I could figure, and I was not above painting stories about Valentine that made it sound like she and Papa were enjoying themselves on a sort of patriotic holiday complete with waving flags and singing. I knew better.

Charles Tyson made the silvered miniature here the summer before George left. The soft sheen of his face stood guard at our table every day, so that he would be present with us whenever we were in the room, sunrise to sunset. Come nighttime, I would carry his picture up to rest on our bedroom bureau.

I see my young husband's character in this image, assured and steady, his expression one of calm confidence. I have always held that Tyson captured the essence of George in that moment. This tintype was the best I could manage to feel close to him once he mustered.

But a picture is only a symbol, a remembrance. Without his flesh-and-bone presence in the house, Sadie and Mollie could not hold on to the sound of their Papa's voice in their heads, and to them my singing was a poor substitute. Heartbroken Sadie cried about this inconsolably for a stretch of nights, until she forgot to cry any more and put up with her mama's voice that was "not as sure as Papa's."

It was not until after the men mustered out in September that I first walked through the doorway of the Union Relief Society meetings. Being newest to the table, the youngest woman in the room, a well-to-do German farmer's daughter—maybe all of that made it harder for me to break into their circle. But I was sure of my skill with a needle, and I was one of only a few in town who owned a sewing machine, quite the newest thing back then.

When I first joined them and shared the news of my Singer with the ladies, I saw two of them steal a glance at each other with their eyebrows raised as if to say, "Well!" I took their suspicion of me as a challenge, and if anything, it made me more determined, more cocksure in standing up to their coolness. The way I figured it, my skills and my husband off fighting on their behalf were enough for me to stand eye to eye with them. Patriotism could come in handy that way.

The women met at the Methodist church three times a week to stitch and quilt, fold and pack up what was finished and brought in from our homes. Get a group of women together, and see how much time passes before a tempest brews. Week to week, there would be disagreements over the smallest detail, from the proper way to attach a collar or sleeve, to the right way to fold a shirt. There were stubborn opinions on how to properly pack a barrel to be shipped off to the troops.

They even haggled over military strategies, as though they understood warfare by reading a newspaper story. Some of those women grew fierce in their disagreements, and there was one who would put her hands over her ears pretty much every meeting when things got too shrill for her.

Lydia Harper read Scripture at the beginning of our weekly gatherings, I suppose hoping to keep harmony in the room. She took her position as secretary of the group very seriously and never failed to remind us that she would not tolerate us picking at each other when we gathered to work. But in the end, she had little power over her volunteers or the tempests that blew up in that room.

I was there the afternoon one of the more august ladies pushed back from the table and stood with tears swelling in her eyes. She looked around at us like we were all as wrong as rain, then marched out in a huff, slamming the church door behind her. She never did return to the group. I cannot remember who she was or the subject of the spat, but I can still hear the sharp chop of her shoes across the wood floor.

I completed more than a hundred shirts that autumn. The steady rhythm of the Singer passed the time and helped sooth me into some calm. It must be what a rosary does for folks, quieting them in the prayers and counting of the beads, again and again, until a sort of peaceful trance sets in.

I needed a purpose beyond the house and the girls to settle me, and sewing fit the need. From the upstairs window where my worktable sat to catch the light, I could follow the passings below—horses, mothers and children, workmen with their tools in tow. Nonie would be at her chores downstairs as the girls played in their room next to me, their voices drifting out into the sunlit hallway.

From the start, Sadie and Mollie were most times the pleasantest of playmates, content with each other's company for hours on end and seldom misbehaved for Nonie. George and I were blessed with the girls' even temperaments.

I believe that my machine made me the finest and fastest shirt maker in the circle, and it was just as well that I was not singled out for it. It would only have led to the spark of envy flaring up and igniting another argument. But I knew what I knew.

Ma was a fast quilter and proud of her neat work, but quilting was never for me. It felt like going in slow circles, working the needle around and around, piece after piece. The forwardness of a straight, long seam was more to my liking, neat lines of connection and completion in short order from one point to the next, like working a row of carrots or beets. So I was not among the quilters who had a longer history of teamwork.

The Relief ladies could finish a coverlet faster than I had ever seen. Leave it to them and their quiet voices rising and falling with the gliding climb and descent of their fingers, drawing the needle through the colors that would keep some Union man warm on an icy night. There was a grace to it, like watching a band of dancers move in unison, each move adding a new piece to some ancient story. A finished quilt would be sent off to some unknown soldier to comfort him in circumstances we could only speculate on.

As autumn took a turn toward winter, summer's patriotism

had lost much of its steam, at least for me. With each passing day the papers made it clearer and clearer to us that the fighting was not going to be over and done with by Christmas, that in reality there was no end in sight for the mess we were mired in, no end to the mounting threats pushing at us from the South. Lists of the dead and wounded, the missing and captured, began to appear in *The Sentinel,* and even though I seldom recognized names, it made my heart sink to scan the page.

George wrote of the cold weeks they were training in along the Potomac, of missing his warm bed on Baltimore Street, how his group had taken on the name "Keystone Rangers" and how he liked the sound of that. His company had a new captain, a distant cousin he had never met, an Albert Hunter. By then our letters were no longer mentioning the possibility of a homecoming.

The letters grew thinner as we read of the pockets of fighting in locations unfamiliar to our ears. The papers listed an Emmitsburg man as the company's first death, also something George never wrote to me about. Where was my husband the hour this first man died? Was he witness to his comrade falling?

I never cared much about the details of the endless battles in the news. I do not care now. But I knew that George was in harm's way. I read that once his company left Frederick it was charged with guarding telegraph lines. Then… let me think…Bunker Hill, Winchester, Shenandoah, Harpers Ferry a second time, Charleston—places that once would have sounded like exotic destinations but now took on a charge of danger for me, powder keg spots where our darlings might meet their end.

I wondered if George caught a glimpse of the famous general people still talk about, Thomas Jackson, outside the town of Martinsville the same time the papers said George's unit was there. Years later, I heard more than once about "Stonewall" and how close a bond he had with Robert E. Lee, that had Jackson not died when he did, he may have led the Confederates to victory in the Gettysburg melee and turned the tide of the whole business.

My prayers for George at what seemed a great distance began to feel flat, even though I tried to keep a vision conjured in my thoughts of him straight-backed in Valentine's saddle, earnest and alert, his sack coat cinched and his hair smoothed and crowned with a Union hat. *Sehnte*—such a longing I had for him to be warm enough, fed enough, well enough, rested enough, safe enough to make it back to us. ❧

Chapter 10

THAT FIRST CHRISTMAS without George beside us was *duster*—a somber affair for me. In December I hung greens in the parlor as everyone else had and brought in a small tree to decorate for Sadie and Mollie's sake. But the gay decorations brought me scant pleasure.

I was glad to have us be in my folks' company for the celebration, if you could call it that. Pa drove into town to transport the girls and me out to the farm, where Ma had covered the table with her best damask soon to be set with a feast George's company, miles away, would have lusted over.

By then the shelves of the town's shops had thinned of some goods, what with the war effort, but Pa surprised us that day with oranges for the girls' stockings. He had cut their Christmas tree from the copse out back, and it stood at attention on the table in the big room, hung with ribbon and paper chains, much to the girls' delight.

That afternoon, I helped set out the Weikert German china heaped with some of my husband's favorites—the *Himmel und*

Erde that George proclaimed the finest potato-apple mash he had ever tasted (and believe me, my Ma drank up his compliments), ham-hocked green beans, the pickled peaches and beets she spiced and canned in the heat of summer's end for her Christmas table, cornbread, and as always, a plump goose, mince pie, and bread-and-sorghum pudding. You can imagine my drinking in the beauty of her bounty, breathing in its fragrance. I find myself thinking more and more of her tables. Nothing could ever measure up to the feasts Ma laid out.

My brother Levi had not yet signed up to fight, so really it was only George's whereabouts that hung in the air as we gathered at the table. Here we sat enjoying Ma's offerings with our clean hands and warm feet while my husband was eating who knows what in some cold army tent far from his family.

To think that we planned to be on Baltimore Street together, the four of us, this very Christmas day, and I could not even be let in on the details of where he was posted that December.

St. James and a couple of the other churches in town sent off barrels of frozen turkeys and canned goods to make the camp Christmas a bit homier for the beloveds missing from their gatherings. I posted a smaller box to George with a ham and his favorite fruitcake and more socks, but I never heard if it even reached him or if he was ever to enjoy the contents.

After dinner we gathered closer to the hearth and lit the tree's candles long enough to sing *"Tannenbaum"* and *"Stille Nacht."* My brother had carved a little pine donkey for Sadie and a lamb for Mollie, and that evening they both fell asleep by the fire's glow clutching their manger animals.

Pa carted us home in the bitter cold the next day. The town was buzzing with news that a trainload of some eight hundred cavalrymen from New York had arrived Christmas night and stayed at the station to sleep in their barren train cars. Not much of a holiday celebration for them, would you say? They were known as the Porter Guards, with Henry Hayes, their lieutenant, at the helm of the company in training to make their way to the battlefront.

That Christmas, (for that matter, the whole of December and January) was too frigid around the countryside for what it took to set up camps, and in the afternoon David McConaughy came to our door to see if I might let a batch of the soldiers billet in the tenpin alley. I was not the only one in the string of households he approached. Well, of course I said yes. I would hope someone might do the same for George somewhere if he were in these boys' shoes on a winter's night.

The men were no bother and took care of themselves out there, even hunting down and loading in their own firewood and vittles. People like me all around town who boarded them felt the same. They were a handsome, polite bunch to have around us.

The Witherow girls a few doors down from us—now, what were their names... They were not the only ones to catch the soldiers' attention. Happy gossip on our streets was of nothing else that January, as though this was a weeks-long party thrown solely for the young ladies of Gettysburg. The Guards' band of musicians put on evening concerts here and there as a show of their gratitude for our generous hospitality. The Porter boys refueled a patriotic fire that had begun to languish in our breasts over the bleak months.

That summer, before George left, he had lined up the slaughter of the one pig we would fatten behind our new house, and at the beginning of November, I had enough meat put up to last us through the winter. More than once my girls and I lugged supper out back to our boarders, a pot of stew and a basket of breads still warm from the oven. You would have thought I was setting out a fancy Christmas banquet, the way they praised us.

A woman needs to hear that she is appreciated, and with George's absence, compliments over my food were scarce. But that day I was grateful to be the lady of the house, to sense their protective presence around us, to share what we had and to field their kind words. I suppose it made me feel like I was making some small contribution to the war effort. Serving a hot supper to them breathed some warmth into my cold winter.

One frigid night mid-January, I hosted supper for my eighteen, all of them coming through the doorway groomed and tidy in their uniforms, including Matthew Avery, a kind man of rank with a sad and handsome countenance. The sound of the men's voices in the parlor was a welcome one on a winter's night, and they reeled in Sadie and Mollie with their stories and games.

Likely some of them were missing a younger brother or sister, or maybe their own child. I felt such a sharp pang as I stood watching my unlikely guests in the parlor. I can remember the weight of that evening, as real as a blow to my gut, a fresh reminder of George's distance from us since September, and a longing for him to see his hospitable house and its mistress holding court.

After the eating, one of them stood to sing, and the rest joined in. Considering the hours they spent holed up together in the alley out back, they must have sung a great deal like this. Their harmonies went straight to my eyes brimming with tears, as I leaned against the doorway, my girls pressed into me. Sadie recognized the tune her Papa sang, and she looked up with her honeyed smile and squeezed my hand. We were still as statues, the whole houseful, till they finished their slow lullaby. Do you know this one?

> *I gave my love a cherry without a stone*
> *I gave my love a chicken without a bone*
> *I gave my love a ring that had no end*
> *I gave my love a baby with no crying*

After a bit, one of the younger boys stood and cleared

his throat and let his voice go clear and dulcet as a meadow bird, a new song he said he learned from his auntie in upstate. Such beauty.

> *My latest sun is sinking fast, my race is nearly run*
> *My strongest trials now are past, my triumph has begun*
> *Oh come Angel Band, come and around me stand*
> *Oh bear me away on your snow white wings*
> *to my immortal home*

I took in the soldier's gift of song, but I dared not let my thoughts go to George being born away in the arms of an angel. I would do my best to put the boy's beautiful tune out of my mind. But of course, there was that pure voice etching his music right into the center of my thoughts when I lay down to sleep that night.

By the end of the month, the men's barracks were readied on the edge of town, but the soldiers lingered on our streets until spring—March, if I recall. We came to depend on seeing them suited up and milling in the Diamond and stopping in to chat up the merchants and customers, especially the young pretty ones. I suppose they made us feel safer than we should have. I can tell you, it was sad to see them finally pack off for the front.

The day they were to depart, Captain Avery showed up at my front door. He had taken up a modest collection from the boys who stayed out back, a kind of token in gratitude for my hospitality to them over the weeks. I will admit that I felt a snag of guilt about inviting him in, as he doffed his hat and wiped his boots at the entryway. It was not proper for me to be alone with a man like that. But already by then I was regarding the opinions of others less and less. Let the neighbors think what they would.

Sadie and Mollie raced down the stairs when they heard his voice, and they were shy and pleased with the sight of our familiar guest. He had candies in his pocket for them that they carted back upstairs like precious jewels when I sent them off to play in their room.

The moment presented itself as an opportune one for sharing a parting gift with someone headed into what he was, and I fetched the bottle of Pa's peach brandy from the kitchen, the one he sent home with me that Christmas. I would offer a proper send-off to the good captain.

As he and I settled across from each in the parlor, we talked of his young betrothed and the bookshop waiting for his return in Vermont, of my husband and our girls and our hopes for George's businesses opening when the war ended. When he lifted a glass, I joined him in a toast: To the swift end of sad separations. He seemed a tender man, and it warmed me to be in quiet conversation with him for that hour.

At the door, he took my hand in parting and did not say goodbye, but only paused, then finally said, "Thank you, Mrs.

Shriver." Only that. I stood on the stoop in the crisp sunshine, and my eyes followed his form heading up Baltimore Street until he turned, and then was gone.

He would gather his men to leave that afternoon for some killing field unknown to the rest of us, and in their wake, a deep melancholy would settle alongside the town's gratitude that would linger for weeks. To no longer see them uniformed and milling around us, to hear their music and laughter and polite greetings—their departure left a gaping hole in our spirits. There were more than a few young women bereft with a beau's farewell.

I sorely missed the presence of a man in the house with George gone month after month. I was never to receive any further word from Captain Avery, nor was I ever to learn of his fate. I long wondered if he made his way home to his books, if he married his young woman, if he raised a New England family after the fighting ended. Or had an angel band interrupted all that might have been for him?

There are few veterans to speak of it anymore, and at any rate I am glad to not hear their stories, those who care to speak of it. I have always avoided even walking past their "temples," those fine Grand Army of the Republic gathering houses. They come and go and sit for long stretches in the sun out in front of their meetings halls—frail, bearded old scarecrows who have aged right along with me and are not a balm to my senses or to anyone else's. Even the sight of one of their military medals hanging on a lapel brings to mind unwanted memories I would rather not dredge up.

It is not that I think their sacrifices were worth nothing. On the contrary, what was taken on by those men, those boys, for the sake of preserving their young country's unity was no small thing. If anyone went the extra mile, it was them.

But how many Georges died for the cause, without knowing what the fate of it all would be? How many women like me were widowed? How many children would never see their fathers again on this side of life?

I can get a bitter taste in me thinking of what the lawmakers in Washington were up to while the fighting dragged on and on—those soft-handed men who likely enjoyed a proper Christmas dinner in their warm homes, returning to rows of tidy, important law-making desks to cast their votes and keep the war churning for months on end. I wondered, did they ever put pen to paper to tally the cost of their edicts before they lit the fuse of war? How many of them had to lose a loved one and grieve like we, the left behind, did?

No, I do not want to hear the death tallies, and I never did. But in the end, the stories cannot all be avoided. I have read enough to know that I cannot take in the notion of that many deaths. So many of them still boys, really; so many of them dying from disease a world away from their kin, suffering in filthy army camps before they even got the chance to take up a gun.

I know that more words have been written about Gettysburg's week of hell than anyone could possibly read, most of them written by men, with their various details seldom lining up about the where's and when's of it all, re-living the horror of it years later as though they were writing about the glory days of Rome.

The town women saw little of the actual fighting, you know. Like me, they were busy keeping watch over those who took the bullet's blast and did not die outright. Our stories would not be nearly so exciting to read.

Like obedient servants, we did what we were expected to do: cooked, fed, washed, tried to comfort the ones who were still alive, lined up before us in churches and barns, on school room and parlor floors, our senses burning with the nightmare around us that would take root in our minds for the rest of our scarred lives.

So I cannot write with any certainty about what general ordered a charge, what banner bearer fell on the fields by Pa's woods, who was a hero and who was not. I can only tell you what I *think* I lived through that week. It was so long ago.

I do not know where George was stationed during the brief and unending hours that stripped our family's dreams and hopes bare. And what if his unit *had* been part of the town's grisly fighting? Would it have changed a lick of anything? In the end, what did George Shriver's life count for in the Great Civil War, or on the quiet streets of Gettysburg?

By that summer, I had long given up counting the days, the weeks, from the autumn morning when we watched George's company shrink into the horizon. I had stopped attaching an end date to the morass. I had no choice but to keep toiling on, trying to stir around the fading embers of self-assurance inside me as best I could and maybe draw some warmth in the flickering thought that my husband might soon return and put an end to our separation. ❧

Chapter 11

As DAUNTING AS IT FEELS to be writing my remembrances of that sad week, I am somehow driven to lay as much order to the carnage that put civility on hold from Pa's fields to Baltimore Street. Was there ever a darker time in a farm town's history than those savage days?

You cannot imagine how still summer mornings were in Gettysburg back then. Nothing like Harrisburg, or Baltimore, or whatever this place is I am kept now. It seems that here no one sleeps any more, and the street lamps are seldom dimmed.

Ah, but back then...Then you could hear the buzz of a bee across our back gardens, working its way from rose to rose and looping in and out of my squash blossoms. The lilt of a neighbor's voice, the seminary bell, a horse's whinny down Baltimore Street, the bleating of lambs from fields far outside of town. I seldom stopped to drink in the peace of it all.

But like the worker bees in my gardens, all that June folks were spreading disquieting rumors of the war coming to our town, of soldiers—Blue and Grey—about to appear with their mighty army machines to threaten our tranquil streets where our children played. You know this, that similar to gossip, speculation can spark quiet fears into hungry fires of terror, whether or not any of it is based in truth.

I slept poorly from the time George first left us to join his company. I did. But those late summer nights before all hell broke loose and we heard that the rebs had crossed into Pennsylvania, I seldom found any real rest to speak of.

I would hear the peaceful rhythm of my girls' breathing, tucked in and deep in sleep in their room across the way, while I lay in my bed, eyes staked wide awake in the darkness and my insides racked with a trepidation I have never known since. Thinking back, those sleepless hours became the foundation for the sadness that my life would become, nightly premonitions that I would lose more than I could muster the courage to consider.

Our bedroom, George's and mine, had been such a focus of pride for me, long before I had paged through the *Godey's* magazines to gather ideas for all my new rooms. Butter yellows and royal blues, sunset pinks and gossamer greens—its pages described a candy-shop of color for me to choose from and imagine onto our walls. And each time the goods came in, I cannot think I ever was disappointed with what I had ordered. I have already told you this, but that space was such a dear haven to George and me.

The room came together like a landscape, with Mother

Shriver's wedding gift—the Hausman coverlet—gracing our bed, its colors enhanced by the paper patterns that hung on the fresh-plastered walls that I can still smell in my mind. There was something so lyrical about that room, especially when I pushed open the windows to usher in the morning breeze. I lavished the sun on my arms when I gathered the drapes back for a look down Baltimore Street. George would be working away in the cellar two floors below while the girls played in the hallway. Nonie would put away breakfast and sweep the kitchen and sitting room. Such order, such peace. This was my young life, and it was beauty to me.

But in the sleepless nights of late June, alone in our bed and worried over my husband's well-being and what our fragile future might not hold, the room had once and for all lost its charm for me. As though holding its breath, the hue of the wall covering, the feel of the linens against my skin, all of what had once brought such pleasure was now a colorless winter's gray to me, heavy and lifeless in the night's stillness.

"If it comes to it, what shall I do when the Seceshes return? What if they burst their way into my house? What would George have me do?" My mind raced around like a crush of bees swarming a hive, with threat upon threat darting at me. Fear is such a powerful thing. There is nothing else like it in this life.

The town teetered endlessly between disbelief and terror. But the war coming to our streets should not have been a surprise to anyone, when I look back on it.

Gettysburg was at the center of a great circle with a good ten roads leading into it.

People would describe it as spokes on a wagon wheel that led straight downtown. We were a bullseye, really, a perfect target and a short crow's flight from the imaginary line that separated the North from the South.

Catherine next door would show up in my garden and set out a full serving of the worst possibilities: the enemy returning to stave in our doors, holding knives to our throats, menacing our children. "They passed through to get a lay of the land," she warned. "And you think they will not come back!? Mark my words!"

Catherine was sure she was on to something, because she could not get her mind or her jabbering off the rebs' visit earlier that week. Truth is, it was a fright, half of them whooping and hollering and pounding through town like filthy cowboys, some of them shoeless, tearing down our streets, kicking up dust and shocking us into our houses. They worked their way from shop to shop, looting what they could if no one was present and its goods not yet removed for safekeeping to some other town.

But if a merchant should meet them at the door, there would be some manner of bargaining and goods "purchased" with worthless Confederate money. Boots and hats, sweets and coffee, the whole scene like a carnival of armed clowns lumbering around town on their horses, juggling their ill-be-gotten goods.

We all more or less stayed out of danger that day. I know some folks actually invited a few of them in to sit at their table for supper, if you can imagine that. By afternoon, the streets grew quiet and the rebs were holed up here and there. You can guess how unsettled we were, as though we could feel the very heat of their breath down our backs. By the time they left town the next day they had set in motion a new wake of fear that was well-fanned by hearsay.

We had three days to worry ourselves sick at the thought of their likes returning to Gettysburg to do worse. But then at the same time, enough hours passed for the *Gerüchte*—rumors and more rumors—to come to nothing. And once again we exhaled and began to think we might not be in harm's way after all.

That last morning in June, before things all boiled over, I remember lying already awake in a leery dawn, like the daylight knew something was afoot. After breakfast, I combed over the gardens as I did every morning. Not that what day it was or what the weather was should matter to anyone—but Tuesday is burned into my mind. The skies had been weepy for a good long while, and that morning, the last day of the month, you could feel the heat settling down into the streets like a brooding hen. When the ruckus started up again outside of town, the fear demon reared up its ugly head.

Nonie had not shown up at the house to work for more

than a week. I saw her people packing their lives out of town and up into the hills. They had a greater price on their heads than we could imagine, and as much as I wished she were there to help me tackle chores, I think already by then I understood and forgave her absence.

That morning the familiar cadence of marching and men's voices in the distance drifted toward the house. But quick as a wink, word spread on the streets that this was not the rebels returning. Catherine called out to me, and we both could see across the way that it was the Union boys coming to town, Buford's cavalry passing through, *our* troops coming to protect us. I called the girls out to me from the back steps, and with their hands clasped tightly in mine, we scurried out front and over to Washington Street to join a congregation of folks fiercely cheering for the Union.

It seemed the whole town was turned out, and what a sight it was. The uniformed must have outnumbered the civilians ten times over that morning. Girls were singing, handkerchiefs and flags were waving, spirits were high.

The troops marched in endless columns straight out of town, a long, impressive parade of them, smiling and waving back at us as they passed. We naively assumed that if there was going to be any fighting, it would be far enough away for Gettysburg, our children and homes and gardens, to be duly protected. Surely now with these troops nearby we would not be drawn into the unimaginable.

I was silently full of hope that I might scout George's company in that trail of soldiers, but they were not among the marchers. Disappointment and nagging questions were all that I returned home with.

But, what did I know of military strategy or of what lay ahead? We went to bed that night clueless about how our life on Baltimore Street was to be turned on its head. Our safety was not to be. The "elsewhere" we had in mind for gunfire and the clash of swords would be right there on the streets of our quiet hamlet.

Without Nonie in the kitchen the next morning, the Wednesday chores were again mine alone to take on. Before I even finished the sweeping, I was stopped short by rumbling clatter and the squeak of the wheels of a long line of Union cavalry wagons moving down our street. You would think we would be prepared to hear it, but we were not.

By 9 o'clock, the crack of guns being fired from Seminary Ridge filled the skies and within an hour was joined by the jarring of cannon fire from further outside town. Fighting in the fields west of us was close enough to rattle our windows, and in the distance, tufts of battle smoke began to hang in the skies like clouds of lambs wool.

Sadie and Mollie were now thistled to my skirts, their countenance pale, eyes wide, and their innocent faces frozen in fright. If George were there with me, what would he urge us to do?

Panic mounted on the streets out front, with shouts that we were in the direct pathway of the shelling. And then the rebels were back on our streets, shrieking warnings for us to take shelter in our cellars or, better yet, to clear on out of town.

All night long I had weighed thoughts of getting us out to Pa's farm, far enough south that the girls and I surely would be safer than we were on Baltimore Street. It seemed the whole town was trembling as though it was on the verge of exploding. Now I scurried into action to pack a basket. "We'll picnic on the way to Oma's," I told the girls, hoping to put their fears to rest. I grabbed George's picture and pitched in the bundle of jewelry and household money I had gathered days before, should this moment come to pass.

The girls stayed perched obediently on the parlor loveseat while I hastened over to the Pierces' to tell them my decision. Their youngest girl, Tillie, was standing with her parents in the parlor, pale with fright. I asked them if they would like their daughter to go along with me, and without hesitation, it was decided that she would be safer away from the chaos. She and my sister were acquainted, and out there, companionship would be a comfort to them both.

I could see behind them that they had already bundled up some of their belongings to stash out of the rebels' grasp. But in the rush of the moment, we decided she need not take anything along. After hasty farewells, Tillie and I retrieved the girls and I made one more quick survey of our house. I remember to this day how that moment seemed much like when I stood with George at the front door a couple of years earlier. I was leaving our "fine place," God be with it.

It could have been an ordinary July first as the four of us set out that hot morning. You could still see a few birds flapping in the branches above us as the sound of gunfire swelled. Down Baltimore to the cemetery, a great gathering of Union army men occupied the anxious grounds, scurrying, shouting, as chaotic a scene as I had ever in this life beheld.

We turned onto Taneytown, and an ambulance wagon rattled past us. Thankfully my girls could not see up inside where the jolting passenger lay motionless. I knew at once that the gray-skinned officer caked in drying blood could not be alive. You could gather as much by the faces of the two soldiers bent over him. It was a frightening foretaste of what lay ahead.

All the comings and goings of troops and wagons had rutted those muddy roads along the way into what seemed like canyons. We marched on, staying up on whatever grass we could manage. We were about to pass the Widow Leister's house, and you could see it had already been taken over as some sort of Union headquarters.

A young soldier came flying out the door and beckoned us to scurry in, out of danger's way. Quick as a wink he was back out to the road and ended up badgering a passing wagon driver to pile us into it and deliver us out to the safety of the Weikert farm. The cart was already filled to the brim with muddied soldiers, yet somehow that driver relented. We sat cheek by jowl with the rest and soon felt as though our very teeth were being jarred loose by the wheels plunging in and out of the deepening gullies.

But soon enough our wagon pulled up at Pa's gate, and there came Ma dashing out the door to gather the girls to her and rush us inside to safety. I was distressed to find the pounding cannon fire to be even worse at Pa's than it was in town. An unending stream of Union infantry was pouring past as we clamored into the house. With the army's protection, you would think we would be safer here, spared of the gunfire we had escaped on Baltimore Street.

But the pounding of cannon fire was only growing, and we felt anything but safe.

The swirl of explosions in the fields around us swelled more threatening by the minute, and already wounded soldiers were being carried through the gate and into the house or out to the bank barn. What in the world was I thinking to leave our nest, our haven in town for this bedlam?

In Ma's dining room, a surgeon—the first one was called Dr. Billings—was seeing to the wounded, some of whom were dying before they made it through the doorway, some still alive and heaving in pain. He directed the hefting and hauling of the injured, and you could hear his sharp commands to his assistants who, I am sure, were doing the best they could manage.

We kept threading our way through the cluttered chaos of

what had hours earlier been an ordered and clean house, kept up to Ma's demanding standards. Traipsing down the steps into her cellar kitchen, we joined my sister toiling away at bread-making, the stove fired up and Ma's slices of the baked loaves already lined up on the table.

I would take over for Beckie as I set her and Tillie to watch over Sadie and Mollie, to distract them from the horrors growing around us while I helped at the stove. As was the same for me, Ma's Colored girls were nowhere to be found that week. Those people had wisely flown like a flock of crows before the first shot was fired.

Poor Pa, his shirt soaked in sweat, rushed in and out of the house, something he continued all that week, while Ma held the reins over the pressing business of feeding the growing mass of wounded. Eventually we sent Beckie and Tillie off to make themselves useful elsewhere, since my girls would not venture to leave my side. The drama swirling around us inside the house was nothing they could make sense of. And outside the cellar windows, it was no better.

Between the baking and the girls playing under the table and the wails of the wounded pouring down on us from upstairs, this is all I can recall with any clarity of our first day at the house.

The whole farm was pounded and trembling with the explosive cracks of battle. But, oh, the horrifying shrieks of the wounded being carried off the fields and in and out of the house for the surgeon's work. It was unlike anything I had ever heard. I can hear it inside me as I write these words.

Around dusk that first night, a wounded officer was hauled through the cellar door to be laid out across from us in the corner of the room. A young soldier parked himself there, dutifully holding a candle in the dying daylight, the scene like an old painting that could have been titled "Vigil of the Brave."

Even by the dim light of the lanterns, you could see the man's fine uniform was soaked in blood and mud. From where I stood by the stove, I watched Tillie kneel down twice to linger over him, once while the attendant went out to relieve himself.

Those nights were not for sleeping. The sultry air was heavy with the rotten-sweet waft of chloroform and pooling blood in the house, and with the stale cannon smoke that hung above the fields. Gunfire and cannon booms may have been quieted by nightfall, but the unbroken wails of the wounded swirled around us so steadily that we could have sworn the very treetops were pulsing with the howls of spirits.

How the surgeons toiled on into the night without rest I never understood. But they did. It seemed to never cease, the rasp of those *verdammt* saws from above us that severed the shattered legs and arms that got tossed into mounds outside the dining room window and, come daybreak, to get moved and piled alongside the picket fence.

There was no room for us to bed down upstairs, and I made

a nest of flour sacks for the girls to sleep at my feet beneath Ma's table. Tillie and my sister trundled up to the garret to try to find a spot to sleep. The best Ma and I could manage was to lay our heads down on the table for whatever rest might come, despite the distant sounds of men's voices and wood being chopped for the campfires dotting the landscape all around us. And, of course, the unrelenting commotion of suffering that ringed the house.

I woke to the officer's soft gasping from over in the corner, and without a thought I rose and made my way to his side, where his attendant still kept vigil. What else could be done but to ask if there was anything he desired. The words of that dying gentleman are still in me. "Yes, m'am. Could you pray the Our Father with me?"

His hand kept roving between his neck and his side, back and forth almost as though he was trying to make the Catholic sign of the cross—not a part of our Lutheran ways. But then his fingers found my hand to grasp hold of it, and I held on as together we murmured that worn-out prayer.

And then something I never did in front of anyone except for George and my girls: I sang. To a dying stranger in the middle of the night.

George liked singing even more than he liked rhyming. He told me he fancied my voice, even though I was shy of it. I saved my singing for alone times in the garden or for hanging the wash, and now for the girls' bedtimes. But that night, I sang steady and clear to this man, like it came natural, un-ashamed, as though I had known him all my life.

> *What wondrous love is this, O my soul, O my soul!*
> *What wondrous love is this, O my soul!*
> *What wondrous love is this that caused the Lord of bliss*
> *To bear the dreadful curse for my soul, for my soul,*
> *To bear the dreadful curse for my soul.*

"Please….." he whispered. "Please go on…"

> *When I was sinking down, sinking down, sinking down,*
> *When I was sinking down, sinking down,*
> *When I was sinking down beneath God's troublin' frown,*
> *Christ laid aside His crown for my soul, for my soul,*
> *Christ laid aside His crown for my soul.*

I leaned in close enough to feel his shallow breath on my cheek for my final verse, for the man's ear alone:

> *And when from death I'm free, I'll sing on, I'll sing on;*
> *And when from death I'm free, I'll sing on.*
> *And when from death I'm free I'll sing His love for me,*
> *And through eternity I'll sing on, I'll sing on,*
> *And through eternity I'll sing on.*

A few moments of quiet passed before he rasped, "Thank you, sister," and after a pause, "I am thirsty." The attendant handed me the cup of water he fetched hours earlier, but the officer was staring off to some place distant to us. Still he gripped my hand as though I might have the power to keep him tethered to this world.

Who knows where words come from in a moment like that? I turned to ask the attendant his officer's name, and then I whispered, "Stephen, all will be well. We are here with you, and the morning is not far off." With my other hand I dipped the corner of my apron into the attendant's cup of water and dabbed his officer's face. His breathing had all but stopped. Then his body shuddered, only to settle back into stillness, his grip loosened, and he was gone. I remember thinking, "Oh the appetite of war! Oh the sting of death!"

That poor, wearied young guard had a time of it pulling himself together. With his dirty sleeve, he wiped the tears from his face over and over until he heaved a heavy sigh and staggered to his feet to go for help to move the body out of the cellar.

The horizon outside was not yet smeared with light. I must have sat there in the holy darkness with Stephen for another hour before a bloodied stretcher was wrestled in the cellar door. The three young soldiers, without a word passing among them, struggled to hoist their officer's broken remains onto it.

I did not know this dead man, but I felt as emptied as if I

did, watching them lift his body out into the night to lay it to a temporary rest on the front stoop with the others. It could have been George. It could have been him that passed into glory in the lantern glow in some stranger's cellar miles from Baltimore Street.

Tillie woke later that morning. I watched her come down the steps and look to the corner for the officer. From across the room I told her that he had died peacefully in the middle of the night and that his body was lying covered on the front porch. She broke into a mighty cry and went on and on about her promise to talk with him in the morning, how she should have been there, as though her very presence might have changed how things ended for him.

That poor, young, foolish girl! I told her to hush her voice, that her weeping was the last thing the others needed to hear. But at that moment—and she surely was not aware of this—I think she wept for the both of us, and maybe for a family waiting somewhere, a hopeful mother, or a wife very much like me, or two little girls, a Sadie and Mollie, who would never again hear their father sing to them.

Up there in the breaking dawn, Stephen Weed lay shoulder to shoulder with a dead comrade whose name I would learn of years later. Patrick O'Rorke was a colonel from New York that Pa read about. He said the Irishman was known for having helped lead the flank that pushed the rebs back down the smaller of the hills by the farm, the one we called Sugar Loaf.

Some say the two of them and their acts of bravery were a key turning point in the fighting. Weed and O'Rorke had fallen near one another in battle, and for a time they rested side by side, covered in the early morning's brief silence on Pa's porch.

Stephen Weed was a brigadier general from New York. That is all I was to learn of him. Had he a wife or children? There was no way for me to search out more about that, or what his work or his life outside an army uniform was. Men like Stephen and the Irishman had "gone twain" as it says somewhere in the Bible. They fought the second mile to the finish line. And with their final efforts, they were ushered from this life.

*   *   *

By the time morning broke hot and clear, more troops were teeming past the farm and heading north toward town. The barn was jammed with bleeding men, army nurses scurrying to make useful what paltry supplies they had. Empty, clattering coffins were delivered, stacked alongside the front fence, like stalking animals of prey, hungry and still and waiting to be filled.

Ma oversaw the unending baking that was emptying her barrels and larder. I stood by the stove overseeing pots of beef tea to send out to the barn for those able enough to swallow it down. Pa kept muttering about *bankrott*—that his "bank was being broken" and that the armies would leave us all in the poorhouse. I kept the girls in the cellar beside Ma and me, since there was no room for us anywhere else in the chaos of the house. Certainly Tillie was of little help in keeping them distracted from what their young eyes and ears were taking in.

By noon, the yard behind the house, churned up and rutted by the prior day's shelling, was overflowing with rows of dead soldiers. None of it seemed real, but there was no escaping that it was.

In the sweltering midday, the cannonading swelled to its heaviest, and we could no longer hear each other in the house. Union dispatchers came to the door and insisted we clear away from the farm since where we stood was the center of the fighting. No sooner had we started out the cellar door on foot than bullets were whirring all around us. Can you imagine the chaos that surrounded us? In the walls of smoke and gunfire we could not hear, we could not see, we certainly could not know what to believe or whose orders to obey.

But we marched on across the field and were about to reach the door of the neighboring farm when a cavalryman charged up and shouted for us to make haste and return to where we had come from. It was clear that there was no safety to be had anywhere for anyone, least of all for the spread of dead men on the fields and thicker yet alongside my folks' barn and all around the farmhouse.

I have often thought about the nurses who tended the wounded in the middle of that mayhem, numb with sleeplessness and no supplies to speak of. They were awash in blood, like the surgeons they labored alongside. Tendon, flesh, bone, blood and more blood—it seemed they all were swimming in a mighty wave of suffering. When would their strength and resources be once and for all drained away? How long could this hell endure?

And those poor wounded ones begging for the surgeon's help, their prayers and curses flowing out sometimes in the same breath! I remember thinking it may well be the dead lined up behind the house who had been shown the greater mercy.

Friday dawned much as Thursday had, with the battle building to a frenzy before the first batches of bread were put in the oven. Pa rushed into the cellar and said the family was ordered to get into the carriages waiting outside to take us down Taneytown to a farmhouse over in Two Taverns. We were so dazed by then, we obeyed like sheep going to slaughter as we left our posts and piled into the buggies together.

Oh the ghoulish sights surrounding us on that ride. In every direction, the fields were strewn with an equal mix of the dead and the walking dead. And those filthy, exhausted rebel prisoners rounded up and standing idle and dumb, as though they were waiting for a train. We wondered if there was a Union prisoner gathering like this nearby, where our boys stood staring and downcast in the hands of their Southern guards.

Now, with the sounds of battle at their loudest, we sat in

that farmhouse crowded with others like us, bewildered and listless, with very little talk passing among us. What good would complaint or argument or discussion have done anyone at that juncture?

By late afternoon, with the fighting subsided, we were hauled back home. The the bodies were so thick along the roads that in places we had to get out of the carriages to make our way around them while the drivers tried their best to get clear of the macabre blockades. As far as the eye could see, all was desolation. There were even more wounded and dying waiting for us at the house, and fresh mounds of severed limbs beside the barn and outside the gate. I tried my best to shield the girls' stares from the bodies we had to step over as we threaded our way through to reach the front door. Instead of the whir of bullets and cannon boom of the afternoon, the sounds of suffering took on a new pitch inside and outside the house. We could do nothing but take up our duties and toil on.

The din of battle had given up the ghost, and in an eerie silence, twilight blanketed the farm. After three eternal days of killing, the fighting was finished. A tiny sliver of a moon hung above us that night when a soldier, who could not have been old enough to grow a whisker on his mud-smudged chin, stood at the cellar door boasting that the skies were clear of bullets and the Southern army was retreating, "limping out of Pennsylvania with their tails between their legs." I remember his scratchy young voice like it was yesterday.

The next few days were a blur of mindless activity, trying to clean up what we could (something that would take months, really), and more of the same endless baking. Ma managed to scrounge bits of cloth from her baskets for us to tear into bandages. Our efforts hardly made a dent in the need.

We all took turns lugging bucket after bucket of water into the house and out to the barn for as long as the well could offer up its holdings. Pa was occupied with his inventory of the ruin, from orchard to barn, field to dining room, bound and determined to tally a good account of all that the Union owed him for the use of his homestead and the loss of livelihood.

Six days had passed since I latched the door of the Baltimore Street house and set out for my folks' farm. In a week's time, the battle had begun and ended, with the armies marching away, leaving the ravages of war in their wake. Like a backwards Bible story, in seven days, all creation had been uncreated in the fields and streets of Gettysburg. ❧

Chapter 12

GETTING MY MIND STRAIGHT and gathering strength enough to leave the farm for town was another story.

"When can we go home?" My girls chirped and nagged at me, like those nestlings you hear every spring, tucked and hidden up above an eave. What could my children understand out of all of that we were mired in? They needed to be plucked out of that nightmare, rest safe and quiet in their own bed, three miles and a world away on Baltimore Street.

It was of no use trying to keep their senses averted from the ravage—the blood caked like batter onto Ma's table and floor, the stacks of severed arms and legs leaning into the fence and teeming with flies, the rattle and slam of coffin delivery, Pa mumbling as he tore around from room to room, wringing his hands with despair over his well, his orchards, his barns.

I could not protect my poor fledglings from the suffocating stench of rot coming off the fields and seeping into Ma's kitchen, into the whole house, even with the windows shut against it in that stifling heat. Nor could I muffle the continued rhythmic draws of the surgeon's saw in the dining room and out on the porch, or the groans pouring out of every quarter. Death had set up camp all around the farm. Surely this landscape of suffering would be seared into the girls' dreams, into *my* dreams—a vault of nightmares to visit us against our sleeping wills.

There was no way the girls could wrap their innocent minds around the hours of horror that had soaked deep into us uninvited. And certainly, they must have believed their home in town would be a safe and quiet nest to return to, that their bed would be waiting exactly as we left it. I had no such expectations, and the sickening ache my gut had taken on only worsened with fears of what would be waiting.

Three days—three endless days—from when we first took shelter in my parents' house, that mud-covered boy of a soldier smirked what we suspected and hoped for. I am not sure there was any relief for us in his edict. For the time we could only carry on, keeping on with our efforts for the dying and dead encircling the farm.

The soldiers who continued in a constant stream by Pa's house were of no use for passing any news we could count on to be accurate. They could not manage to get their stories straight about the state of affairs in town. We gathered that Gettysburg was fast to empty of the lot of soldiers—North and South—who were left whole enough to march away for their next performance in some other unsuspecting town.

My head was in a fog of exhaustion, but I plodded through three more numbing days—hours of baking, stirring, lugging, doing what I could to keep out of the way but still be of use in what was clearly not going to be fixed. The rains continued on and off, drenching the fields into a stew of bloated bodies waiting to be carted off or poorly buried in shallow mudded troughs.

All of us were a sullied mess, and there was not a place or an opportunity to steal away and get cleaned up. The only good thing you could say was that our odor was outdone by the stench of infection and death that won out even over the rankest pig manure you could fathom.

By Monday I knew it was high time to return to Baltimore Street. I could not stay put another day. Ma packed the four of us off with some bits she could scrape from her larder. No one knew what was left for any of us in town. We wondered if there even were passable tracks left for the trains to make their way to Gettysburg. We had no idea what roads were open and safe or what the two armies had left behind in our streets for us to face.

Between the sodden skies and the endless procession of supply wagons and ambulances, cavalry and infantry, the ways leading from the farm were an abyss of rutted mud. Pa's carriage, nobody's carriage would be of any earthly good in the carnage. It was quickest for the girls and me to walk back home.

The four of us took to the newly tamped footpaths alongside the road to best keep our feet from sinking too deeply into the churned up mud that ringed us. We had so often made our way out to my folks to the sound of contented cows and birdsong, surrounded by wildflowers and hayfields. But now as we trudged our way back across the very countryside we came through a week earlier, what we traversed was surely how the highway to hell must appear.

Any distance, any direction we looked, nothing but devastation met our tired eyes.

The land was rutted up into endless jagged heaps and crevasses, trees were split apart and felled, fields trampled and rotting horses and livestock carcasses on all sides, chunks of artillery and abandoned knapsacks and clothing, and as far as the eye could see, mound after mound after jagged mound. The rains were doing their best to wash away enough dirt to display a protruding hand or a blackened foot from a too-quick burial.

I could not believe the sight of the field gleaners, thick as thieves—sweat-drenched curious in groups of two or three who must have followed the rampage in the newspapers. Was the rain and the mud and the stench really worth making their way to Gettysburg? And here they were, prodding at the gore we were walking home through, stepping over death itself to pluck up a button, a hat, a boot. One woman—imagine this if you can—she stood chatting with a man while she wrapped a dead soldier's severed hand in her shawl. What a morbid, shameful thing for us to witness.

There were the others with anxious faces solemnly searching for a son or a husband or a brother, sorting through death's droppings in vain, I think. There was too much ground for them to cover in those sopping fields, too many bodies, blackened and swollen beyond recognition, many of them already being moved elsewhere. It was a scene of confounding confusion, grievous with the heavy odor of death and rot.

Almost right away there were undertakers who flocked to Gettysburg's battlefields to set up their tents and maybe even put an embalmed soldier's body on display to better hawk their services. I did not understand the science of what they were selling to us, but grieving families lined up to put their money down and have their loved one's body preserved by the machines and potions waiting inside. A coffin would then be better able to make its way home in the summer heat for a respectful burial among kin.

I saw only one buzzard in the distance that whole week, tugging at the wool of a soldier's uniform like a spring robin would a worm, undoing someone's pathetic attempt to cover a body in a poor excuse for a grave. Perhaps there were more of its kind working over the dead. I did not return to those fields of flesh for a time to witness nature doing its regular business.

On all sides of us, flies hung in humming curtains, fanning and fueling the sickening odor that would settle over town for weeks to come. The July heat was merciless that day, speeding up the rot of the two armies' leftovers. The stench would take its own good time to lift from the streets of Gettysburg, waiting outside our doors and peering into our closed windows for weeks on end like a drunk beggar.

Lee's army may have been the one that caved in that week, but the Union boys had paid dearly for their victory. And so had the rest of us. Despite the townfolk sounds of celebration—great cheering roars that reached us out at the farm that July 4—I hung back, filled with such anguish at what we had slogged through. I could not find a stitch to cheer about.

When I first learned Tillie Pierce had written years afterward about being a witness to our dark adventure, I found myself somewhere between anger and amusement. I never read her book. I never intended to. She had been a tiresome girl all that week, flitting from soldier to soldier with cups of water for the columns marching past on the road out front. I remember her jabbering and whispering with my sister in the kitchen, giggling one moment, then all weepy and wagging on and on about the wounded in the barns and the dying she tended. She was not of much use to me or my girls. But then it was my idea that day to bring her out there with us. And, frankly, in those circumstances, what use could she have been?

That afternoon I instructed her to do her best to distract Sadie and Mollie on our walk back to town, and she chattered away at them with stories and riddles. I could not tell how well it helped to avert their attention, but it certainly was Tillie's best effort for me that whole week.

They tell me she and her lawyer husband live over near Philadelphia. I would rather not read what she wrote about me from her eyewitness chair. Perhaps if my own story had turned out differently, I would have no qualms about reading the thing.

They say she donated what profits came from her account to help the veterans. Too many soldiers who survived the war could not work because of their injuries and their state of mind, and I would imagine any help on their behalf was welcomed. That is, at least, what I remember of the talk around Tillie and her book.

It was early afternoon when we made our way over cemetery ridge, a sweep of carnage, gravestones toppled and shattered, and everywhere soldiers sitting, standing, bandaged, dirty, wrung out. The seminary's museum building had been turned into a hospital, and more stacks of severed limbs and bloodied rags alive with fly colonies stood heaped as they did outside Ma's window.

Nothing we were walking through was new from what I had already witnessed over the week. Trapped inside for the duration of the fighting, I watched out the cellar window as someone's wandering cow was blown apart in the field across the road, foisted into the air by a cannon ball. I saw a young soldier outside Pa's barn—no more than a boy, really—whose eye caught a bullet, and he labored to scratch out a note to his mother. He was dead by nightfall.

The soldiers laid out their fallen comrades to bury them in Ma's back garden, like so many logs, for *Gott's* sake. I witnessed cities of maggots working dead horses in the fields on our walk back home.

But as we looked down Baltimore Street that day, the buildings peppered by artillery fire, the heavy air putrid and at the same time filled with the sounds of a band playing patriotic songs in the Diamond, I had to step away from the girls to empty the contents of my stomach. Thinking of this now, it was a most appropriate response to the death we had tasted over the past week and now were bathed in that afternoon for our macabre homecoming, strangely set to jaunting music.

The ruin around us was nothing short of Biblical, a smoking desolation teeming with strangers in a strange land that used to be our quiet town.

Up and down the streets, yellow banners hung limply against houses and churches and shops to mark makeshift hospitals holding the wounded. From a distance I could focus my vision on the front of our house with one of those flags hanging from our upstairs hallway window, as though it were part of a citywide laundry day.

Tillie asked if she could run on ahead of us, she was so anxious to see her family, and I was glad to release her to them. They would get an earful of what their daughter had encountered in the "safety" of the Weikert farm.

We were a sight, to be sure, with our ruined skirts, dirt-streaked faces, matted hair, shoes heavy and stiff with mud. I thought Tillie's mother might not recognize her own girl through the haze of filth she came home in. I was soaked in sweat as we approached our front stoop, Sadie and Mollie silently gripping my hands.

A week ago I left our home tucked in and tidy, praying as much for its protection as for ours as I closed the windows and latched the doors behind me. And now we had come home.

Dread. It is the only word I can bring to mind when I think of that summer. It was all an unbreakable chain of dread, beginning long before the days that led to our week at the farm.

All along I had been filled with fright at the thought of the harm the rebels might inflict should they break into the house in our absence. It had not occurred to me that wounded Union boys might be the ones to take up residence once the enemy fled. But really, what did I expect, that both armies would wait until the mistress of the manor returned from holiday before they asked her permission to cross the Shriver threshold?

I swung open the front door, and standing in the hallway that afternoon, I had the oddest first response: that the place no longer smelled like my house. The same clammy staleness of sweat and blood, astringent and suffering that I had walked away from in Ma's dining room hours earlier hung in the air of my refined Gettysburg home, like a heavy, sopping vale. I felt my spirit wither with a new reality slamming into my senses.

The wounded were laid out on my parlor floor like a row of

pencils, a soldier nurse holding up the head of one of them to offer a drink—from my china cup! Ahead of me, the stairway held a wide swath of dried blood. I had seen enough of that at Ma's to know what it might lead to. At first I thought it must have been too much of a challenge to manage hoisting the wounded up to the second floor, where surely the stifling heat was worse yet. But I remember in those first moments trying to puzzle out that rusty trail dragging down my stairs and hallway.

The girls and I stepped over to look into our sitting room and kitchen, and I must have held my breath for a very long time in disbelief. What looked to be a paste of porridge was strewn across the walls and mounded in the corners like cow manure, my dishes scattered and broken, my larder stripped and emptied of the goods left from last fall's canning. Havoc encircled me as though it would swallow me alive.

As we stood there in silence, a second nurse trudged up from the cellar and, realizing who I was, quickly told me that there were six more men being cared for down there and another ten in the building out back, for how long he could not rightly say. But, he hurried on to assure me that a proper camp was being set up on the east side of town at the Wolf farm near York Pike. "Letterman" was not yet receiving the wounded, he went on, but word was the trains were already bringing supplies and teams from Washington to work around the clock to get their hospital up and running.

For now, the wounded were being cared for like this all around town. It was how he found my house, he said, in this mess of a disaster. The Seceshes had done this to any space they found empty, lifted everything they could and destroyed what they could not pack out. "Damned plunderers..." he said, and I thought it a fitting description.

It was as though he was apologizing for what I returned home to, as if he had some part in the destruction. But what did it matter who did this ravaging and to what purpose? The damage was done, and done thoroughly.

Houses like mine would be emptied of patients as soon as it could be arranged, and there was nothing I could do to hasten the trains and their deliveries needed to get the hospital properly appointed.

In the end there was never a precise, agreed-upon figure, but the papers said there were some twenty-thousand of these men left behind in need of care. The number is too big for me to take in, even today, but especially back then when there were only—how many?—two thousand-something of us living in Gettysburg. We were being asked to care for ten times our population, as though there were enough of us who had the means to do that.

It was a matter of how bad a man's injury was, how fast the equipment came in at the station and got set up at Wolf's, how quickly the ambulance wagons could make their endless rounds from house to church to shop to move out the wounded. The peaceful hamlet of Gettysburg had become a beehive for the crippled, buzzing with construction, delivery, departures, and depositions. For a time our streets were not our own, and the situation was out of our hands.

The girls would not leave my side as we stood struck dumb that day, the reality of our surroundings seeping down into my tired body. A man wailed from the back wall of the parlor—his leg was on fire, he kept crying out. The nurse beside me murmured under his breath, "His leg is long gone…" and shook his head and turned to go on to his duties out back.

I shepherded the girls up the bloodied stairway to survey our bedrooms, and it was a cold comfort to find that their space had been shown more mercy than the kitchen below. Every chest drawer had been pulled out and emptied, and toys and books had been strewn across the floor. Their bed was laid bare and not a stitch of clothing was left behind. At the farm I watched Ma scavenging for any cloth that could serve as bandages, so it was no surprise that our window swags had been yanked away as well. Across the hallway, my room had fared much worse.

Not only was our bed stripped and the carpets gone. The mattress had been pulled onto the floor and slashed open, the innards pitched around us like drifts of snow. Most of the ticking had been ripped away and taken. Our feather pillows were nowhere to be seen, nor was Mother Shriver's wedding gift, that beautiful coverlet. Next to the shattered chamber pot at the foot of the bed, a soldier or two had left what should have been deposited in the thing, or better yet, left in the privy out back. Oh the odor, the shame of such an animal act.

I glanced into George's workroom, ransacked like the others, but my sewing machine stood right where I left it, I suppose too new-fangled an object to be of value to them or too heavy a nuisance to heft. Someone had randomly ripped the books and magazines apart that two summers prior my husband had so carefully arranged onto his shelves. Why they did not destroy the little Byron collection he gave me I could not guess. There it lay intact amid the ruin, to make its way into the box here.

I sat the girls down in the hallway to wait while I followed the trail of dried blood that began downstairs and carried on up the steps. I climbed the stairs alone to the garret, and of course, the rebs had been in my attic! Some soldier's wounds must have painted that pathway of blood as he was carried down and out of the house.

I stood outside the space and surveyed what had been our ordered storage area. The floor was strewn with gunpowder papers and bloodied bits of rags. They had chiseled a couple of large gaping holes into our young brick wall to give themselves a good vantage for firing at the enemy along Baltimore Street. As it was in Ma's dining room, blood, and plenty of it, had soaked in puddles and swirls into the floorboards. And the metallic stench of gunpowder and grease still hung in the suffocating air of the top floor.

I remember thinking (as clearly as if it were yesterday),

"Where is George? Why is he not here? He has abandoned me and the girls to suffer this disaster alone."

And then right away came my most regretful, my most re-visited thought, "Why in heaven's name did I leave this house?"

It was not the first time that week that my husband's familiar adage flooded back to my mind: "Fear is a poor advisor." I had succumbed to the terror that was on fire in the streets of Gettysburg the first day of July, and it was that fear that drove me in the exact wrong direction.

Had I stayed put and not fled out to the farm, my home likely would still come to serve as a hospital, and I would surely be more willing to work alongside the two nurses tending the wounded. But my larder, my drawers, my furnishings would be safe and intact, and I would be willing to play the patriotic nurse. As it was in the ruin we had come home to, I could not gather myself into what it took to be a gracious host.

I went back down to the girls, and in the growing darkness, the second nurse, the older of the two and the one who cared mostly for the wounded in the parlor, brought me a lit candle, knowing I would have to figure out how to bed us down for the night. We gathered the strewn toys and books to a corner of their room and sat on the floor to eat from Ma's basket in the flickering light before I lay down with them.

The heat had not lifted, so there was no need of a covering. As we settled side by side on the bare mattress, they began their tired questions, and I tried to ease their restless minds. They had lived through a hellish week and trudged through three miles of horror only to reach home and find it in a wreckage they could make scant sense of.

That night, and for many to come, we lay tucked together like spoons, Mollie, then Sadie, then me with my arm draped over them, as though they might feel harbored, as though I had any success in sheltering them from the unthinkable of the past days. It is how it would be for a long while ahead. Their spirits exhausted, they slept soundly while I dozed in short bits alongside them, the murmuring of men's voices drifting up the stairs in the darkness as though we were caught in a social gathering gone very wrong.

Those times, I could not lay down to rest without the fear of the dreams coming on, skewed scenes that made no sense, splashing with the blood of dying soldiers, eyes gouged out or ragged legs hanging by a thread of muscle. With deafening explosions, or a gaggle of us struggling to run away from the farmhouse, or my losing one of the girls in clouds of smoke and hearing them scream for me. It was that way for weeks that summer, and it seemed I seldom slept longer than an hour at a time. Every now and then those nightmares return, but less often these days.

I woke before dawn that first morning back home in a continuing swell of dread, aware of what I was yet to discover in the hours ahead.

I would go to the Garlachs and the Pierces to try to piece

together the story of our street in the week the girls and I had been absent. They had the same yellow flags hanging from their houses. Catherine and Margaret would send me home with enough to make do—a blanket and the scraps of food they could spare.

I learned that Catherine and her children took shelter in our cellar for a night because theirs had a foot of rainwater standing in it; that the Pierces witnessed my house being broken into it by the Confederates, who must not have had an ounce of good in them to do what they did. They told how the men chose our garret as their sharpshooter perch, knocking those ragged holes beneath our eaves to shove their guns through and rain gunfire down onto the Union fighters below.

And, yes, James Pierce was sure that at least one, probably two, Confederate fighters had taken a bullet and died up there. He saw a limp, bloodied body being carried out the front door to a waiting wagon.

Before the week's end, the legless soldier in the parlor would die, as would two more in the cellar on their rough planks laid across George's tables, and two more out back, men who were never to make it over to Letterman. George's tavern and tenpin shed had become death caves.

So what was the worst of it? The hellish days of fighting that raged on around Pa's farm sending the countless wounded to Ma's dining table? Or the weeks that followed, the endless wagons rumbling down Baltimore Street to cart off the living to Letterman or the dead, the lifeless bodies, the ones who hung on for too long and needed to be laid to rest in their graves? Was it the sopping smell of fresh decay and burning rot that took up residence in the summer air? Or my plundered home steaming and dirtied with infection and loss and hopelessness?

I cannot rightly say what was the worst of it. The whole lot left the bruising tooth marks of war sunk into every part of me, as though I had been mauled by the fangs of some fantastic vengeful wolf. ❧

Chapter 13

SUNRISES AND SUNSETS came and went in the trampled fields around us, like nothing had happened the week before. The smell of rot and smoldering ash may be hanging in the sultry air. But the pink and blue and gold-painted skies of Gettysburg went right on ahead with their shameless show most mornings and evenings, as though we were not suffocating from the stench in the streets.

The beauty of early mornings and days end used to capture me as a girl. Now the hours seemed a tableau of despair to me, with us posed and mired in something unfathomable. How could death and beauty continue to thrive so effortlessly, side by side, day after day, in our shamble of a town?

Birdsong returned, flowers went on blooming and dropping their petals in all the spots where they had not been trampled into the mud by military boots. All around Gettysburg, nature pushed past the mess of war and refused to be defeated by what human hands had brought down on creation.

I confess that I was not one of those generous-of-spirit women who laid everything aside to selflessly nurse the wounded billeted in my house. As I did in Ma's cellar, I steeped quantities of beef tea and baked bread for the men with what the army supplied the likes of us. But I never was one to linger beside a soldier to feed him and offer encouragement. I had no stomach for it.

I must have walked a good hundred miles in endless loops to haul in buckets of water from our well, up and down the back steps, in and out the door, over and over. You could say I served begrudgingly and did not have it in me to play the angel of mercy.

Did I ever feel haunted by my lack of compassion? No, I think not. By then, standing in the ruins of my home, what I felt was put-upon by some force far beyond my control, an insulated political machine miles away from Baltimore Street. Had any senators' homes been desecrated by strangers? Had even one of those men stood sweating and stirring in a hot kitchen so that a soldier got fed?

How many of their backs ached from bending over the wounded to offer drinks in the dank summer air thick with flies? I could only guess the answer. Since our homecoming, I felt drained of goodwill, of tenderness or concern for anyone beyond my family. I was wearied to the core.

Inch by inch, working around the occupiers of my house as best I could, I scrubbed and reclaimed and sorted out our nest for myself and the girls. Or perhaps what I was doing was creating a different nest altogether, a different life. Now my raw hands were seldom at rest, and this time, the work was on my shoulders alone. There was no Nonie, no one I could hire or call in for help. We were all swimming in disruption.

Each morning I would set right some small detail, collecting jars and bowls from around the house, washing them and returning them to the table to be grabbed up and filled again, a ceaseless ritual of washing and returning. For some curious reason, the high shelf by the stove had not been torn from the wall and stomped to pieces as the rest in the kitchen were. To again see at least a few of my things lined up against the wall held a seed of satisfaction in it. I wrenched any comfort I could from the smallest act like that in the long road to getting my house back into a semblance of order.

By the end of the month the last of the wounded were hauled away from our neighborhood and driven over to Camp Letterman, where proper medical supplies and trained doctors and nurses were plentiful. It was said that four thousand or more soldiers—Union and Secesh—were cared for over there until they were either transferred to an army hospital up north, or patched together enough to board a train to somewhere and maybe even take up a gun again, or buried in the growing military cemetery that now hugged Ever Green, or embalmed for the lonely trip home to a grieving household.

I walked the girls over to the camp one early evening, a strange outing to say the least. Letterman stood a vast ocean of orderly peaked white tents, workers coming and going with hushed purpose. If only the good generals had the foresight and power to plan ahead, they would have put that city of healing together before the Gettysburg killing began, not weeks after.

Every new day, I put Sadie and Mollie to some special detective work around the house, to find broken and scattered items on the three floors and in the back yard, and, once the last man had been moved to Letterman, out back in the desolation of our gardens and in George's alley with its scuffed and dirty tenpin floors. The deadly garret remained off limits to all three of us in our daily recouping.

The girls would present me with some odd item so that we might puzzle out a story about it together—how a piece might have ended up broken or in such a corner as it was found. It became quite a game with them, and it lifted me a bit out of my valley of preoccupation.

I was not alone in making a daily burn pile. My goodness, every street in town was in the same state, with trash and bloodied bandages and rotting horses that could not be moved. Of course, a vision of Valentine's body burning in some unnamed street haunted me and turned my stomach every time I saw carcass ashes or smelled the smolder of meat and horsehair.

The rains punished us all that summer, and they were not about the business of washing away our burn piles or the remaining rot. No, what they did night after night was to leave behind brackish puddles that invited the flies and mosquitos to extend the misery of it all, a nagging, itching pestilence, Gettysburg's own plague of Egypt those months. To say I swatted ten thousand flies in the house that summer would not be an exaggeration. I did feel sorry for how the wounded were nagged from dawn to dusk by the critters.

Carry your lavender-soaked handkerchief or rub as much pennyroyal oil under your nose as you cared to. There was no real relief from the odor. The wafting of death and decay in the humid sunshine made its way into our hair and skin and clothing for weeks on end.

Fire was our only resort for so much of the destruction. Every evening behind the house I lit my sad burnt offerings. The girls slept above as I lingered over my regrets and worries and watched the sparks fly and then the flames die down into smoldering embers. I wondered how it must feel to be a bird flying above Gettysburg those evenings, with a host of fires glowing in the streets and gardens below them, the smoke rising like a graveyard of spirits come out to observe the spoils of war.

I remember that word "refinement" coming to mind one night as I stirred the last ashes of the day's burn. Our town would have a long row to hoe before it could return to the fancy notions of refinement that seemed so confounded important in the years that led to our grim pyres.

Pa's Bible reading came to me, a passage he would recite over his own fires in the autumn fields: "*But who may abide the day of his coming? And who shall stand when he appeareth? For he is like a refiner's fire.*" I never really knew what the lines meant and, for that matter, still do not. But the fires we built the rest of that summer helped refine naught, as far as I could see. There was simply nothing else we could do with the rotting ruin.

With Sadie and Mollie tucked into their room above me, night after night I sat at the table to return to the tallying of my shrinking remainders, trying to tease out a different path forward from what our life was before July. Listen, all of Gettysburg was reconfiguring their lives that summer. Placing value on our losses would be a daunting task, and not just in terms of money.

I suppose I was foolish to end up replenishing all that I did that autumn, the bedding, kitchenware, floor coverings, the Hitchcock chairs that could not be repaired, the window dressings—to replace all that was shredded and smashed, all that we had so carefully carried over from across the street in the beginning, all that came with us from our kin and our country lives, into town and onto Baltimore Street, where our children would grow up surrounded by their ancestors', their parents' history.

Of course, what I purchased could never recreate the meaning of the lost items, and I was wrong to think any of it could. What I thought would assuage my guilt would only drain our coffers.

Not to go down that lonesome road again, but to think of all the schemes George and I shared, those lofty thoughts of a life together bursting with abundance, from tavern to tenpin, handsome profits for investment from season to season, the four of us sitting down to supper together, a clean and ordered scene played out hundreds of evenings, serene and satisfying.

Instead, from the moment I stepped into our shambles of a home filled with the bleeding aftermath of battle, our family's destiny took on a different hue altogether, one that would not include paid help or afternoon teas. It was the beginning of my realization that the Shrivers would not find their names among the rolls of Gettysburg society.

Gone were my hours of paging through *Mrs. Beeton's*, the leisure of pondering a detail like changing a hallway paint color. There was no space in the daylight hours to keep a diary or fuss over a dress design. That summer, hired help had all but disappeared from town. And who could blame the Coloreds running for their lives to go who knows where? That autumn, some of them would suddenly show up on the streets, only to disappear again in a heartbeat. Nonie never again stood in my house after that killing July, nor was I ever to learn of her fate.

I should have asked her more. I did not try in the least to know her better, to learn of her beliefs or longings, to hear of the fears she may have lived under in her young Gettysburg life. I should have asked her aunt before her, when we worked beside each other in the Shriver farm kitchen. I should have asked my own kin more than I did. Then one day they slipped away, one by one, and whatever opportunity there was to hear more of their journey was gone forever. I should have made the effort with Nonie, and I am sorry I did not. Most likely her story remains untold to this day, much as mine has.

My tallies were never the same, but always they showed me that, for now, I could not afford to pay or trust someone else to do my work, at least (I thought) not until I got the household sorted out and cleaned up and re-set. It would be my hands that would grow chapped and swollen from scrubbing and scouring, my knees that would thicken and groan with calluses, my back that would ache from the bending and lifting that someone else had been paid to take up only weeks earlier.

That summer, the chandlers, one after another, came off the highways to work the streets of Gettysburg, peddling their essentials door-to-door that so many of us needed—soap, knives, candles, lucifers, lamp oil, kitchen cloth. They would stand on our front stoops, sweat trickling down their necks and soaking their soiled shirts, their carts holding what we were eager to hand over our coins for.

Somehow my barrel of soap in the cellar had survived the rampage. I think the scoundrels did not recognize it for what it was when their filthy hands were ripping apart the rest of my house. It was one of few godsends, lifting the lid at that moment and finding my blessed amber liquid waiting, its promising smell of cleanliness wafting up to meet me.

Between Norbecks' and Boyd's and Mary McAllister's, I was able to restock my kitchen with necessities, from linens to notions, and the essentials stolen from the larder. Even though the town was in the throes of caring for a needy sea of wounded "guests" left behind, not to mention families coming to search for loved ones and all those curious field scourers who crammed our hotels and boarding houses, I do not believe anyone went hungry that summer.

Train tracks had been repaired in short order allowing supplies to flood in from aid societies up north right away. Food, bandages, bedding, and, yes, more soap—every bit that came off those trains was put into service. It was not a comfortable thing for me to stand in a line like a beggar in the early days of aftermath to accept donated goods, but I did. Vittles and bedclothes for my teeming house of wounded would not appear out of the thin air. I struggled to put pride aside and stand with the others to collect what I did.

Our stock of vinegar stored out in the shed survived as well. I had on hand what I needed to work myself to the bone. Mollie and Sadie stayed at the simple tasks I conjured to keep them occupied while I toiled. They would find a scrap of cloth and bring it to me proudly, knowing I would use it for a scrubbing rag, something I desperately needed. It was the item I would put a penny in their hand for to send them off to Winter's

Confectionary for their sweet reward. They were brave and determined, my girls, and they did their best to be obedient and cheerful for me.

Collecting and counting buttons and bits scattered around the upstairs, carrying buckets of trash out to the burn pile, hunting down missing items—a cup handle or a bobbin of thread—my girls became my "hired help" and did a fine job of it.

Like my folks, I aged a good ten years those few weeks. I was no longer a pampered, well-to-do young wife with a fine house. I had grown haggard, circles beneath my tired eyes, my fingernails dirty and jagged.

Weeks passed without a word from George, and I wondered if his hands were as full as mine were with the mess of war. Or was he lying on a dirty cot somewhere, suffering from a wound and smelling to high heaven like the boys carried out of our house? What had he heard about our plight? There was no way of knowing of his whereabouts or his circumstances.

What is strange is that I was so occupied with the house and so bone-tired at the days end, I think I worried less about my husband those weeks than I had over the two years since he left us. I could not complain about his failure to write. I had done no better.

The night I finally gathered the energy to sit down at the table to write my first letter to him, the thoughts came hard for me. The only good news I could think to write of is that we were alive, the girls and me, that only one Gettysburg death came out of that dark week, the Wade girl who was helping at her sister's house, not far from ours. Oh the stories that came from that one death! I did not know her beyond seeing her at market, and I do not know if George had an inkling of who she was.

I did not go into much detail in my letter about the damages, what had been ruined or stolen from our home that he put so much of himself into. I was knotted with regret for leaving Baltimore Street in the first place, with the nightmare of coming home to the wreckage, sick and tired of the stench outside our windows that refused to lift. I was lonely to the core with long nights, little sleep, and no one to talk with.

It took too much effort to make that letter any more than it was. We were alive, yes, but I felt dead inside, void of small talk, with no sense of how George would take in what I wrote.

It was the second or third day after we got home that the girls found what was left of my treasured rosebud in a pile of bedding I had not yet swept out of a corner in my bedroom. How they spied it I will never know. But I had told them the story enough times, how their Papa was just a boy when he put the flower into my young hand. They knew how dear it was to me.

And at the moment I spied its ruin, I could not help but sink to the floor and cry. Both girls joined me. We must have been a sorry sight. My rose, my rose, my rose.

This hard time was what it was for many of the town folk, and we had no choice but to get up in the morning and go on, emptied out, no longer complaining of the stench that hung in the air, no longer speaking of hope when talk of war's end would come up. We could not ignore or avoid the gaping hole in our lives inflicted on us by this morass.

With all the withered possibilities that confronted me every night at the table, it was a long time to come before I realized that the world would go on no matter what I did or did not do. How did I miss that simple, solitary fact for so many years?

Whether we lived with finery or patches on our clothes, whether George returned to us or not, whether the Baltimore Street house would continue to hold the Shriver family, whether I lived or died—in the end the world would go on. I am not sure Ma and Pa did much better than I realizing that.

All this while, I watched from a distance as the two of them struggled one day at a time to get back on their feet, to clean up their own ruin that was the prosperous Weikert farm. On my first visit back to see them, I found my folks had suddenly taken on old age, looking bent and worn. *Gott*, it was a pity.

When the smoke cleared from Pa's fields and the dead and wounded had been gathered up, it was as though they were left with another farm entirely. Fences were gone, animal carcasses were left to rot in the rain, and the gardens circling the house and barn were trampled and pocked and mounded from battle destruction and temporary burials.

In his reckoning, Pa believed his orchards never really recovered from three days of being peppered by artillery and hurled into by cannon balls. His stands of trees were left with gapes and holes, like a crone's missing teeth. It took weeks to gather what the dead and wounded soldiers could not carry away—bits of uniform, ammunition boxes, artillery shells buried in the mud, ripped-apart boots, pieces of weapons, the boys' personal items some gleaner's eye missed, any small thing that might have helped identify a body that had fallen there.

Levi retrieved Pa's horses from their hiding to return home and take on triple work, retracing their slow passes over ground that had been packed hard as stone from foot traffic and wagons wheels that soggy week. It was July, but he hoped to somehow get another crop in for fall harvest. And always there was maneuvering through the remains of war, stopping to discover yet another soldier's rotting body left in a shallow grave, either overlooked or ignored—you never could tell which.

Poor Ma. It seemed her world was left soaked in blood. Her sacred altar of a dining room had become a death ward where a good many men had arms and legs hacked off by the surgeon's saw. Whoever could have imagined those horrors? Over and over she scrubbed the floor and rubbed bees wax into her oak table until her hands grew swollen and raw. But the surgeon's knife had opened the bloody fountains in their patients that would imbed death's trace deep into the wood, sealing the rusty remains into the grain that I am certain must still be there as I write this—wherever that table ended up.

My childhood home, Ma's pride and purpose, like my own home, would no longer be a serene haven of *Sauberkeit*—of cleanliness and peace and safety. It had become a house forever branded by the filth of war, a reminder of a curse no one asked for or could have imagined.

You know all of this, I am sure. I am not the first to write about what a woman like me or my Ma is left with at the end of a man's war.

Late autumn brought some welcoming relief to us, with the air cooled and the odor finally beginning to lift. The leaves provided us some sorely-needed color, and the rains did their final washing away of the stewing ash of a thousand fires around Gettysburg.

Then word appeared in the newspaper that President Lincoln himself would come to our streets to help dedicate the official military cemetery that was pushed for and carved out over the months by some local zealots. No one could have guessed how many more "war tourists" would flood our streets. Oh, I know there were grieving widows and mothers and families coming to honor their dead. But even though the pockets of gawkers picking over our fields had lessened by summer's end, they would return as well, and stand among the throngs crowding the ceremony.

Looking back, you could say that the last-minute scramble

of preparations along Baltimore Street and everywhere around us was a blessing. It was a refocusing of strength and energy on a new chapter, one that promised a profit on the tail of what was left behind by two armies bringing down their death hammers on each other and leaving it up to our little town to do the cleanup. If I could fathom a scenario where money might be made from that death-dripping war, well, I say so much the better.

Even before we found out a President would be among the town's guests, it was clear there would not be nearly enough beds between hotels and boarding houses for the dedication. So a great lot of those visitors would pay to sleep in the homes of any Gettysburg citizenry willing to open their doors to them and take their money.

As worried as I was about my dwindling resources, I was not in the frame of mind to serve as a hostess so soon again to strangers sleeping in my house. Looking back, I was probably foolish to not have bedded down a few of them and taken their money.

It was a big *Affare*—an event that drew a lot of attention from the newspaper people. Imagine how much extra food had to be shipped in to feed that many visitors, how much bedding hung on clotheslines afterwards when the town emptied, how many new trash fires burned in the cleanup once the last of the flag wavers boarded the trains that would carry them off.

On a cloudy November morning, I stood at the upstairs

window with Sadie and Mollie to witness the procession inching down Baltimore. The girls caught a glimpse of Mr. Lincoln, but I am certain they did not really understand who he was. Even though it was history happening in the streets below, to be a part of the milling crowd gathered to hear speech after lofty speeches and patriotic music was not for me.

I read the President's address long afterwards. Most people said they thought it was too brief, as though he had not put enough effort into his preparations. We are not an easily satisfied people, are we, ready to take apart something like the sad graveside comments of a tired leader.

If you want to know my mind, I would say that what happened during that sweltering July week in our fields was a miniature of the horror that went on in the country's far-flung corners during all four dreadful years of war. I think it was too great a sacrifice for that many souls to lay down their lives for the sake of a lofty idea like preserving a Union.

Mr. Lincoln may have had righteous intentions and meant what he said about the soldiers not dying in vain. But I will go to my grave wondering if it was worth the cost. I will forever be nagged by the notion that what happened in the fields of Gettysburg was one more pointless spectacle of men urged into killing other men at the command of yet other men. So many fought to the death and never saw what the killing brought about in the end.

Not a week later, I held a telegram from George. He would

make his way home from his unit for a four-day furlough. I cannot figure right now if I was nervous, or excited, or scared. I had less than a month to get things in final order, to prepare for the homecoming of the husband I had not seen for more than two years, the one who entrusted our house into my care, the one I had let down. ❧

Chapter 14

DID GEORGE COME HOME TO US that Christmas still loving me? It is a silly question, I know. Love had struck up a new tune for so many of us by then.

I asked him once long before we married why he loved me. "Love" was a subject our families did not see fit to openly discuss. That can be a dangerous question, but then George and I were too young to stray from such talk. He told me he loved my kindness and my hair, and both those things came as a surprise to my ears.

I sometimes think that what was left of my kindness got on the train with George that last cold December morning. I was a good mother, a caring mother, and I kept an ordered house and held my complaints to myself. But I would not say much charity remained in me once I became George's widow. My supply of kindness and lightness got covered over and smothered, and I have lived a good forty years without sensing much of it in my soul to speak of.

His letters at the beginning of our separation were tender,

with kisses to his girls, details of his various sicknesses with no one to offer him comfort, the wretched living conditions of camp that made him miss my soups and his bath, unending days of waiting for battle action, and at first, the promise to be home soon.

From what he wrote, I could not discern if he took to being an army man, despite his growing expressions of discontent. The inconveniences must have been balanced by the hope for victory and a commitment to his unit. It was part of that inherited sense of responsibility and purpose George carried in him that by then felt to me like a curse the father had bequeathed his son.

As for me, my worry over what might be, about how I could keep hearth and home together without him, must have come through in my letters to him. That fear of not having enough set itself up in the house, in my kitchen, in our bed. I had such a fist of loneliness in my chest, and now the gnawing fear over our dwindling means for survival.

And then, after the smoke of battle lifted from Gettysburg and the stench settled over the streets, George's letters grew even thinner. It was not until the house had been cleared of the last soldier that I gathered enough wits about me to write a second letter spelling out more clearly the reality of what I saw as the remains of our former lives. I was filled with shame for having left the house for the rebs to strip and batter and bloody. All around me the others had stayed put and held the enemy at bay, but not I. As he warned against, I succumbed to the fear that indeed was a poor advisor.

When I eventually wrote to him of how badly the house had fared, it was weeks before he replied with a terse note to say he would return to Gettysburg when he could, but he could not even begin to guess when that might be. He wrote that he was disappointed to hear the details and that he was tired.

And there you have it. I was piecing together the shambles of our home. He was miles away with his unit thinking, "She was not to be trusted. She has let us all down." At least that is what I read into his silence.

Despite the efforts to return the town to its former order (especially around Lincoln's visit that cold November), one needed only to step through the Shriver doorway to know the extent of grievous loss I was sorting through. By then my hands were thoroughly calloused from scrubbing, stitching, lugging whatever I could to bring some order back to the shattered rooms.

For a long time afterward, I re-wrote his homecoming in my mind that last Christmas. The train would come to a steamy halt at the station, and he would step out into the winter air, and we would run to him with open arms to welcome him home. He and I both would have the color and light of innocent youth back in our faces, our smiles warm and deep.

Instead of the drawn, unsteady frame who appeared before

us that afternoon, my young husband would be overjoyed to see us, sweeping us into his embrace as we stood at the platform. We would trundle home with the girls, coy and shy as they got reacquainted with their long-missed papa. And within the hour they would be regaling him with stories of all they had seen and done in his absence, and their Papa would reward them with songs and tales of his adventure.

The house, our bed, would be as it was when he left two years earlier, the scent of greens hung about us and the parlor Christmas tree perfuming the air. I would light the candles at the table and lay out the spread of foods he had dreamed of for months miles away in his cold barracks. I would spare no expense preparing the special dishes I patiently fussed over for hours in our kitchen. The four of us would join hands for the table blessing as though nothing had changed in our two years apart.

Instead, George stood in our hallway a bruised, not an angry spirit, as I had read into his letter. The spark in his eyes was dulled. His countenance was gray. And he was too thin. I struggled to recognize my husband behind his tired, sagging uniform.

Listen, I know I was not the only wife who was taken aback by her soldier's return. Even then, I kept reminding myself that there were women aplenty who would have no loved one to welcome home, women who could not manage to find a body to bring back for its final rest, women who were left with a legless or faceless or mindless man to care for 'til death did them part.

There he stood, leaning against the wall of the hallway, slow of step and with a lessened voice. In my mind he was failing, like a sapling, all scrawny and wilting for lack of water, and it was a struggle for me to see him as the same man who left two years earlier. The new dimmed, haggard version had lost the light of George's presence.

Even as he sat at table or lay with me those three nights, loneliness stayed put in the house, almost like a third person, standing alongside my husband and me, leaning into me and making the hurt burrow even deeper inside.

The ledger and a handful of papers that somehow escaped destruction from the rampage after we fled were what was left of George's dreams, the drawings he enjoyed laboring over, receipts for equipment purchases, his book with its columns of neat figures. He would slip upstairs and spend long stretches behind the closed door of his workroom, and it seemed to me he spent more time closeted away up there than with his family the floor below.

The cellar door was kept closed after a single visit down those drafty stairs.

"We will have to start over…" he said quietly more than once, as though it was something he did not quite believe himself. All I could seem to find in me were replies of worried apologies, as though my mind went blank of any other words.

The first night, when Sadie asked if Papa could sing for them in bed, he looked at me and said, "I have no songs in me tonight. Mama can sing you one." I watched from the doorway as he pulled the covers under their chins and kissed their foreheads. I went in afterwards to remind them how tired their Papa was, how he needed to rest after so hard a trip. I was the one who sang *All the Pretty Little Horses* to them those three nights. Sadie did not ask him again, as though she understood her Papa's distress.

He had a long bath that first night and stepped into pants and a shirt I sewed for him as a Christmas gift. The clothes hung on his frame as though he were a coat hook. I would hear Sadie whisper again and again to her sister to not stare, because it seemed all Mollie could do.

The girls could not reconcile this thin, quiet presence with the man they remembered their father to be. It was not so easy for me either. While George rested, I took up his uniform, fussed over it to bring it about, mended and cleaned as best I could. At least I could be useful to him in that way.

"We will just have to start over." And how would that look, that starting over, I thought. Indeed, when could starting over begin?

When he left for the first time, the necessity of new beginnings for us were not a concern. The Union boys would send the Rebels running back home, and George would return to open the doors of his business before the New Year. This is what we all believed when Lincoln called for the last big batch of volunteers and George answered. That lofty belief in a swift defeat of the rebellion was like a soap bubble that popped as it rose in the air. How wrong, how blinded by patriot talk could we have been those early days?

The new reality was that there was no end to the fighting in sight, no opening in the constant stream of bad news that lay right alongside the victories, battle after battle, loss after loss.

Our last night together we readied for bed in the room we had rejoiced over the first night we slept in it not three years prior. Back then we were giddy, playful in our new doll house. But this night we stood in silence, eye to eye for perhaps the first time since he had gone off to war, strangers who once stood in my Pa's apple orchard and so earnestly pledged our love to each other.

I waited for him to offer a few crumbs of words, but nothing came. And like a strike of lightening, something snapped in me—some brittle branch of anger—and what flew off my tongue stunned even me.

"Who are you to blame me, George? You have enough dedication to the flag and to your army comrades but not to your wife? Talk to me! Tell me what has kept you from us!"

I was unleashed. "Why have you abandoned us? Why did you leave me and the girls to make do on nothing? Nothing!"

I railed on about his shrinking letters, the longed-for words of encouragement and forgiveness that never came, the furloughs that in two years' time never happened, the measly army paychecks that came sore late most times.

"And you show up here now to judge me with your silence for what was lost?"

This! This was coming from the very center of me, that taut string of fear and anger in my gut that had not been set loose in a very long time and was now snapped asunder. I had been left too long wondering what his thoughts were, if he worried about us, if he cared for me, his leaving me to guess about his whereabouts, his safety, all except for what I could glean from a newspaper or an army letter.

Gott, I was on a tear, red-faced and unstoppable. I paused long enough to get a breath, and we stood facing each other again in silence. And his quiet reply? "I am going to lie down…" Only that, and he turned his back to climb into our bed. And still I could not let go of my rage.

"Thoughtless, George, and cruel! Shame on you!" And here is where I broke into the most tears I had produced in a very long time. That poor, dear, broken husband of mine! I watched him struggle to hoist himself up off the bed, and then he came to my side and, without a word, put his hands on my shoulders as if to steady my shaking frame.

At that unfixable moment, I cried through a choked speech of final apologies, all the things I had said before, but this time I let them flood out of me like one of those burst wineskins in the Bible. He put his arms around me and listened without replying a word. There was never another time after that last night when I defended myself or aired my regrets to another living soul as I emptied my tears at George's weary feet.

Exhausted and with no tears or fight left in me, I helped him lie back down. Before I joined him in our tired bed, I crept over to the girls' room to tuck their quilts under their chins. Their soft breathing in the chilly darkness helped slow the pounding in my chest. My swollen eyes grew accustomed to the surroundings as I stood surveying their recovered room, considering my visitor-husband across the hallway, reviewing all the venom I had released into our bedroom walls moments before, and, now, feeling a great weight somehow lifted from my shoulders, as spent and resigned as any widow must feel.

When I slipped into bed next to George for the last time, he was already asleep. I inched in close to him under the coverlets, and I whispered my love to his slumbering ears, words I had not been able to speak over those three days. Then I joined him in sleep, feeling somehow at last *verziehen*—a forgiven woman.

After that night and George's departure, I seldom slept in our bed again, mostly trying to find rest in a chair by the parlor window or by the bedroom window above. I would use up a storehouse of candles those vigiled nights, longing for peace to come over me in the midst of the waiting.

I cannot find a way to explain myself here. The soldier we stood with on the platform the next morning had been my steadfast, assured, dearly beloved husband before a war was declared. But now the man we were sending away seemed a familiar stranger in a tired army uniform, so deeply, deeply changed, tentative and distant, quiet and sad.

The lonesome wail of the train whistle in the distance that marked the hours of Gettysburg signaled our final goodbye. I had used myself up in the tirade the night before. I was spent and chilled to the bone but somehow strangely quieted, and I watched George put a hand on each girl's head as a goodbye to them.

Then we turned to face each other, and the sadness in his eyes sank into mine. If I were standing here with you right now, you would see it is still in me, his final look. "Hettie. Listen to me. We will figure this out. We will," he said quietly. And then in almost a whisper, "We can begin again. We can find our way..."

A kiss to my cheek, a brief embrace, he doffed his hat and climbed onto the train and was gone from us.

In hindsight, when George returned to his unit the thirtieth day of December, 1863, I think I must have known in the deepest part of my being that it would be the last we would sleep together in our proud bedroom. By the end of the summer, our fate would be sealed in a lonely plot far from Baltimore Street. Still, I kept the hope in me that it would be otherwise. ❧

Chapter 15

IS THERE ANY ROOM IN THIS WORLD for an old woman like me? Do any of them know who I was? Do they care about the things I miss? I sit here listening to their clock chime out there, hour by hour. What more can I do but stare at these gnarled, idle hands of mine, restless and fidgeting in my lap. I think my fingers must have memories of their own, of how they once were so capable and needed. *I* was needed. I cannot set my mind on how my work, my meaning, slipped away from me.

There was a sureness in my time as Mrs. Shriver that long ago escaped from me. My edges are fading and frayed, like an old shirt, cast off and left out too long in the sun and rain, worn weak and thin, good for not much of anything. It is as though my self got left behind somewhere.

I miss my sewing machine, the steady rhythm of the working needle, the way my hands guided the fabric so confidently, how my foot rested into the pedal's grooves. My eyes took delight in the straightness of a neat seam marching longer and longer before me as I fed the cloth through the thread's even tracings. My machine and I sewed more dresses for my girls and for the fine women of Gettysburg than I could count. I would like to sit before my Singer again, my peddling foot in a confident stroke, to feel the peace of the quiet work we did together.

I miss the kingdom that was my kitchen. Pots and jars, towels and spoons, the steady heat of the stove on a winter's day, the sun's movement from table to basket to floor, the sound of the sitting room clock.

I miss the moonlight flooding the farm fields on summer nights. The supper dishes clean, the kitchen put back in order, my sister and I would lie on our backs at the edge of the gardens and count the stars. We would chase after the glowbugs by Pa's barn, squealing with the delight of it all.

When Ma called us in for bedtime, our regular perch was at the upstairs window where Sarah and I cooked up crooked tales of goblins rising out of the trees, of moonlight treasures and strange beasts, until Ma would holler up the stairs and shush us to bed.

I miss the comfort of George's voice, his singing to the girls, yes, but even hearing him instruct the workmen on the house, or sweet talking Valentine while he drew the brushes over her withers. I miss waking up beside him early mornings before the day's work began, and come nightfall, of falling asleep to the details of his day. I cannot conjure it this moment, but if he were to appear outside my door today, even a murmur from George's lips would be as familiar to me as the sound of the rain.

I miss his hand on mine. From his first real kiss out by Pa's gate the afternoon we were promised, to that last tentative one on the train platform at our final goodbye, I miss George's mouth.

I miss my young body, when I could walk free and light instead of dragging these heavy limbs about, my steps as painful as if someone filled my old shoes with jagged gravel. There was a time I could rise in the morning and be dressed and stoking the kitchen fire in quarter of an hour. These days it is a struggle to hoist myself out of this chair. It aches to bend down and pull up a sagging stocking. I can barely squint out my own hands in front of my face. Oh, how it would be to look in the mirror and recognize the young beauty I was.

I miss the autumn sunlight through the tall kitchen window George lingered at to gaze out on his land, admiring the turning seasons over those brief months our family shared in the new house. I miss knowing his eyes were on me from that spot the spring I spaded the ground for our first real gardens. When I smiled back at him, I could take in his whole form waiting there. It pleases me even now to remember those mornings.

And my gardens! Oh, how I miss my gardens and the promise they held year after year. I miss taking in the fresh smell of March after the earth had slumbered all winter. I miss the dirt under my fingernails and sowing the wintering seeds that rested ready and waiting on the shelf in the cool of the cellar. Those sunflowers and I knew that in their own patient time they would stretch and lean up to catch the sun and one day tower over me like some haughty older child.

Year after year, once the snow melted away with winter's passing, again and again, a garden would become my orphan child—tangled, down-at-heel, resting through the long months to come to life again, to be tamed, to have her weeds combed out, her wrinkles pressed, her seams straightened. My tidy plots welcomed the narrow pathways stamped between the new rows, and the first seedling buds would hold so much promise of color and food. Those staked-off pieces of my world took my name and wore it so proudly.

Even the miserable puny strip of earth behind the High Street house became my ward and got transformed into a decent "Hettie's garden." I needed that balm for my soul even more those later years.

The ritual of putting up the bounty from the fall harvests for our winter table, the daily ordering of my household, sunrise to sunset—this was the work I did well.

But still I look back at that time, and it seems as though I managed to pick only the low-hanging fruit in my tree of life once George left this world. It was as though I could not reach for what hung higher, whatever sweeter, richer fruit might have been waiting there. I think of all that I miss of my younger days, and I am filled to the brim with a longing for something I cannot quite put my finger on.

You might read this in a history book somewhere, that the January when George was captured was a wretched, raw one. People bemoaned the news that so many of the boys who went off to fight ended up dying in the throes of the freezing cold. I found myself staring out of George's window time and again that month after taking in the news from *The Sentinel* that his company had been ambushed on the first day of the New Year. His name was listed among the twenty-some men captured and missing.

Some mornings, the clock would chime the hour, and I could not think how long I had been standing where he once stood in the kitchen, staring out across our property, on over to Washington Street. As though I was in a trance, I could seldom recall later what my eyes had rested on for so long. I could no more tame my distraction, my sorrowful worry over George's whereabouts and fears for my daughters and for me, than I could make the wind stop blowing.

By and by, as it does after every deadening winter, March blew in, and on one brisk morning at the window, I watched a crimson bird alight on the head of my clothesline post with the weightless grace of a snowflake. He seemed to me a free-floating flame, a color so bright it liked to burn a hole in the air around it.

Have you ever stopped to listen to the song of the red

bird? A rounding call that can pierce the skies like an arrow, so loud and clear your ear can pick it out from one end of town to the other. Pa used to say that the bird was either letting his mate know where she could join him for dinner, or he was warning the rest of the birds that they had best stay clear of his staked territory. Oh, they are a kingly sight, crowned with a soft feathered crest that looks sharp as a razor's edge.

When my firebird showed up that morning, I realized it was the first real beauty I had stopped to rest my mind on since George's furlough ended at the train platform in December. I was hungry for something like the sight of that crimson bird and grateful to focus my attentions on it.

As I stood there mesmerized, for no reason I could account for, the bird suddenly fell from grace, keeling off the post, plummeting like a whirling maple key, lifeless to the ground. I could not believe my eyes. I plucked my cape from the hook and threw it around my shoulders, scrambling out the back door, down the steps to where he lay, like a blood stain in a tangled patch of weeds, his eyes pinched shut and a seed of some sort clenched in his nut-brown beak.

Never in my life had I so much as touched a red bird. But that morning I bent to gather up his lifeless, weightless form and cup it on its side in my palm. Up close, his crimson feathers glinted with an indigo sheen in the slant of the morning sun. Ebony feathers ringed his beak like a tiny fur mask rustling in the morning breeze, almost as though he were outfitted as a wee outlaw.

I pried the seed from his mouth as naturally as I would have picked a sprig of hay from out of Mollie's hair. Had the bird's heart given in? Had he been hurt before he landed in my garden? Had he swallowed some poison from a farmer's plot? I knew the girls had their eyes fixed on me from inside as I stood stock-still, studying my handful of treasure.

A long while passed as I held his lifeless form, and then, without a move, the bird half-opened an eye! I gently tipped him upright a bit onto his chest, as a hen might settle to brood an egg, my palm cupped into a moment's nest.

With both eyes now wide open, the bird sat motionless, stunned and staring glassy-eyed, and I began to speak to him: hushed word-songs of praise and reassurance and encouragement, whispers of wonder. How long I babbled on I cannot say. For those brief moments, time took a deep breath and held it.

After a bit the bird rustled ever so carefully to refold his crimson wings, tucking one, then the other, into its proper lay, much as I would fold a clean sheet from off the clothesline, the edges straight and flat, the folds neatened and properly lined up. And once he had rearranged himself, he lifted off my hand with a soft flap and floated up without the least bit of effort to perch again on the head of the post.

I could have reached up and captured him, he was that close. We stood there, the two of us, regarding each other for a long pause. And then he silently rose into the skies, higher and higher until he became a speck of red, and I could no longer see any sign of him.

I squinted up for a very long time and did not, could not move from the spot, as though I had been granted a visit from a spirit, my own winged messenger, come and gone in a moment's flash.

I saw a red bird in my new country garden the year I became Mrs. Shriver. It landed not an arm's length away from me on the handle of the shovel I had just jammed upright into the spring dirt Flora and I were about to sow seeds into. As I eyed him, he floated down to where we had cut a fresh row into the soil for planting. With a sort of haughtiness about him, he surveyed me as though I were the trespasser, not him. And when he had enough of us...poof! Off he flew.

Flora watched with me that morning, and, as she was wont to do, she launched right into her folk wisdom about seeing a red bird rise into the skies—a sign that good luck is on its way—and seeing one come down to earth as this one had just done—a sure sign of bad luck aiming to strike where it would, an omen of the worst order.

Her stories never took much purchase with me. At least not until five years later as I stood in my own garden that morning contemplating my red bird visitation, with the knowledge that George was in the enemy's lair.

"Only a red bird catching his breath," I told the girls afterward as I brushed past them to the stove, "flown off now to look for his breakfast." And they asked no more until that night when I tucked them into bed. I wove some story around it all to put their questions to rest, a tale they would ask me to repeat for at least a fortnight.

You might think me daft, but I was left undone by the morning, as though that bird was a harbinger, a prophet delivering a coded message I could not quite decipher. That night, after I set the kitchen in order and trudged upstairs, sleep would not come. And there they were, the questions rising up and flapping around inside my tired mind like a whole swarm of red birds volleying for my attention.

"Where is George tonight? Is he alive? Is he ever to return to us? Am I already a widow? What will happen to us? How will we manage? What must I do next?"

These were not new questions by any means, but their urgency had been reborn by a morning portent.

That bird and I were together in one set-apart moment in my morning garden. He flew away without a fear for his fate, without a worry over his tomorrow or how to order his next moves, free from fret over his supper or his mate or his nest. He was absolved. I was the wingless one, tethered by guilt and by fear of the unknowns, gripped by a dread only a widow might be acquainted with.

Can you see my bird's tail feather here? It is the very one left behind in my garden that morning. I found it the next day and hid it away in my apron pocket for the rest of the week. It has faded some, but that morning it was a burning scarlet, glossy and fine as could be, when first I spied it.

Red is the color of courage and longing, of passion and love, of fire and blood, of roses, and as far as I can think of it now, that was the time for me when red became the color of death.

I have a faded picture in my mind of the three of them standing and watching me as I worked the garden that first spring, Mollie up in her Papa's arms, Sadie pressing into him, all eyes resting on me. Even with my back turned, I knew they were there, and it was beauty to me. ❧

Chapter 16

WE WERE NOT A CONFESSING LOT, the Weikert clan, and maybe had we been bred faithful Catholics, we could have knelt for regular confessions before a collared priest who would assign us the secret code to recite that might lift the weight of regret from off our shoulders.

I confess that I was only a shell of a wife to the second husband. I confess that I have lived my life missing the rest of me, the one who laughed and played and dreamed such vivid, colorful dreams, as though I took up a pallet and brush in my sleep and daubed delight into being. I never stopped missing the first husband, the part of my life who stood before us in tattered Union Blues on the station platform at the end of his last Christmas in Gettysburg, my twenty-seventh year.

I confess that my anger sometimes got the best of me in our early months of absence from one another, before George, my true husband, left his final farewells at our feet that day in the blowing cold. I confess that there was never another bond on my heart like the one he set there square and straight. It was something you could almost touch, a proud, untearable weave of strength and loyalty and tenderness, and a strange indebtedness. I was devoted body and soul to the man.

But even the strongest of bonds, the richest of loves, can be rent apart by a betrayal, or a failure, or a loss, or a war. My undoing was born out of a decision made less than a hundred miles from my kitchen table, by a band of elected men sitting in Washington, every one of them strangers to me, the comfortable, self-assured gentlemen who would send the "other"—the younger, the braver—out to do their work for them. The thousands of lives undone by a government decree that started that war is too big to realize. It could have as easily happened to you. It still *could* happen to you.

You people today cannot know how important a letter was back then. Oh, the *verdammt* letters! I clung to George's like they were my food and drink, my air, my lifeline. Without his written voice in my hand, despair could grab hold of me at sunset and nag at me all the long night.

In the end, the letter that came to tell me he was dead arrived many months after the fact. Long before that notification, I read my husband's name in the *Sentinel,* one among the many names of the dead that we came to expect as a regular part of the news in those days.

You could say I took in the information with a great measure of doubt. Mixed in with my disbelief of George's death was a sort of magical sense of peace, almost as though I assumed the papers got the information wrong, that he might still be on his way home. We had all heard stories like that, of soldiers' identities getting mixed up and a loved one showing up at the door weeks after his death had been reported.

I had surmised George's whereabouts without the army or the President, or even some soldier sending me word, as so many families received from a stranger, written after a fallen comrade's death in a midnight field. Always there were assurances that their relative died a hero with his loved one's name on his lips. The grieving back home needed some hopeful word to hang onto as they read about the death they feared all along.

See in the box here his last heart-rending post? I took that poor soiled envelope from the postman's hand on a spring morning in this sad state, the pathetic, sullied paper, the scribbling that was so unlike George's careful script. The ink was not from his father's good pen he had packed off when he mustered, I can assure you. See there, he scratched out only a few lines to tell me he was alive in a Confederate prison somewhere in the South. Beyond knowing that he was able to pen these words, what measure of comfort or hope could his post have afforded me?

See all the lines blotted and blacked out? That must have been done by the captors who feared a prisoner might give away any one of the camp's pitiful secrets. George wrote this, yes, but this is not his proud, neat penmanship, nor is it his familiar voice. Over the winter months, he went from "missing," to "captive" in the newspaper, and now I read the grim news of his plight directly from his hand.

Months earlier, a week or so after my encounter with that bird in the back yard, I first sent a letter to the War Department asking them for help in locating my missing husband. That letter was never answered. But soon after I got my answer with this last post from George that managed to make its pained way to me, in spite of the military's unforgivable failure to respond to my earlier letter.

It was almost a year later and the war all but over when the papers announced that some general (whose name I cannot bring to mind just now) sent an army team to visit the Southern battlefields and prison grounds to try to search out and identify as many of the missing dead as they could, a daunting task as anyone would admit.

It took a woman to see that all of us waiting to hear of our departed loved ones' fate deserved a proper letter. Her name was Clara Barton, and she would come to make quite a name for herself. She had a reputation for being a thorn in the flesh of the government men, a persistent presence who refused to give up caring for the wounded on the front lines. And then after the fighting ended, she did the courtesy of contacting the likes of me, the widows, the mothers, those of us left waiting.

I think her show of strength made the generals look weaker than they fancied themselves. Why had they not taken the reins to demand that families of the dead be extended the courtesy of the government's regard? Why did it take a lowly woman nurse to grasp the urgency of the thing and set up her own office in Washington? All those congressmen who were willing to fund the killing were not so apt to take on the hard business of contacting those left behind, to face the death their war brought on a nation of grieving remainders.

I heard she came to be called the "Angel of the Battlefield," and there was one of those stories about a bullet entering a tent where she was tending to a man, that it tore through her shirt sleeve and struck her patient, killing him on the spot.

I do not know if this really happened. So much grim myth rose off those fields, like throngs of cawwing crows taking flight. Even today, all these years hence, there are flocks and flocks of far-flung stories still coming out of that war, even though it is long past and fading in memory. You cannot trust which tales are fact and which are fancy.

During my months of waiting, I sent three letters to Barton to better grab her attention among the thousands of others like me who were desperate to know more. She had the help of a young clerk who himself had been a prisoner at Andersonville. He was educated and had good penmanship, and the prison guards right away put him to work keeping records of the sick and dying.

His name was Atwater, and likely it was his hand that wrote George's information in the death ledger on the day my darling died. I always wondered if the two of them ever spoke face to face, before the clerk jotted my husband's name on that dreadful list.

While the fighting was still going on, Atwater was packed up along with a trainload of prisoners to be transferred out to some other Southern prison. He smuggled out his own list under his shirt, an exact copy of the daily tallies of dead he had so carefully recorded for his captors, kept hidden away and safe, as though he knew of its importance. After the South surrendered, that list eventually ended up in the hands of the army in Washington. Or at least that was the story.

Barton and he spent weeks in the summer heat toiling alongside each other on the wreaking prison grounds of Andersonville. I was to learn that more than ten thousand men like George died there. I imagine the nurse and the soldier sorting through Atwater's list while the sweating army men worked along beside them.

Thousands of stakes were pounded into the gravesites that had been left helter skelter by hasty prison burials months earlier. Now the digging and rearranging and setting of official markers over row after mounded row might offer a more honorable gravesite to the departed.

Just weeks after their work was finished as best it could be, there was a ceremony to honor Andersonville as an official military cemetery, something like what had been done in Gettysburg two years prior. I read of the gathering in the *Sentinel*.

Mr. Lincoln would not attend this event, for he already had been resting in a coffin since spring, cut down by the assassin's bullet just as the fighting ended.

It was not until December when Barton's official letter reached me bearing the final word that, according to the Atwater list, George Washington Shriver died in August of 1864, seven months after his capture in the bitter January cold at Rectortown. He was one of a dozen from his company sent to a Georgia prison where the Confederates oversaw an unthinkable multitude of men perish in filth and misery. My husband's rotting body lay among an ocean of dead, each man from a household like mine that stayed soaked in mourning for a good many wretched years after the war ended.

I once heard Andersonville referred to as a "harvest of death." All of those sons and husbands, fathers and brothers penned up and starved in conditions unfit for cattle.

My George had suffered in squalor, his life drained out of him drop by drop. I had bid my husband goodbye on the train platform four brief days prior to his frigid capture. Oh, if he had only stayed on with us a day or two longer that Christmas. What might have been...

The Army form that Barton sent listed *scorbutus* as George's cause of death. I was later to learn more from Dr. Huber about the strange word that took my husband's life. He called it scurvy: a disease of the blood, probably brought on by starvation and infection, from bad water and weakness. Oh, did my heart ache to hear those particulars. Still, it was probably for the best to learn the truth of the matter.

Do you know I once was handed a picture by someone here in this house, a photograph clipped from a newspaper of a soldier who survived Andersonville. These things were printed out and people passed them around, images of men starved beyond human understanding, propped up, naked and crazed before a photographer and his camera box. I pitched the thing onto the floor. It was too cruel to merit looking at, even for a moment, too awful to imagine George in the starved skin of that picture.

A number was assigned to a sort of honorary gravesite for George, for how on earth could they really *know* where his body lay among the thousands identified the same way and buried in that hellhole? Plot 6816 was the symbolic resting place for my dear husband's remains in some long row of trenches and mounds of desecrated Georgia dirt. Back on Baltimore Street, when I had quietly observed his twenty-eight birthday passing, I did not the know he had already passed from this world.

You would think, would you not, that with all the unanswered questions stuck to me over the months of The Great Civil War, with all my festering fears and unknowns, you would think that holding Barton's letter in my hand, a piece of paper that settled out the worst news once and for all, that this would be the final drop of water to drain out of my leaking bucket of calamity.

After all, now I knew with certainty that my husband was not off living a different life with another family, or suffering and fevered in an army hospital I never heard of and with a leg or arm missing, or wandering lost and crazed and filthy as a cur in some far-off countryside, unable to remember his name or make his way home to us.

You would think I was mourned out, that this news should have been a benediction to my troubled mind. But there was no relief for me in the letter's official wording, no balm to rest in on the day it arrived. That letter was my end and my beginning, for to me it was when I officially ceased to be George Shriver's loving wife, and I began my life as a war widow with an unknown future that would never measure up to what had been lost.

Oh my heart, my heart, my heart. I can still feel the weight of that moment of knowing inside my chest, for it was the final departure, the severing of our marriage vows. Death had officially parted us asunder. George would be forever absent from us, and his absence would be forever present at the very center of things.

I remember suiting up the girls and taking them by the hand that December morning for the long trudge out to the farm. But I do not remember talking to Ma or Pa before I fell into their bed and could not be woken.

They told me that I did not stir up there for a full day and night. I remember nothing until waking with a song running in my head, one that George brought home from a meeting when we were first married:

> *And if on earth we meet no more,*
> *oh may we meet on Canaan's shore.*
> *I hope that you remember me*
> *if on this earth no more I see.*
> *An interest in your prayers I crave*
> *that we might meet beyond the grave.*

Beyond the grave—whatever that might look like, however far off into the horizon.

The certainty that I would never behold George's face again in this life leaned into me like one of those toppled, broken tombstones we walked by at Ever Green after the melee. There would be no more denying my status as a widow from Gettysburg, and now I had to go on with my life like an amputee, missing the part of me that was George.

Ma was waiting in the kitchen when I inched down the stairs, and she said not a word as she set coffee and *kuchen* in front of me. Her gingered apple bread was always the first food she set before us children when we crawled out of a sick bed.

That day I ate in slow silence, studying my girls outside the kitchen window as they played near the chickens circling in the winter sun. Sadie might remember him, but Mollie will not, I thought. His presence in their memories had already begun its fast fade.

Within hours I gathered my wits back to me and asked Pa to drive us home to Baltimore Street that very afternoon. Evening came on and the girls and I did a proper prayer for their dearly departed Papa, without a body to prepare and sit beside in the parlor, without mourners coming to the door to offer condolences. All that we had was his picture and our memories and now the certain knowledge that he would never again stand at his kitchen window, never again sing them to sleep, never again sit at the supper table with us.

Much later that night, after the girls were asleep, I would observe my own solitary wake by the window I had spent so many months in front of in my long waiting. A single candle and my thoughts were the only other mourners to keep me company.

It was the putting to rest of our marriage in my tired mind, a completed thing with an ending neither of us could have fathomed on the January wedding day we stood facing each other before Pa's hearthstone. I had already come through the long months of losing him anyway, and now this was how I would make my final peace with George's death, alone in the darkened parlor he and I took such pride in.

The next morning, my chores done, the girls reading on the floor beside me, I set out afresh to sort through the decisions that clamber for a widow's attention. What before had been only the worst possibilities were now settled and sure realities I needed to take charge of and act on.

I remember breaking into a laugh late one evening, stuck once again staring at my ciphers and still not seeing a clear path through the darkness that was to be my future. It suddenly occurred to me that Mrs. Lincoln and I had become members of the same cruel club, the Abandoned Widows of the Civil War. We might meet to talk over tea about how unwise it was to spend beyond our means. Or perhaps what was the better way to lose a husband: by the strike of a swift and certain bullet, or by the slow drain of starvation.

The President's widow suffered her burdening grief on a public stage of scrutiny and criticism. I suffered under a hidden terror of uncertainty, of losing my home and livelihood. We were two lost ladies, peas in a strange, sad pod. Both husbands were murdered (a dark word, is it not) for neither were lawful killings. John Wilkes Booth knew what he was up to, and so did the men who starved my husband to death at Andersonville. Mrs. Lincoln and I lived with our men's wrongful endings sewn into our skirt hems.

I have to ask, what might have transpired before 1865 to change our fates, Mary Lincoln's and mine?

What if the Union had successfully held Fort Sumter at the start, and the standoff had gone down in history as the beginning and end of a two-day Southern rebellion? What if the South had figured out on its own by 1860 that slavery's time had run out, that the world was changing and they had best learn how to navigate their way forward without relying on unpaid labor? What if John Booth had collided with a wagon as he scurried across the street in darkness on his way to the theater that night? What if General Lee and his boys had chosen some other Pennsylvania village to plunder?

What if George's furlough had been for a week instead of four days? What if he had not ended up at Rectortown the freezing hour Mosby's cutthroats captured him? What if, what if, what if. The widow of a President must have been driven mad by the same sort of questions, unmanageable, circling and swarming around us without ceasing. I was doing a poor enough job of swatting the unknowns out of my face those nights, I can tell you.

Not even a week before Mr. Lincoln's head took the deadly bullet, two generals from the opposing armies sat across from each other at a table in a farmhouse parlor hours south of Gettysburg. Both survived the long trudge through the death, the ruin that four years heaped on the country, North and South. And finally, finally, they agreed it was enough. What took them so long to come to that moment of understanding?

At least the President had been informed that the worst of it had ended with the Appomattox signing. I think of him heaving a mighty sigh when word of the surrender reached his desk. He stepped into his theater box that night knowing the war that plagued his every day in Washington was all but history, a cold comfort for the missus who would watch his life bleed out hours later.

You know, in the middle of the whole mess of war, Lincoln issued his infamous Emancipation Proclamation, a fine and lofty sounding phrase: "…That all persons held as slaves are and henceforward shall be free." But I could not see how it would all fit together, how in the world it could work out, that such a notion could be swallowed by a country that had lived with slavery from the start and then set out to tear itself apart over the institution. A proclamation by God Almighty could not have changed the climate of the country those days. Likely nothing could have changed Mr. Booth's twisted mind by the night he pulled the trigger.

Sure enough, not very long after the war between the states ended, a sort of club sprouted up around the country—the Klan, they were called, chapters of crazed hooligans dressed up in costumes and spreading their own deranged gospel of evil.

They worked all manner of wrong on the Coloreds who were supposed to have stepped out of slavery and into new lives of freedom and liberty. Freedom and Liberty! Big ideas with different meanings for the likes of the Klansmen who could not grasp or swallow what Mr. Lincoln had in mind.

The killings they accomplished were nothing short of butchery, worse than any animal should have suffered. It took far too long, but their scattered chapters were squelched by federal police, even though the killing must have continued here and there, I am sure, with crowds gathered to watch like it was a sporting event.

I would bet my last coin that evil like that will continue to resurface. Equality can be a hard thing to swallow for some soul-infected folks who would not recognize the common good if the meaning of those two words was written on the palms of their hands.

After Lincoln, two more presidents were murdered like he was, you know. Let me see, there was Garfield, when I still lived on High Street, shot down right there in a Washington train station and going on to live several weeks after he took the bullet. And more recent, it was McKinley who was surprised by the assassin's bullet while he stood at some exposition up in New York—was it Buffalo? Both men would wring out a few more hours of life than Mr. Lincoln did. The minute Booth took aim, the President was as good as dead in that theater box. And like me, his wife never got to hear a dying word from her husband's mouth.

Oh, this is a strange house, a strange town, and no one out there knows my stories. I am not from here, you know. These are not the sunrises I grew up with, not my birds or my streets or my people. Every bit of who I was got left behind in the town that was my home and where I lost everything, save the bits in this box. Perhaps Mary Lincoln had a box of her own remembrances she left behind when she passed. ❧

Chapter 17

PRACTICALLY EVERYONE KNEW everyone else those years, all of us good citizens of Gettysburg. D. worked for Solomon Powers, the man George hired to lay the foundation for our house. Back then you could not step out over your threshold without rubbing shoulders with the rest of the townspeople.

Solomon Powers fathered a brood of girls—six daughters and not a son in the lot to carry on his name. Daniel Pittenturf blew into town, a young buck ready to learn the stone trade from the man who would end up becoming his father-in-law.

D. must have been like a rooster in a henhouse. He was three years older than the Powers firstborn, Cynthia. With this apprentice showing up, old Powers had to keep a sharp eye on his brood from dawn to dusk, and especially after dusk.

You would not say the Powers girls were a comely bunch, but Cynthia was probably the easiest to look at of the six. It would be no surprise that she was the flower that D. would pluck from the bouquet. After they married, the couple stayed in the Powers nest, and I can tell you, it was a tight circle of hens studying that man's every move. At least this is what D. harped on years later, when he had very little to do with the Powers clan. When the time came, D. and his bride were able to take a house, it ended up being smack next door to his in-laws.

As much as the North was profiting from the war effort, Gettysburg was not. The carriage business that employed so many went into hibernation. Posse after posse of the town's younger workers went off to fight, and any kind of business growth stalled out. House building was part and parcel of that. With tightened belts and a growing uneasiness over the fate of the Union, who could afford the luxury of new construction?

The Powers, like the rest of Gettysburg, had to make do with less. D. and Cynthia were no different. His work had dried up, and they could not keep up with what they owed on their house. They were forced to rent it out and move over into the Powers henhouse again.

What D. must have thought back in the day when he was laying those stones for the young Shrivers' fine new house! I remember watching them work from across the way. Suited up in his good waistcoat, George would stand in the circle, his hands clean and cocked on his hips, his pockets holding the workers' wage, holding D.'s livelihood.

With his stonecutter's arms and rough hands, D. probably could have picked George up and slung him over his shoulder. The only time I saw the man properly washed up and presentable those days was in the pews of St. James when we all happened to be gathered for Sunday service at the same time. He was only five years older than George and me, but he had a hard-used look about him, seldom clean-shaved that I can remember, and I thought then that his rough way in the world came hand in hand with being a mason. Still, he was not a bad looking man.

We were of different worlds, the workmen and the young Shriver couple. It came down to this: George was a gentleman who felt it was his God-given duty to present himself to the world as one. D. would say he was not raised as a fop and had no need or desire to pretend that he was.

Why he did not muster with the rest of them that year I never really understood. He was already thirty years old when the call for volunteers came, but he had the strength of a much younger man. He stayed behind and eked out a living in town. Years later he would not even talk about those times when the subject of war came up in conversation, except to question the sanity of the boys who went off to fight for a "warlord" like Lincoln—the very word he would use.

Like the rest of the townspeople, D. heard anything I would hear about the war efforts and men like George's whereabouts, from capture to prison death. It was a time of precious little privacy, when we knew too much about each other's affairs.

As a new widow, my loneliness those months was like a lake, and I was drowning in the thick darkness of it. All the tallying and listing and resetting I took on that year of unknowing might have helped keep another woman sane at the center, but I was barely keeping my head above the murk and doing my best to maintain a sunny disposition for my daughters.

I had more or less made up my mind that I could not spend another unwelcome year in that house now that my husband would not come back to his life with us. Every corner held a reminder of what was lost, of George's shattered intentions for our family, of the death the place was stained with.

I tallied and refigured for months trying to tease out a reasonable next move, hoping and praying all along the way that the war would end and a miracle would happen, that somehow George would walk through our door, that there had been some mistake made in the records. But eventually, I accepted the reality of a graveyard like Andersonville, and all hope was as buried in me as George's remains were in a numbered plot deep in Secesh territory.

It was not really only the matter of putting a roof over our heads. It was the rest of it: living out the next six, seven, eight years, or until I got the girls married off, in a house that reminded me every hour that I was George's widow. I began to resent the very doorways, the walls and floors that held his careful design. You could say I was sick at heart.

Of course, everyone knew the details of Cynthia's illness. The Powers' house was one of the full-up hospitals after the battle, with every corner of the place occupied by the wounded.

And why not? There was a ready-made staff of girls to take on the press of constant nursing duties.

Months before the battle, Cynthia had given birth to their second son, close on the heels of firstborn Frank. Now here she was, bending over the wounded, lifting their heavy heads and limbs, trudging up and down the cellar stairs that were so dank and knotted with disease. She could have done less, but she had a strain of martyr in her, as D. once told me in the early days of our marriage.

By the time Gettysburg and the Powers house had long been emptied of its wounded "guests," Cynthia herself had become the infirmed one in need of attention. The sisters took full charge of firstborn Frank and baby James' care. Her breathing and coughing grew worse and weakened her to the core, and she did not live to see the baby's first birthday. D. was left a widower with a two-year-old and a baby not yet on its feet, and all the grieving Powers milling and clucking around him.

A year that I can barely remember had passed, and here I was, with a dead husband, a dwindling purse, my growing girls, and a big house that would never again be the home it was built to be. And I was suffocating in a paralyzing loneliness.

Then one early evening, there stood D., unannounced on my back stoop to tell me he had brought over a load of firewood and asking where would I like it stacked.

It had been one of those days George would have called "Indian summer," and now the smell of autumn was seeping into the warm air of September. My garden was still heavy with beans and squash, and the muted pinks and golds of primroses and black-eyed Susans dotted the growing dusk with color. I fetched D. a cup of water, and we settled onto the stoop as darkness fell.

We were not the same people who had first spoken in that yard years prior. There were no stars in our eyes and whatever pride I wore when first moving to town had long ago been shed. But a conversation naturally opened up about my thoughts on selling the house, and it was a surprise how almost right away we were considering how it might look for us to pool our pasts and futures. Still, it was a slow talk that felt to me like a door being nudged opened barely a crack.

The girls were asleep upstairs, and his boys were under the watchful eyes of the Powers sisters a few streets over. I thanked him for the firewood, and we rose and shook hands in parting. I was too tired to be surprised by any of it. For the first time he referred to me not as Mrs. Shriver, but as Henrietta.

I was tired of trying to figure out the road ahead, and soon D.'s proposal somehow became the only reasonable path to consider. The man was certain he could invest what the house would bring to turn a profit for us. And without further thought, I began to consider the reality of moving my old life out of George's realm and into a new chapter as the wife of another man. In those times, it was what you had to do.

And really, by then I had already concluded that there were

no reasonable alternatives. I must have come to that understanding long before D. showed up that night. I could not
think another month, another year out, let alone ten or fifteen
years. I have come to believe that many a widow moves too
soon, the heart still blinded by the fear and confusion grief can
breed in you. I can say now that this was the case with me. I
should have waited.

Instead I found myself asking, why not marry him? It
would be a quick move into the security I was hungry for. It
was not clear reasoning, but I was stranded in a well of desperation. It was as though my desolation was choking me.

We would reclaim his High Street row house that shared
a wall with the Powers henhouse. I would cling to what few
pieces I could not part with, the Shriver part of me, and
squeeze them into cramped quarters as the new Mrs. Pittenturf. The girls and I would move from the ample grace of the
home George gave us, to the cramped row house that would
hold D. and me and four children.

The word went out in short order that I was considering
selling, and Daniel Trimmer showed up at the front door
within the week to talk about buying. He and Henry Garlach
had designs for putting their cabinet-making business on the
property. In short order, I brought in a lawyer to do an inventory of my possessions, from garret to cellar, cup to chair.

What I did not know was uncovered by that attorney's
scouring of the deed, that George's brothers had borrowed

some sizable amounts from their father before he died. Perhaps life would have been different for me if the loans had been paid off before I became a widow, as surely as they would have been had George come home and opened his business.

But I never saw a cent from those notes, and I figure the brothers did not consider me to have a right to any Shriver assets anyway. It was men's business, it was paper, I was no relation to them, and what was owed would not affect the sale of Baltimore Street.

Look, by then, so much had fallen apart anyway. All the music that once was my life with George, all the possibilities that lived in our once-fine house, all of that was as dead as my husband. I needed to take up a different life, that much I knew.

The spring morning that I handed Henry Garlach the key to my front door lock, I walked away from the house that held my greatest joys and my deepest sorrows. For a time the girls and I stayed at the farm, but by summer I would stand in the St. James parsonage beside D. to become his wife. We were two widowers grasping at some sort of a future together.

And with that act, my name fell from the veteran widow pension rolls. You see, the good folks in Washington had not yet sent me so much as a cent, even though they knew their war left me a widowed mother, with George already dead for close to two years. As far as I was concerned, there was no guarantee that any kind of government support might ever make its way to me.

Was I to remain frozen there, husbandless and down to my last coin, my larder empty, my girls hungry, patiently waiting for the lawmakers to decide it was time to send me my rightful pension money? I was one of those widows you would read of in the Bible, and no one was pleading on my behalf. I was alone and in a bind, jammed into a corner with no prospects.

There were times down the road when D. would throw it in my face, how he had "rescued" me, and where would I be if he had left me there to end up in the poor house and watch my girls wind up in rags. But I never thought of him as my rescuer. I came to believe that I had given up, surrendered too soon, taken the wrong turn at the wrong time with the wrong man. ❧

Chapter 18

LILLIAN MAE PITTENTURF CAME INTO this world a strapping, hungry cub, not like Sadie and Mollie, my scrawnier newborns. I was barely nineteen when I first gave birth, a young farm wife with a future lying before me like an unread letter. Maybe it was George who planted smaller babies than D. I do not know.

By the time Lillie came along, my treasure chest of joy seemed to have toppled over and emptied itself. I was no longer a comfortable young woman with my beloved beside me. At thirty-one, with a man I had not planned to marry, this birth was not something I anticipated with joy. I was with D.'s child too soon, and I reckoned that was what I assumed the townspeople thought when they looked at me.

From my first months of confinement, when I could barely keep food down, the mornings were something that I had to grit my teeth and get through. But despite that early sickness that made me appear a weakling, I apparently had grown tougher with age and weathered the rest of the pregnancy to the finish line. D. was surprised at how quickly I would spring back onto my feet after Lillie was born. He must have feared I might follow in Cynthia's wake, languishing in my birth bed only to leave him a widower again with a baby and my girls on his hands.

I am not saying Lillian's birth was a picnic. What birth is? But mine, even with a big baby, was not as dire as some that I witnessed, where a woman's pains were more than her body could bear, or a limp, blue-skinned child would come into the world with its life already passed and gone.

I remember like it was yesterday. I was nine when Ma birthed her last, a puny, gurgling baby girl who lived only a few hours. Children cannot forget fear in a father's eyes, or the sounds of suffering that come from their mother.

Ma had a hard, hard time of it that final birth, and I was afraid to go to sleep for many nights afterward, so worried I was with how gray and spent she was, then with how quiet she grew, like her spirit was wandering in some far-off country. She was forty years old, and she was laid up in the borning room for weeks. She sank into a well of sorrow for a long season afterwards, as though all her hopes had been dashed away with the loss of that one.

I remember Pa trying to comfort her again and again with assurances of those babies resting in peace somewhere—"Suffer the little children, for of such is the kingdom of heaven,"—and about it being for the best and all. Even though we knew of the fickle chances of our wee ones surviving, the losses mattered to us mothers, and we grieved inside for longer than any-one noticed. Women still do, to this day. It is the way of nature.

I was younger than Ma in this third pregnancy and maybe of hardier stock, I do not know. But after a quick birth I was soon on my feet with a baby slung on my hip and my girls to care for in the crowded High Street quarters. The big sisters treated Lillie like a princess doll, dressing and coddling her when they were not at school and other times when they fig-ured it was a good way to weasel out of a chore or two.

The times were changing, and for Sadie and Mollie, it was a freer, lighter way compared with my growing up. I wanted this for them—not only to learn how to run a house and raise children. How to have fun with my own citified friends was something I seldom experienced as a country girl. St. James was a stroll away from High Street, a nest for families and young people, with picnics and parties that wove my daughters into a busy social calendar.

D. was gone long hours those days, which I figured would be good for the family purse. But then he would come to the supper table too wrung out for small talk, even though it was about the only time we all sat down across from each other. To his credit, he more or less tolerated what my girls gabbed on about with little complaint. Still, he was never much interested in drawing them out. I will say he was happiest when his own darling girl scrambled up onto his lap.

Even though by then D.'s boy Frankie lived right next

door, father and son saw little of each other, mostly because it was what the Powers had decided was the way it should be after the accident. Have I written here yet about baby James and that dark day?

From the start I felt the coldness of the Powers clan toward me. When D. told them he was marrying the Widow Shriver, they must have silently finished his announcement in their thoughts with, "She is taking our boys away from us."

It must have come across as wrong to them, to have Frank and James under their roof from the start, changing nappies and wiping noses and doing the things the boys' mother would be doing had she lived. And now to have them taken away, moved out to become another woman's children! To them I was an undeserving imposter standing in for their Cynthia, not so long cold in her grave and deserving of something better.

But there we were, living our lives next door to them, my belly already growing with a baby not related to them, their boys no longer eating at the Powers table or sleeping beside them.

I cannot remember that D. ever began a sentence with an inquiry as to what I might be up to and if I could be interrupted. It was his way from the start, and so it was that morning.

My weeks of sickness with carrying his child in me were shorter but were worse than my other three confinements put together. Well into the afternoon any smell of food was enough to set me off. That day was a particularly bad one, I remember, and I struggled to keep my stomach from emptying right there on the kitchen floor. If I knew what he had in mind I would have told him to wait for a spell till I got my stomach settled.

But D. got it in his head that he should butcher a chicken before he went off to work.

The girls were at school. The boys were churning around under foot. Without so much as a word to me, D. heated up the dunking pot of water to scald the bird in after he killed it to make the plucking easier.

I was never quite as fast as Ma at that, but that morning was not a good one for me to be pulling feathers off a dead chicken. I suppose he thought he was being helpful, or maybe he was irked with me and my queasiness. Maybe I was not working fast enough to suit him. I will never know.

D. moved the kettle of scalding water to the floor before he stepped out the kitchen door to do the slaughter, and almost at the same moment, little James decided it was just the time to step up onto a chair behind me. In one fateful second, he lost his footing and tumbled into the steaming pot.

I do not have to draw you a picture here. You can guess how it was, with D. tearing back into the kitchen with a dead bird dangling from his hand. I had yanked that poor boy out of the water, horrified to see his scarlet skin already trying to pull away from his body. I can hear that child's screams in my head as I write about that morning.

D. flew out of the front door to get the Powers, and in a

moment there they all stood huddled and frantic in our kitchen, fussing and weeping and shaming. Catherine lifted the boy into her apron to move him to their house with D. and the others in tow. One of them ran off to fetch the doctor.

D. stayed next door for the rest of the day. At suppertime, he came home cold with anger toward me. His boy had drifted into unconsciousness, his chest heaving with fever. There was nothing to be done, and it was my fault. Sadie and Mollie took all of this in from their room upstairs, where they often hid from D.'s tirades.

Moments later, he hefted confused Frankie into his arms and swept out the door to join the rest of the Powers keeping vigil through the night beside their boy. Little James was dead before sunrise, joining his mother in eternity. I had not yet had enough time to think of that boy as my own. To me, he was Cynthia's baby, D.'s son. The Powers clan probably was right, that I was not fit to care for him.

For endless hours all that long night the weeping came through our shared wall. The lament would rise and fall, then there would be long stretches of dead silence, only for it to all charge up again. I felt as though I was a witness to hell, that I was the door tender, holding it open for everyone to peer in and feel the heat. I had caused the death of that innocent.

You can imagine how thick the air in the rooms of the High Street house hung with blame and sadness for weeks after the accident. That was a warm October, and I remember standing at the edge of the group in Ever Green in the late autumn sun as James was lowered into the earth beside his mother. He had not yet reached his third birthday. No one spoke a word to me about it, but I felt the sure stares of my accusers from that moment on.

The Powers wasted no time filing court papers to take Frankie under their roof where they figured he rightfully belonged. I refused to even look at the letter from the lawyers that D. silently read at the kitchen table. We did not have the money to bring an attorney of our own into it. I sometimes thought D. agreed with his in-laws, that we, no, that *I* was not fit to watch over his boy.

We were required to stand in the courtroom proceedings the morning that Solomon and Catherine Powers were awarded custody of Frank. D. was ordered to surrender Frankie and any rights connected to the his son's welfare. The grandparents would end up calling the boy "Powers." And I thought, old Solomon finally got his wish granted to have a son of his own.

Of course little Frank did not really grasp what happened the day the Powers became his legal family. But I figured there would come a time of bitter realization in that boy, of how his brother James died, of being given away to his grandparents, of how his pa had not lifted a finger to fight for custody, of what kinship was lost to him. The boy deserved better than what I had given him. I can tell you that there was no hesitation in

Frank to switch his devotion away from D. and return it to old Solomon and his wife.

I can see now how it must have looked to them. I was not their long-suffering firstborn daughter. I had not provided good enough care for their precious treasures—those two little boys. I was a poor substitute who now shared their son-in-law's bed, where their dear Cynthia should be laying her head at day's end. And I was so careless as to have let the baby she kissed goodbye die on my watch.

So it was that Lillie Mae came into the world to become D.'s only child. Despite the sad drama that preceded her, she played her part as well as any actress, a plump *Engel* whose smile I can recall more than any crying she may have done.

There was another baby, you know, born two years after Lillie and far too early, and dying far too soon. We called Emma. Right off, I could see she was too sickly, too small to hang onto her life. She was barely a month old when she joined the angels and was laid to rest just as her half-brother Jacob had been over in Mt. Joy.

But really, as for the angels, it was a fool's wish to think that these children's lives went on in some other heavenly realm. All I could say for sure is that Jacob and Emma were no longer in my realm, or in my arms. Suffer the little children…

Lillie Mae was the angel who stayed put on the earth, and no one else could soften her father's sour moods like she did when the darkness came over him. She was the easiest baby

I ever knew, and I miss that time with her. You see, by then Sadie and Mollie and Lillie Mae had become the whole of my universe after so much had shifted. In them was whatever future lay ahead for me.

There is much that is forgotten in a lifetime, but there is much that I remember, all that is stitched into my being and will go to the grave with me. Whether or not I know my own name by the time I close my eyes in death is of no concern to me today. But I remember their names, those dear children. My babies are gone, and to this day, I miss the feel, the sound of them. ❧

Chapter 19

IT WAS A SUMMER EVENING before her eighteenth birthday when Sadie's voice first took on a hoarse quality and her coughing started up. At first, she could go a stretch without a problem. But it would happen more often that her speaking grew raspier and her breathing would become labored for longer stretches.

When it got bad enough, she took to her bed, and I made cabbage poultices and rubbed cubeb salve onto her chest. I cooked up quantities of horehound syrup and bergamot tea and *Stachelbeeren*, the gooseberry tea Ma used to force into us. I sat her in the kitchen with her feet in buckets of hot mustard water—anything to help give her some small relief. I simmered apple cores and cinnamon on the stove and brought cut balsam branches inside to freshen the house air. And she would wrestle her strength together and be all right for a week or two, only to have her chest fill up again too soon.

Ma always kept a couple of bottles of horehound syrup on hand. She would traipse out to the far edges of her garden, up against the stand of trees, and bundle up bushels of those leggy, hairy weeds to hang high above in the cellar. When the plants dried to her liking, she snipped off what she needed to steep in boiling water for a good long time to reduce the liquid into a bitter, dark brew. She would add a healthy pour of honey or sugar or sorghum syrup to the strained liquid. The smell would drift up from the cellar as she continued to cook it down to a dark, amber shimmer. I never much liked the syrup, but when she hauled out the bottle and made us swallow a spoonful, I admit there was relief to be found in its bitterness.

Better was her horehound candy. She would sweeten the pot even more and plop a scoop of butter into the bubbling syrup to boil it all down further. Finally the thick syrup would be poured into a greased pan to cool and be cut it up into chunks to wrap and twist into paper. We would gladly accept a piece of that whenever it was offered. Chandlers sometimes would carry those candies in their carts, but I have not seen the plant or the candies for a good long while.

My poor Sadie would have her coughing spells and she would swallow spoonfuls of syrup for me, squeezing her face up like an old cat. In the end, she opened and swallowed obediently, although by then there was no elixir that would be of any real use to her.

D. and I stood alone in the kitchen one night, and he handed me a bottle of Allen's Lung Balsam he brought home from a peddler. That was the first he confided that Sadie's sickness was what he had seen in Cynthia. Even though I had long harbored that very fear, his bringing the notion out into the room was like a fist to my chest.

Only four years earlier my younger sister Beckie took sick over in Harrisburg with the wasting disease. She and her husband—another George—had two little ones, and like D.'s Cynthia, after her baby girl's birth, Beckie grew so weak she could not leave her bed. Their Harry was four years old and daughter Carrie had barely passed her first birthday. My widowed brother-in-law, so devoted to Beckie, went deep into mourning after her passing.

Their story was like so many around those years. George had survived the fighting, even being locked up for a time in a Virginia prison. The war was not yet over when he was discharged from the army, a captain and a decorated hero. Right away he and my sister married out at the farm. He was a kind fellow, a good father to their little son and daughter, and Beckie's passing broke his heart.

The man died a year after he lost his wife, almost to the day. His orphaned children were taken in by their grandparents on the Kitzmiller side over in Harrisburg.

The same *verdammt* disease that took him that spring had already worked its evil in my Sadie's body. You would think I could have read the writing on the wall, but I was deep into denial over my girl's state.

Dr. Huber came often enough, urging us to get her out into the sun as much as we could manage. But by then winter was coming on, and really, what could he or anyone do about the wasting disease? I was on my own making her comfortable, trying my best to help her find her breath.

Beetons suggested warm baths as a good remedy for a tight chest cough, and by then folks were not so afraid of the dangers of bathing, of immorality and disease seeping into the body through the bath water, all of that nonsense. These days, I am told there are people who take more than one bath in a week in water drawn especially for them, emptied out before another climbs into a tub of fresh water. But in my time no one would dare do that. Our Saturday baths were sacred, all of us using the same water. I broke the rules for Sadie and lifted her into a warm bath almost daily toward the end, praying to see if it might loosen her chest up. There were times it seemed to do her some good.

That summer she grew a great deal gaunter, and even when a fever would rise, the color stayed drained out of her cheeks. September was the first she coughed up quantities of blood, and a few weeks later, the doctor shook his head as he put his hat on in the doorway to step out into the autumn rain. What could he do? What could anyone do? She had picked up considerable speed on her slow road to the grave.

To lose a daughter who had soldiered on through what Sadie had—childhood sickbeds, the horrors of that week of war and the months of stench and burying all that was left behind, the loss of her father, leaving the house on Baltimore Street that she wept over for weeks and probably never got over. It was wrong for her to have to take on this fresh suffering, and it was written in her stars.

She had sat through confirmation classes at St. James and stood tall and beaming with the others the Sunday morning they got their certificates. She finished her studies with her two best friends, and I will say she was a smart one. She had even been kissed by the Danner boy on a church outing, news that her sister trumpeted with glee one evening at the supper table.

Autumn was taking its last breath when we moved her downstairs and propped her up on the divan as best we could. I will not go into it all—the last of the endless nights, me trying to doze in the chair or on the floor beside her, my own chest aching as I took in her ragged wheezing, sounds that made me think of a broken pump organ.

On Sadie's final night in this world, while the others slept upstairs, there was no denying her tired body was about to surrender. She had not murmured a word for a good three days, and her sweet eyes that so often pleaded with me for help were closed to life as her spirit struggled to do its final work.

My firstborn died before dawn on a Friday morning, with an early winter snow floating down as if to cover the sins of the world outside the parlor window. After Sadie's rush across her finish line, it seemed all was covered in a mournful, silent peace. I sat in the stillness of that room with her body and thought, "What is the point of this life?"

Mollie woke up before D. and Lillie to learn the sad news of her sister's passing. I remember she did not cry that morning, and I suspected she had shed many tears in the nights of sleeping alone upstairs after Sadie had been moved down to the parlor.

Together we set to work in a hush side by side, bathing her thin arms and legs and wresting her wasted frame out of her nightdress and into her blue gingham, her first and favorite long skirt. I brushed and plaited her hair for a final time and wiped her thin face, her neck, her hands with lavender water. I had bathed and dressed her like this almost nineteen years prior, when she was my firstborn, my only treasure, toddling around the Shriver farm kitchen.

She was the baby who taught me how to be a mother, arriving in this world to transform George and me into a family.

I remember so much and so little of the day she passed. But as if I had to act all at once, I grabbed my purse and charged over to Baltimore Street to lay down money for my daughter's coffin, right there in the cellar where Sadie played as a child. The air was heavy with the smell of fresh cut pine and lemon oil, almost as it did when it was being finished by the builders years before, with George standing there, overseeing the work. Trimmer, well-versed in offering condolences to the likes of me, would deliver Sadie's casket within the hour.

By the time I traipsed up High Street, I could see our door had been hung for mourning. Without a word, Catherine Powers had put up the white crepe that we kept on hand in those days. I stepped into the silence of that room, my Sadie as I had left her, sleeping there in her Sunday best and free of suffering.

To be fair, I must say they turned out to be tolerable good people, the Powers.

They were. I knew I was a poor substitute for their firstborn, and Cynthia had managed before she died to give them the thing they so desperately wanted—those two little boys. How many children had they ended up taking into their home to foster over the years I could not count.

But even after all the sadness of James' accident and the courtroom drama, it was not so many months of silence when they softened to us, as was their habit. They stood beside us in Sadie's passing, young Frank—their "Powers"—in the midst of them. They did not owe that to me, and yet there they were.

Word spread quickly in a town like Gettysburg those years. D., knowing my state, stayed at home that morning and slipped out to put a notice in the papers. The minister showed up at the door to offer prayers and settle the details for a quiet service the next day. We would gather beside my girl in the room where she breathed her last, with her family and the Powers and her two good friends present. Both my folks took sick that week, and there was no other family to stand beside me in my mourning.

Poor little Lillie. I was focused on her dead sister and had nothing to say to her, and she clung to Mollie like a burr, trying to make sense of big sister Sadie being lifted into her coffin that afternoon, the air heavy with the fragrance of sorrow.

And dear Mollie! She had never woken a day in her life without her big sister in the world beside her, the one she whispered her secrets to as she fell asleep and argued and giggled with and copied everything, from manners and hairstyle to all those other things girls do growing up together. Now she stood alongside us, abandoned by Sadie and promoted to the honor of being the oldest child.

I kept the wake alone that night, a candle lit, singing lullabies soft enough so no one upstairs would hear, talking to George as though he were sitting right there beside me with Sadie, keeping vigil in the darkness. I conjured up his voice whispering "Our girl is gone." And for all I know, he may have been there mourning with me that night. What do we know of the spirit world?

But as I sat those long hours, I remember being filled anew with regret that I was not able to keep this very vigil over George's body. Sitting in the dimness with our girl, I was fresh consumed with such guilt and anger over his parting. If only I could have seen his face once more, to bathe it as I had Sadie's, to comb back his proud hair, to clean the soldier's dirt from under his fingernails and tie his cravat just so. These were things that mattered to him. Instead I was bound to be forever haunted by the image of his skeletal body rotting in the mass grave he had been tossed into without benefit of a prayer or a shroud.

Sadie's prayer service was brief the next day. I insisted we walk behind the hearse, a slow, shivering procession all the way to Ever Green, through sloppy streets of melting snow. The girls moved me along, Lillie Mae with one hand, Mollie the other.

I stood in a fog with a handful of mourners, watching the box that held my girl be lowered down into its cold cave. And I thought, "That's four." Baby Jacob over in Mt. Joy, George in a military grave a world away, baby Emma from D., the one who came out of me as good as dead, and now Sadie. And then there was D.'s baby James sleeping across the way beside his mama, and sister Beckie and her George in the Kitzmiller family plot.

Was this my own personal punishment for some unspeakable sin of pride or lack of charity, to watch all who I love die, one by one, before me?

It is a curse of a thing for a mother to bury her child, and worse yet when that baby has grown up into womanhood. All the nursing, the diapering, the illnesses, the feeding and disciplining, all the teaching and bedtime prayers and comforting of night terrors, past all of that early work, to the time when she stands eye to eye and shoulder to shoulder with you by the kitchen stove and makes you laugh until tears fall. And then to have to say goodbye and watch that child depart before me.

Despite how regular the deaths of our kin are, deep in me I believe a child going before her mother is wrong, and I wonder where God stands in that kind of mixed-up order. Is He standing unmoved off to the side watching disaster unfold, or does He lift his mighty hand to stop the child's beating heart Himself?

And we, the left-behind women, we put on our mourning dresses and prod ourselves on through the motions of living. The day after Sadie was lowered into the ground, Mollie helped me rearrange the furniture in the front room and move her sister's things into the trunk upstairs far away from my eyes. We put away the medicines and aired out the bedclothes on the backyard line in the icy afternoon breeze. That evening, there was one less chair at the kitchen table as we tried to swallow our quiet supper. Death hung around the house like a sulking intruder.

I have this one tintype here from Will Tipton after he took over the Tyson studio on York, when Lillie was four, I think. Sadie was about fifteen, and you can see her father's fair hair and ebony eyes. Mollie always favored me in her coloring, you know. The girls were fidgety that morning, fussing over Lillie's hair and trying to steel up for the long pose when they needed to be stone still before the camera box.

Will learned his trade as Tysons' eager young apprentice. By the time the little studio became his, he had grown into a smart businessman with notions on how to better turn a profit. He ended up well known in those parts, you know, for his battlefield and monument pictures, recording all the drama of the war's biggest battle. People would come from all around to buy his Gettysburg images.

You must agree that this is a fine miniature. I remember Will kept urging me to step into the scene he was about to capture. But I said, no, this one was for me to remember my girls by.

After Sadie's passing, it seemed to me that the dying and death became as regular as Christmas. As Pa would say, "Dust thou art, and unto dust shalt thou return." I had already been standing knee-deep in the dust by then, and I had no notion of how to make my way out of it. ❧

Chapter 20

MA COLLAPSED IN HER GARDENS on a warm spring morning. Levi tore into town to fetch me and stood before me, hat in hand. It was a Wednesday, washday, and Lillie Mae was in school. I was hanging laundry, as Ma herself had done that morning. I find it strange how you forever remember where you stood and what you were doing when bad news came knocking.

By the time I made it out to the farm, they had set a cot for her in the borning room. I held vigil at her side, but she never wakened to know I was there, and by sunset, she passed. Levi and Pa and I wept our quiet goodbyes, then together we murmured the *Unser Vater* in the stillness, not in English as I had done in Ma's cellar kitchen with the dying officer years earlier, but in the quiet beauty of her German tongue.

Were Beckie still alive, she would have helped me wrestle Ma out of her housedress and get her bathed. But I was on my own, tugging the linens up over her again and again to keep her covered as I worked. I remember being shocked to see my mother's frail body, suddenly withered in death, naked as a baby and so vulnerable. It was as though I was washing up a sleeping child.

We kept watch a long while beside her as dusk came on and mourners came and went. I made tea and invited folks to step into the kitchen and have some of the last bread Ma was to pull out of her oven that very morning.

Later, in the hush of the lantern glow, I found myself glancing in at her furrowed face and wrinkled lips sealed in a still peace. I remember wondering where all her lifetime had departed in an instant—seventy-two years of habits and receipts and wisdom and stubborn opinions—all of it gone in the blink of an eye, vanished to leave behind the frail, lifeless shell that once was my hearty, outspoken Ma.

Poor Pa could not be persuaded to go up to bed for sleep. I tried to nap in the chair by the hearth, but Pa stayed beside his wife in the candlelight the whole night, bent over for his head to rest against her side, his hand covering hers.

The two of them had their share of differences. What marriage can avoid rough waters in that many together years? Ma was nine years younger than Pa when she married him at nineteen. Strong-tempered and quick-witted, she could be a demanding one, and as children we would snicker at the sound of her stomping foot from their room above.

Moments later she would be the coy, playful one, whispering some sweet nothing to him in her hushed German in the kitchen, and he would walk away with a smile. The thing is, the two of them stayed the course beside each other, and as far as I know, were loyal partners for all those decades, faithful until death parted them, as the wedding vows declared it.

I have often wondered what it would have been to grow old beside George, he and I a couple of ancient crows cozied at our table, the stove warming our feet on a November evening. These days, squinting through my clouded eyes into a looking glass that holds a stranger, I find myself wondering if the years would have treated him kindly. How would an "old George" appear to me in this tired world?

Some might say my George was the lucky one, to never grow old and feeble. But if he had, would we still see each other through the eyes of youthful love? Would our loyalties be as unwavering as my folks' were the day death parted them? Would there have been more children born to us on Baltimore Street? Would we have prospered to grow into the loyal, respected family he intended the town folk to look up to? Perhaps George would have become mayor of Gettysburg or even a senator, like one of the men I blamed for the killing fields.

At least my folks were graced with a long life together, with time to finish out the story of their marriage.

My widowed Pa went on for a year more. Ma's passing was a sledge to his spirit. They were a couple of old geese, those two, loyal and bound together by some mystery a human cannot explain, slowed and limping around their farm in the final years.

Long before her death, Pa had been so undone by the summer of the battle, witnessing his farm being blown apart by that *verdammt* week of fighting. Even fifteen years hence he lamented that there was no "peace that passeth understanding" in him, having not gotten an ounce of satisfaction from Washington, not a cent of *Zahlung*—no payment or so much as a word of gratitude for the sacrifices those three days forced on him. His government's disregard irked him to his last breath. Even after all those years of replanting and repairing and harvesting, he was never again to find the same proud satisfaction with his fields that he held before 1863.

Within days after the fighting ended, Pa filed a reckoning with the army people in Washington, a list of all that was lost during the battle week, tallying the cost of destruction at $2700, or close to that. He was obsessed with the notion of getting something, anything repaid for all the carnage left by a war that five years prior no one could have dreamed would come to Gettysburg.

It was, I think, a dozen years and at least that many back-and-forth correspondences before he got the last thin letter from the government saying they would settle for $36. They said he had no "proof" of his damages—no receipts, no officers who witnessed what he claimed. $36! He had spent ten times that on attorneys who ended up being as worthless as their calling cards. As it was, the meager money they promised never reached Pa's calloused hands. A couple of months after

Pa was buried, Levi stood at the post office and held a government check made out to Jacob Weikert.

With Ma's death, all the energy, all the purpose had drained out of him. By then my brothers had taken the reins and were doing a fine job with the farm anyway. One early evening after chores, Pa missed a step at the bottom of the barn stairs and, in the tumble, broke apart his hip bones. A week later we were lowering him into the ground next to Ma. The goose and the gander finally rested beside each other again.

Cemeteries did not used to be as fine as Ever Green, you know. But Gettysburg got bitten by the refinement bug, and part of the city plan was to bring its graveyard closer into town, with gardens and a fancy archway entry. No more country plots where cows would graze around the tombstones.

The same year we married, 1855, is when Ever Green came to be, complete with speeches with words like "elegant" and "civilized" and "inspiring." Imagine that! For a meadow of the decaying dead to be referred to as elegant.

If those good citizens had only known on the afternoon our refined cemetery was dedicated that war would blast the gravestones apart only a few years down the road, that fresh blood would soak into its manicured grounds by the bucketful, that Ever Green would end up being bordered by a military cemetery holding the thousands of soldiers killed in a summer battle that was anything but civilized.

For being so new, the hills of Ever Green had quickly

grown into a gathering spot for my kin. For Lillie, it had become a familiar destination, what with her sister and now her Oma and Opa, all buried there in four years' time. She would go with me on Sundays to visit their graves. But Mollie wanted nothing to do with it and never once came along with us.

The same year that Pa passed, Mother Shriver had been lowered into the earth at the Elias Lutheran cemetery over in Emmitsburg. We had not spoken for a very long time by then.

My mother-in-law—what can I say of that woman? I used to shake my head at her ways, that nobody and nothing seemed to be quite good enough to suit her. My girls hardly saw her face after we moved off the farm and into town. And then once I married D., well, I had dishonored her fallen son and now I was as good as dead to her.

I think now of George's mother and realize I was not much better at seeing the sunny side of life than she was. She never stood in our house on Baltimore Street once George mustered. She never was to see the ruin I had let things come to that dark week.

On the other side of the balance scale was my Pa. You should know that Jacob Weikert was a good father, a decent man. There were some *bedeuten* stories printed in the papers, and it was downright mean talk from the army people and the fools who flooded the town and fields after the smoke cleared. We all read the pieces about Gettysburg's "crazy Dutch farmers" who fled the battle scene to hide with their animals, how they refused to cooperate with the army men and even profited off the needs of the soldiers that dark week.

Well, let me tell you, Jacob Weikert was not crazy. Furthermore, he considered himself a hard-working American, certainly not Dutch or Deutsch, or whatever labels the outsiders slapped on our people.

For *Gott's* sake, can you stop for a moment and put yourself in Pa's shoes? Here you are, trying to protect your family while you watch ruin brought down on everything you have worried and labored over for as long as you could walk, your livelihood, the inheritance, the *Erbe* you were responsible for, to pass onto your descendants.

The farm that was his life was trampled and bloodied and blown apart right before his eyes, dumped on by forces he had no truck with. And then those forces turn around and want him to be grateful for what they had done to him? *Lugen*—lies and more lies, those stories.

When he breathed his last it was the sigh of a gander lifting off for the skies, as though being hoisted upward out of his featherweight body to rise to the light, liberated and set free, never to return to this wounded world. All those years, all that had been broken and lost, all that he had carried around on his shoulders like an ox yoke was finally lifted. Pa was eighty-one years old when he was laid to rest in Ever Green.

Death had been downright busy, and it was not done with us yet.

*   *   *

The year she watched her older sister die, it seemed to me Mollie grew up in a fortnight. At fifteen, she had lost the last traces of little girl in her face and rose up a good three inches to stand eye to eye before me.

By that spring she took on the shape of a young woman. There was a new maturity, a tenderness in how she treated me, as though she could read my sorrow-drenched mind. Mollie understood as no one else how wrung out I was, and in her attention to Lillie and me, she tried to fill a void I could not so much as shape into words.

Of my three girls, Mary Margaret Shriver stood most in my image, even though she was the one named after George's mother. But my Mollie was more a Weikert than a Shriver. Her coloring, her laugh, the way she posed with her hand hitched on her hip. Pa used to say that the girl was spit out of her mother's mouth. And it is true, there was a way about Mollie so that my family would tease and call her Little Hettie, something she never seemed to mind. She was my miniature looking glass self.

Enter Will Stallsmith, a young man with a proper way about him who waited until Mollie turned eighteen to come calling for her on High Street. He was four years her senior and grew up over in Littletown. Will had plenty of extended family in Gettysburg, and once he moved to town for work, he seldom missed a Sunday at St. James. From his family pew, he must have had his eye fixed on my girl for enough sermons to know what he wanted.

Will was a good man, always polite with me and playful with Lillie. I can only say Mollie was the happiest I had ever known her to be from the time he showed up at our door. He was a handsome one, with green eyes and strong arms, and I liked him from the start.

Even before Will started calling, Mollie struggled with stomach sickness—the doctor called it dyspepsia—and we came to think of her as delicate. Not so much time had passed from when she had watched illness take her big sister's body hostage. She must have sensed the worry I harbored, and as each bout of sickness hit, Mollie put on a good face and took to her bed "just for a spell," she would assure me.

She and her young man became inseparable. Her health did not stop Will from proposing marriage on her twentieth birthday, and I believe nothing could have stopped Mollie from giving him her yes.

I had a notion this was in his mind, and that day I went all out and baked a pound cake with heaps of butter and eggs and even fresh lemons I paid dearly for. Those times, we did not go to the lengths they do now to celebrate a birthday. But that evening, we had a fitting little celebration. Had George been with us at the table, he would have been proud of his grown-up girl finding a decent, hard-working man.

It was December when they married on a sunny Sunday morning at the front of St. James. Together Mollie and I had sewn a fine navy blue wool for her thin little frame, the fabric much the same hue as my own dress from twenty-some years earlier. I remember the looks on that couple's faces as they sat beaming beside each other in our pew. Instead of rising to leave, the whole congregation stayed put after the benediction to witness my girl's marriage vows.

The house on High Street being so small, we held a brief reception in the parsonage next door, and everyone got at least a morsel of the fruit cakes I brought over the day before. My Mollie stood there, the new Mrs. Stallsmith, glowing bride of a good carpenter whose rough hands would give her the gentlest of care in the time ahead.

They made their home in a place they had set their eyes on, near the Baltimore Street house Mollie had cried over as a child when we left it to move to High Street. I passed on to them some of the things I brought with me from the house sale a dozen years earlier. I did not tell D. I was doing that, and he would not take notice of what had gone missing, and really, neither would I. It warmed me to think that a linen runner, or Ma's serving spoon from Germany, or the little footstool that survived the ransacking years before—once my treasures— were making their way over to the street they had graced in happier times.

That left only Lillie and me across from each other at the

kitchen table that Sunday night. In the months ahead, her father would show up for supper if he saw fit. Our girl was eleven the day her sister moved out.

As much as she delighted in caring for her husband and keeping house, Mollie's bouts of illness reappeared like field crows, pecking away at her health, robbing her of color and strength. We all thought her thinness was about her stomach ailments, the poor thing having bout after bout of trouble keeping food down.

I admitted my growing fears only to myself, that, like Sadie before her, my Mollie was wasting away from consumption. But again and again she would rally to get back on her feet, only to once more fail and dash our hopes.

I think it was a sadness for them that she was never able to carry a baby. But then again, no one would be surprised there were no children. You only had to glance at her thinness and the paleness of her face. I knew women stronger than her who died giving birth, so it was well and good Mollie did not have to go down that path. Through it all, there was such an unusual tenderness in Will and his care of her that even a mother's hands could not equal.

Mollie's passing was more sudden than her sister's, in the middle of the night after an uneventful day. Will sent a boy over with a note to let us know late the next morning. He was stunned silent when Lillie and I showed up at their door to ask if we could help wash and dress her. He only nodded and ushered us into their bedroom where my daughter's body rested.

But as the three of us bent over together to work in the quiet, he opened up, repeating over and over how good of a Thursday Mollie spent, how she held down the bread and tea she asked for, how she wanted the windows all the way open to hear the July rain wash the air clean. There was no warning, he said. He was held fast in the stocks of fresh grief, and we listened silently as he tried to free himself from what he could not grasp and could not repair.

All the while we labored over her body those hours, I thought of George's piggy-back rides when young Sadie and Mollie would squeal and he would sing. And her song came to me—oh, that precious girl—and I sang it to her when I stepped away from the mourners at the cemetery the next day as she was lowered into the ground. I could hear his voice in my ear, and little Mollie begging, "Papa! Again! Again!"

> *In Dublin's fair city, where the girls are so pretty,*
> *I first set my eyes on sweet Mollie alone,*
> *As she wheeled her wheel-barrow*
> *through streets broad and narrow,*
> *Crying, "Cockles and mussels, alive, alive, oh!"*

"Papa! Again! Again!"

She was buried in the Stallsmith family plot, my sweet Mollie, a month shy of her twenty-third year. She and Will had been married less than two years. As far as I can think, I believe he never married again but stayed in their house and worked alongside his uncles. He had given the girl he loved a life she was simply not able to keep hold of, and he chose to live out the rest of his quiet days as a widower.

There was no warning. Is that not so often how death is? What hung over me those weeks was the reality that with Mollie's passing, the last trace of George had slipped away from me, like a specter. She was all I had left that was blood and bone of him.

Now even that final bit of preciousness was gone.

We three women—my Sadie and Mollie and, I—we carried a shared memory of love and loss among us, unspoken but central to our Shriver name. My girls were the last remnants of a life long past when I was a young mother raising a family alongside the man I loved. Mollie's passing untethered me, and there was only Lillian left to tug onto the thin thread that was keeping my feet on this earth.

By this time, what little color and spark left in me was gone, my reason to be all but drained out of me, drop by drop, death by death. I was left flattened inside, without a care to feel anything anymore. I remember thinking this is what it must be to grow old and die. I was wrapped in a friendly cloak of sorrow, and I had no energy or desire left to shrug free of it. And still, I carried on. ❧

Chapter 21

WHAT HAPPENED AFTER I LEFT Baltimore Street hardly merits writing here. I can tell you that in the decades that trailed on after George, no one baked a better *Sacher Torte* than I did. No one kept a tidier house. No one stitched as clean a hem as I could. But you and I both know this does not add up to a life. Was there any happiness left in the corners of my days?

D. and I were not suited. I knew this even before we two solemn widowers stood in the church parsonage on that steamy July afternoon. He was offering me and my girls a roof over our heads. I would help him raise his boys. But very early in the arrangement I knew I was, I *still* am the wife of George Shriver.

I carried two Pittenturf babies, washed the man's clothes, cooked his suppers, made his bed. I may have given my body to him at the start. But I did not give him my heart.

On many counts this was not his fault. His greatest shortcoming was that he was not George. Over the years I would watch D. loose his teeth and his hair and his sight and take on the wobbled gate of an old man. Meanwhile, George would forever remain a fair young man in my heart's eyes.

We did not speak of it, but I knew it probably was the same with D., that he still considered his heart as belonging to Cynthia, not me, even to his grave. We did not speak much of anything, they would tell you. He provided, in a fashion, and seldom were we without enough coal in the bin, enough stock in the larder, and proper shoes and smocks for my girls.

Together we made Lillie Mae, who grew up to be a fine young woman. She was sunlight to me. I have not seen her for what seems an eternity, and I cannot figure out where she has disappeared to. She filled up the High Street house with her bright laugh and her optimism. But she could not pull together the gap between D. and me that grew wider as she grew taller.

Do you know, I do not believe the man ever told me what it was that made him pursue me, past my possessions. If he ever uttered a word of love to me or complimented me in some small way, I cannot recall it. A woman needs that measure of kindness like summer gardens need the rain. Apparently that way of affection was not in D. to share, or else he had used up his store of praises on his first wife. At any rate, I did not merit high regard when it came to how he spoke to me.

I could not tolerate his love for liquor. I could not abide his hands that never seemed clean. He spoke too loudly and too often, always the first to remind me how glad he was to not be a dandy. And although he may never have said it directly, I knew he was referring to the man who came before him.

Cynthia's picture, the one with all the sisters, was stashed in a box of his keepsakes, underneath a pocketknife, a broken watch, a length of ribbon and other bits. He knew that I knew it was there, and I could not have cared less. We never spoke of it, and only once, in bed one night when he had imbibed too much, he called me by her name. Just that once. Cynthia was as forever young in D.'s mind as George was in mine, while D. and I were growing older and wretcheder by the hour.

Those early years on High Street I learned what it is to live with less, not only fewer material comforts, but fewer expectations and less and less hope. I had gone through my own burial, not of George's body, but of George's spirit, his voice, his gentle enthusiasm, and all that we might have fashioned together.

After the stench of battle finally lifted and I surveyed my losses and what was left—the collection of items not stolen or smashed—well, apart from my daughters, those things were all I had to keep me connected to myself. The new things I purchased to replace the old never really brought me any peace to speak of.

That autumn of recovery, the smallest of items that survived the week of hell took on an out-sized importance way beyond their merit, from a spoon to a thimble. Those were the parts of my past that reminded me of where I had come from and what I once called mine. How I need that sort of reminder as I write here. But then again, they were only things.

What season is it out there? I cannot make it out in this busy city. Is it summer? Is it berry-picking time? Has Ma proclaimed that the bushes are finally weighted down enough with fruit to send us out?

Every year, without fail, we are surprised by them, as though they hold magical powers, those blackberry bushes that one week are all flowers and the next are heavy and thick with their tiny fruit. Here and there the branches tangle and climb and tower high over us, and we dive and pluck at them like starving urchins.

Every time, the minute we return home and Ma sees our stained mouths and fingers, she sends us right back out to the berry paths with her pail and washbasin. The pleasure of our gleaning gets cut in half by her orders to not come home until the pots are filled.

The cellar kitchen stands ready, copper cauldron steaming on the stovetop, jars already scalded and obediently lined up. Ma waits like a watchman as we heave our trove onto the table, cold and glistening from its well-water wash, our arms webbed in scratches and stomachs already satisfied by our afternoon harvest.

In short order, she gets the jars of sugared fruit filled and sealed and slipped into their canvas sleeves to be baptized in the slow, hot bath. The berries will end up coming to boil in their own juices, and as if by more magic yet, in good time you will be holding a jar of preserves that, come the snows of winter, will bless your tongue with a taste of summer.

I see her standing at the stove hours later, jars cooled and resting in the tepid waters. She pulls each one from the bath and unwraps and inspects it, wiping off the drops of moisture as she would a baby's bottom. Each jar gets set on the long table in a growing train of jeweled canned fruit.

My childhood held such sweetness, you know. But then came the rest of it that followed.

Did I ever think of leaving D.? To say it never entered my mind would be a barefaced lie. But the mountain I would have had to climb to get away from my life with him was too steep. It would have meant fleeing Gettysburg, and I had no means to travel, let alone to settle somewhere else far from my kin and find a way to provide for a child.

And Lillian? She would not have wanted to steal away with me anyway. She had her circle of friends, her cousins and her parties, and she seemed to have no idea of how hard my life with her father had become. Besides that, D. would have pursued us like a hound, sniffed us out and treed us, and then I would have had hell to pay.

Divorce was not in the cards. If running a tavern would bring down gossip on my head, imagine how vile the talk would have turned against me if I were the one to end my marriage to D. I would have become an even stronger magnet for scorn.

No, stepping out of a marriage like that was out of the question in those times. I would stay mired in my arrangement, no matter the cost, no matter how bitter the entrapment. I had made my bed, and I saw no other way but to lie in it alongside my numbing choices.

But there were two times I can remember being bound and determined to get free because I could not stand another moment being D.'s wife. It was not all that long after Mollie's passing that I grew to loathe the very sound of his footsteps on the front stoop. By the time he made his way into the kitchen, my stomach would be in knots. It was no way to live.

I was standing alone over in Ever Green one late morning, the skies dimmed and crowded with storm clouds. The town was too occupied with itself to turn its attention to the dead resting over in the cemetery. Lillie was at school, and D. off occupied with whatever it was he did then. I cannot remember.

Over and over I sauntered between the girls' graves, when all of the sudden the notion struck me that I could quit my life with D. right then and there. I could begin walking out of Gettysburg with only the clothes on my back, as far south as my strength would hold out. I might have to beg for food along the way, maybe forage the farm fields and forests that flank the roadways. Along my journey, I would pronounce the names of the trees George once pointed out to me: dogwoods, chestnuts, the pin and scarlet oaks, arched over me like some great cathedral.

When I grew too weary to go on, I would make a nest in the velvetleaf and knotweed to take my rest beneath the stars. The wind cutting through the red cedars and Virginia pines would hush me to sleep, and then a blessed stillness would blanket a benediction over me. That sound was always beauty to me. There are none of those trees with their canopied arms in these parts, none of that quiet to sit in.

I would set my face for Andersonville and ask as many travelers along the way as it took to figure out the route. And if I survived the odyssey and came to stand at the gates of that lonely cemetery, I would end up at the grave marked 6816 and lay me down across it. And there I would finish, to let the remains of my life drain out into the Georgia soil and soak down into the remains of George Washington Shriver.

You see? It was *verrückt* thinking from a woman made crazy by lonely desperation, by my sick heart. A soft drizzle started up before I could think it out any further. It was the kind of afternoon rain my gardens would welcome. I returned to High Street to make supper for my daughter and her father.

But there was that other time, and even though it was a moment's turn, it seemed a more purposeful act, as I recall.

It was the day after Lillian's fifteenth birthday. Why I remember that at this moment I cannot tell you. I was at the kitchen table peeling a bushel of fruit to put up apple butter. She was always off with her circle, and that morning was no different. Before she took her leave, Lillie stopped short before me and blurted, "Ma, you look a mess!" And off she flitted without a notice of what she had carelessly let slip out of her mouth.

Why a hurried remark cut so deeply at that moment I cannot say. I recall pulling myself up from the table and padding over to the looking glass after the door closed behind her. She was right. I was in my stocking feet. Where were those shoes anyway? I failed to fix my hair that morning, something I was careful to tend to at the start of every morning of my life once I came of age. I grew up proud that way.

The Weikert girls took good care of their looks all along, even at work in the garden or caught up in housework. I never went to market without primping and straightening. Ma drilled that into us—the importance of how you presented yourself to the public eye.

But this morning, there, staring out at me, was the face of an old woman, tendrils of hair worked free from their weave, spiking every which way like the veiny branches of one of those berry bushes. My cheeks had begun their settling into creases, to mottle and rut, the likes of the wax rivets on a burnt-down candle. It was the first time I could not recognize my own face looking back at me. I think I was not even fifty years old then.

But my youth had packed up and flown with the deaths of George, then Sadie, then Mollie. I had little desire to keep up the façade of anything other than a woman grown old who had already lost too much.

How had this come to pass? How could that morning have been anything different from all the rest? I had stood before looking glasses a good ten thousand times by then. Why was I seeing with new-old eyes at that moment? Oh, the sight of me, a Methuselahed stranger fading to a gray clayness that seemed to soak right down into my very bones.

D. broke the spell just then, rattling the front door latch to clomp into the house, and he passed behind me, muttering something to the effect that if I stared hard enough at my old ruins I might break the glass. He must have found what he came for in short order, and I was relieved when he flashed away again, out of my presence, gone in the slam of the door. I remained motionless, nailed fast to the spot, my eyes fixed on the image of the stranger before me.

The old litany started up again in the far recesses of my mind. What was left of me *was* a mess. I was no more wanted or needed than a broken cup in that closed-in house, or in the weary world. I was no longer of much use to the daughter or her father. (And listen, you may well find yourself in my shoes someday, hearing this convincing voice in your head and believing every shaming word.)

How can I describe my despair here? Nothing extraordinary had happened those weeks, no ax hanging over my head, no one missing or sick and suffering, no urgent smell of death in the streets. I simply felt such a wave of uselessness break over me. I was left with the last ounce of desire to go on drenched out of me. I was done with the whole business of being alive.

I glanced over at the unfinished apple butter fixings, now framed in the rays of sun slanting through the window by the stove. It seemed to me that the room had become a glowing still-life painting, a beautiful morning kitchen in a sad little house that was so bereft of beauty. The bushel of unpeeled fruit waited on the floor by my chair, and on the table, the peeled apples quietly bobbed in their pot. Mounds of the sweet peelings already grown brown rested alongside on the spread of newspaper.

My eye fell on the paring knife lying there, the one Ma taught me to keep sharpened on the rough bottom of a bowl. She put me to the test often enough as a girl, showing me how to hold the knife at the proper angle and to press it harder against the honing surface. I drew the blade fixed and flat, over and over the potter's unglazed base, down and away, down and away, across the grainy stoniness, until the blade's keen edge was readied to make short work of peeling and slicing. My sharpening skills would challenge the work any whetstone would have accomplished.

If Lillie had not burst through the door right then to grab something she forgot, I may well have succeeded with my getaway that morning. I looked up at her with blood dripping from the cut at my wrist, and she gasped and grabbed a dishtowel to stem the flow.

"Ma! Ma, you have to pay better attention! What were you

thinking!?" She went on and on like that for a time, while she bandaged up the slash with a strip of old muslin from the rag box. It was a good cut, a deep one. But she stemmed the flow.

It could have been so easy, had she not come through the door at that instant.

I do not believe I ever tried to escape this life again after that morning.

Surely you understand. It had all piled up on me—that long parade of loss after loss. I got drained of my tears, finally, after so many years, and emptied of so much that once mattered to me. By the time Mollie was buried, I think I had nothing left to say to D., and he was probably done talking at me as well. I think he seldom took notice of me at all by then.

It was at the end of that year, I think, when D. had an accident working on a house build across town. One of the men brought a sledge down on a chisel he held, and the thing missed its aim, not splitting the stone D. was positioning, but instead splitting bone from bone. D. lost two fingers in a moment's misstep. He worked less and less at his trade after that, it being too difficult to do the hefting and leveling that had been his bread and butter for a good many years.

I was losing bits and pieces of my mind while D. was losing parts of his body.

*   *   *

Business was not his strong suit. Little by little, scheme by scheme, D. managed to deplete the remainder of what I brought into our arrangement from the sale of Baltimore Street. Quite an accomplishment in fifteen years, is it not? And with the money went the few shreds of kindness and patience he held for me, as though it was my fault that he and the dollar did so poorly together. For reasons I do not fully understand, D. never seemed to have much success in his business plans.

More times than I care to recount he would pull a chair out from the kitchen table, plop down and clear his throat, and lay out his newest "opportunity," like the shop that failed to get on its feet. Rent was put down for a space over on York Street that never saw so much as a shelf or a stitch of merchandise moved into it. Did he think he knew enough about business that he could swing open his doors to compete with the likes of the Fahnestock brothers?

D. was one of those people who are fully confident they know everything there is to know about everything, and they cannot imagine any subject they would not be able to offer their advice on. They believe the world is waiting with bated breath for their worldly wisdom, from business to religion, from cures for what ails you to the best way to break a horse. But I can tell you, he did not know the first thing about merchandising, and that deal died before it even so much as took a breath.

And there was the time over at The Union when he became friendly with a salesman passing through who gave him the heads up on a shipload of shoes. They were waiting in a Pittsburg warehouse, and they could be purchased for a song. He and D. would partner and peddle the product in town and parts around and turn a handsome profit. I can tell you I was not happy when I handed over money from our thinning funds for that scheme with his new friend.

Weeks later the shoes arrived, all right, and were unloaded on the station dock, a product too pathetic to convince anyone to buy. The barrels were filled with mouse droppings, every one of them, and the critters must have found leather to be tender to their taste. Every piece looked buckshot. Water did the rest of the damage. The whole smelly lot was ruined, the weasel of a salesman never to be heard from again, the "investment" up in smoke.

By then I was taking on seamstress work, sewing and altering and mending for the folks who could afford to hire out for such things. I would put aside little bits from those jobs, out of his reach, nothing that amounted to much. Still, I could treat Lillian to little things that delighted her—hair ribbons, Warren's rose lotion, good wool stockings ordered in from Philadelphia, a *Ridley's* magazine or two.

She had grown into a lovely girl, full of much more energy than her sisters and me put together. She was like a honeybee that knew no rest, flitting from one flower to the next. I envied her happy way that protected her from being trapped in the garment of grief that I wore tight against me, even long after her sisters' deaths. Despite her father's ever-growing gruffness, she could lighten up a dreary supper table with a riddle or a piece of hearsay.

Without fail, Lillie delighted in drinking up those Sunday gatherings at St. James and her times out at the farm, summer picnics and games with her cousins in the orchards and fields that George and I played in as children. I believe he would have embraced that girl's spirit. I never spoke to her of my first marriage beyond her finding George's picture a time or two and asking about him. Why confuse the situation with stories of my happier days?

By then, D. and I did not grace the pews at St. James. He had long argued against paying rent on a church pew. I was not willing to tangle with him about it any more. And in truth, I had grown weary of sermons and hymns and the people I had to work up a smile for. It had become a worn-out club to me. God seemed to have removed Himself from my sphere, and I did not have the wherewithal to seek sanctity inside those walls or for drawing myself up closer to the Holy. I felt like an orphan child fresh out of *Glauben*—any belief in belonging to a loving God.

But Lillie Mae? She never missed a Sunday in church. She would come home and bubble on and on about what the choir sang, what new hat some woman wore that morning, odd bits of fresh gossip, and, of course, the goings on of her young set, the friends she enjoyed gay times with those days.

In the center of her world was Will Hollebaugh—William Allen she called him. He was never far from my daughter. He had his pa's dark hair and gray eyes, and for that matter, he had my girl's heart from the get-go.

I watched them grow up side by side and so often thought of how it was for George and me—that same sameness of always knowing one another's voice and laugh, then the long goodbyes on the front steps, as though the boy lived in Boston, not on the other side of Gettysburg.

His father Barnabas (they called him Barney) survived the war to return to the hammer and anvil in his blacksmith shop on the edge of town. But Will had no designs to step into his father's trade, and even as a boy, he chirped of bigger ideas that would make for a better life away from Gettysburg. I think Lillie Mae always fancied she would be part of his grand scheme of things.

Their decision to marry surprised no one. She and I fussed together over her dress design. Unlike Mollie and me, Lillian decided to marry in white, the newest fashion in the magazines she poured over at her cousin's house. A gauzy dress with fancy detailing, I figured it would take quite an effort to refashion the thing down the line, not like my navy wool that needed so little in the way of re-fitting.

But my daughter was convinced the white would hold up as well as any wool and could be made into a fine summer smock. I was bound and determined to see her a happy bride in that regard and stopped short of any more disagreement over the color of her wedding dress.

Hours after they stood at the altar in St. James, they left for a wedding trip to see the sites of the Capitol. I watched my only surviving child board the train with her husband's arm around her waist. They were children, really, so young to be starting off. Which is funny for me to write, because George and I were even younger than Lillian and William Allen on our wedding days. I think we grew up sooner then. We had to.

*   *   *

Their first baby came a year after they married. That sweet little bean was named after me, but they called her Pearl. I think it was three years or so before they moved her away from us to Harrisburg, and things were never the same for me. Not that I was surprised about their leaving. With all their restless scheming as youngsters, I knew they were at the ready to start up their lives away from us.

That chapter of my life is a blur to me now. I felt at loose ends once Lillian left Gettysburg, even though Harrisburg was only a couple of hours down the road. Still, it was a loss to me. I recall that I stayed locked away in the house for several weeks, going out only long enough to do quick marketing. I was nothing short of *leer*—lost in myself, lost to the world, and cut off like one of those amputated limbs on the pile in front of Pa's porch. Here I was again, feeling of no use, especially to myself.

When I was a young woman like Lillie Mae, I took notice of things like the last light in the evening sky, the quieting of the birds when the summer crickets cranked up their song at day's end, the smell of washed linens flapping in the sun, my girls soft breathing in their bed, the satisfaction of pulling domed loaves of bread out of the oven at exactly the right moment. These things were my reason to be, my *Schönheit*, my beauty.

But in the quiet confines of the High Street house, empty and void of Lillie Mae's voice and the babbles of that baby when she brought her to me, I felt nothing, as though everything in the world was *leere*—empty as a pocket. And I do not remember anyone caring one way or the other about my state.

We lasted a year or two, I think, from the time they went off to when D. pulled out the kitchen chair and cleared his voice, which could mean only one thing. The new scheme he worked up had to do with cigars and Harrisburg, and our son-in-law was on board with the venture.

When D. announced his intentions that night, you would have thought I would either weep for the grievous thought of leaving everything I knew, or hoot with joy at the prospect of being near the baby again. But I remember clear as day that I felt nothing.

There were no friendships, no mother or father to look after, nothing tethering me to High Street or to the town that was the nest of all my great sadnesses, piled and pressed down and sealed in with mud and tears over too many years to count.

By then Lillie Mae was closer to my family out on the farm than I was. I had long before lost any notion of how to be a smiling Weikert girl. Lillian stepped into my shoes, a cheerful, energetic young woman hungry for the family connection that D. could not provide. Playing that role was simply not in him.

To this day I believe the town looked down on me from the start, the young Mrs. Shriver and her fancy things in her new house finer than the rest, getting taken down more than a few notches. Foolish woman to leave the Confederate thugs free to wreck whatever they could lay their dirty hands on. Wasting no time after her soldier husband's death to jump into another man's bed. Letting that little Powers boy die the way she did. Losing those two daughters, one after the other.

Listen, I could not step out my front door without feeling their accusing stares jabbing at the high and mighty Shriver woman brought down by her pride.

D. had made up his mind that it would do me good to shake the Gettysburg dust from off my feet and start over in a new town. I figured he must be right. People miles away were not privy to my long list of sins. And, he threw in, what about that blessed grandbaby waiting for me there?

I recall holding her once and taking in the baby smell of

her head, and it brought to mind baby Jacob, as though this little one was stepping in for him. I loved that new little girl! Her name was … I cannot remember her name just now. And I cannot bring to mind dear Jacob's face. I have lost even that.

I am sorry to say I simply do not recall all that much about leaving Gettysburg or arriving at the next town. As hard as I try, I cannot gather the frayed edges of my memories back to me. ❧

Chapter 22

I CANNOT FATHOM what got into me. I do not like strong drink and never did, which is curious, is it not, since there was a time I was well on my way to becoming a tavern owner's wife! But it was the same with George. He said the taste of his father's whiskey and rye never much suited him.

With D. it was another story. He liked his spirits. I could smell it on him every time he was late coming home. Sam Herbst over at what they used to call The Union was among his closest companions. The two of them did their share of drinking together and fancied their long conversations to be built on lofty ideas and worldly wisdom. Name any subject, and the two of them would weigh in on it like they were decorated scholars.

If D. had invested as much effort in talking to me as he did to whoever he drank with those evenings we might have gotten to know each other a little better. On the other hand, I suppose I should have been grateful to have him out of my hair those nights.

We had been packing, sorting through what little would come along with us for the to move to Annapolis. Or Harrisburg. Or was it Baltimore? Somewhere. He would raffle through the piles I set aside and pull out what he judged was not worth taking. I did not fight him. Would it have done me any good if I had?

One morning when he was off somewhere, I took on sorting out the little coop in the yard, already emptied of chickens, when I unearthed two bottles of whiskey D. must have hidden there out of my sight.

Listen, I was no teetotaler. I could not have cared less what the man did with his time. But considering how little money we had, to scratch away the dirt around that bottle top and find two bottles there—well, that was a *feine Sache*—a fine thing. I was having to make do with so little funds for the household, while he was out burying his whiskey bottles, hiding his sins like a secretive child!

I decided not to confront him and covered the bottles over again. But the more I pondered it that morning, I came around to thinking why should I not enjoy a bit of his little hidden treasure myself? That afternoon, I plucked an almost empty medicine bottle D. had pulled out of a kitchen pile to leave behind. I tucked it into my apron pocket, grabbed a cup of water and a knife, and headed back out to the coop.

The corks were easier to pry out than I expected. I shook out the medicine bottle and carefully decanted it with D.'s whiskey, a couple of inches from each bottle. Then I topped off his spirits with water and jammed the corks in, pressing them with a shovel blade until not a drop leaked out. Into my apron went my "medicine," and back under the dirt went his treasure. I am smiling as I write this.

I had settled it in my mind to visit the grounds that once held my gardens on Baltimore Street one last time before we boarded the train out of Gettysburg. Those times D. was away more than home, "tying up loose ends in town," as he was fond of saying. That night it was late when he staggered through the door, and as I suspected, he reeked of drink, grunting straight to bed without so much as a word to me.

Once the snoring set up good and loud, I slipped out of the house and into the night air. The summer skies were clear as glass at that hour, the stars and a half slice of a moon flooding the streets as though it was late afternoon. I had not often walked out at a late hour like this, and now I was passing all the familiar, darkened houses that had been the sentinels of my life for—what—thirty years?

By then, I had little to do with the good people of Gettysburg. Children had grown up and gone, folks had died or moved on. Things were forever changing. I was a stranger to so many of them and sometimes a stranger to myself. But I knew my way to Baltimore Street. I knew my house, and in short order I was lifting the latch on a gate around the side where George's orchards once began.

The cabinet business had changed hands again by then and George's tavern now served as a showroom. This was not the first time I had walked down that passage over the years. I never lingered to take it all in, only to steal a glimpse of the house whose face was aging like my own.

As I stood at the entrance of the tenpin alley that night, I could see pallets of stacked timber the woodworkers would craft into tables and benches, hutches and trunks. The woody fragrance of the fresh-milled lumber seeped out into the night air. It had been a long while since I had taken in that sweet smell.

I wrote how my Ma taught me so carefully growing up, and even as a young girl, how my gardens were always a thing of beauty. Even in the midst of the killing summer, I managed to replant and tease a harvest out of the ruin behind our house, my flowers and vegetables trampled by all those crazed soldiers.

When I sold and married D., my lot became such a pathetic little patch to work behind the High Street house. Even so, I managed to draw out a decent yield every summer.

But that night, I stood there and imagined my proud gardens as they were when I was a naive twenty-five-year-old with not a hint of what was about to unfold. I made my way past a stack of packing crates and sank silently onto the stoop of the house, where, once upon a time, George and I watched the sun go down as often as we could. Oh, if I had only known our time together in the new house would be one brief year!

After awhile I drew the pirated bottle out of my pocket, removed its cork, and brought the "medicine" up to my lips.

It took only a bitter sip or two for me to begin to feel the effect, and there was a sweetness to how my fingers and lips started to tingle in the quiet dark. This seems to me as though it was yesterday as I write! I lifted my flask up to the stars and conjured up George for a conversation, or was it a confession, or maybe a litany.

Moonlight glinted off the windows behind me, and I rested my mind on the kitchen window that used to be his and mine to stand before and survey the first season of flowers and vegetables and what would become a healthy stand of peach and apple trees.

The house, the gardens, the girls, his plans, his departure, my failure to protect what we valued—it all poured out as sips of D.'s precious nectar poured in. And then as natural as can be, I began to thank George, calling up the details of my fleeting time with him, from childhood to that very moment.

There seemed to be a bottomless well of memories I could dredge from. Like some great lifting of weight from my shoulders, I felt as though I had sprouted wings. *"Danke, mein Schatz."* Over and over it poured out from deep inside me. *Danke.*

I do not remember finishing the bottle or what my last thoughts were before resting my spinning head into my arms on the step above me. I awoke from my moonlit trance that very way, with the skies beginning to lighten in the east. I stood unsteadily, straightened my skirts and tucked my hair, and headed for High Street, leaving the bottle and my night of thanksgiving behind me on Baltimore Street.

Why D. was already awake does not matter, but there he stood undressed, whiskered and with his hair spiked on end as I slipped through the kitchen door. As would be natural for him those days, he was furious with my absence when he came down the stairs. When the man stepped into his tirades, I had no recourse but to let him have full rein with all manner of cursing and accusation. I remember thinking if his head felt anything like mine that morning, I needed to take little, if anything, to heart from his rantings.

He had said it enough times by then when he went off like this. His anger of late was capped with the familiar reminder: "You are a crazy woman." And I remember saying to myself, "*Ja*, I am *verrückt*. And what is that to you?"

I never did confess to him where I had been the night before. And what is better, he never suspected that I had tampered with his buried spirits, the very ones he thought I knew nothing of. Out of my sight, he would dig up the bottles to stash away in a crate of tools for the move.

I was *verrückt*, and a little proud of myself. I had outwitted D., gotten tipsy on his whiskey and enjoyed a stolen night with my sweetheart on Baltimore Street. All I can say is that it seemed my world was covered in peace for a long time afterward. Do you know, I have never again touched strong drink, not to this day.

I can remember that Lillian came to help finish packing us up and closing out the house that we had held onto for all those strangled years. From the time she moved away, she had become a regular on the trains to Gettysburg with her little one for visits out to the farm. She insisted I go along with her for family gatherings that she clearly took delight in. She had already survived well past her sisters' ages and was able to connect herself to the Weikerts in a fashion that Sadie and Mollie never lived to do.

By then D.'s Frank had grown and left Gettysburg, and only Catherine Powers and a couple of her girls remained next door. Old Solomon rested up at Ever Green with my people. I would guess they that remained were glad to see us load our lives out of that house of gloom. There were no goodbyes from them, or from us.

D. seldom spoke of the son who was removed and renamed next door to become his in-laws' ward. But the townspeople surely must have looked at the boy as a victim of a careless father and an even more hapless stepmother. I would see Frankie around town as he grew up, and we never once acknowledged each other, as though we were strangers, as though the new nickname given him by his grandfather erased D.'s and his kinship and any regard for the guilty woman who let his little brother die.

The day before we left the High Street house for good, I took one more long walk alone, past the shops and businesses I had seen flourish and then fold over the years. Past St. James Lutheran that boasted its fancy gas-lit chandeliers installed at great cost. Oh, the things that church paid attention to and squeezed money out of its congregants for, rather than focusing on the reason folks were supposed to be gathering there on Sunday mornings.

Then I took one more hurried stroll past my house on Baltimore Street. The Timmers had taken it over from the Garlachs by then, and I believe they were no longer running the business in there either. But there it stood, secure and stoic as ever, all of its sill paint peeling and the windows I was so proud to keep polished now dulled by street dust riveted onto them by rainstorms and street traffic. It was the last time I can remember visiting Baltimore Street.

My last stop was Ever Green, and I plodded through the cemetery gates that stood witness to my regular visits. I made my way past Solomon and Cynthia's graves, past the Stallsworth plot where Mollie rested, past Ma and Pa's headstone, and over to the mound that marked Sadie's grave.

In all those years after she passed, we never got around to placing a headstone for that girl. As Pa would have recited from his Bible, each day had enough trouble of its own. Way led unto way, and all good intentions to give my firstborn's grave a proper stone marker got pushed back. Then came all the other deaths and one thing and another.

Sadie mattered more than for me to remember her so poorly. The least we could have done was to have D. cut a slab of granite himself to memorialize my girl. But time slipped away, my will grew weak, and her grave lies unmarked to this day.

This is wrong to me, but there was nothing I could think of to do about it at the time, and certainly nothing I can do about it now. You can see my distress over this, just as I carried with me that last morning walking away from her grave. I do not believe I ever again stood in the quiet of Ever Green. Or if they took me there, I cannot remember.

My belongings came down to what I could fit into my trunk, and that chair right there next to the window, the one Pa gave us the week we moved onto Baltimore Street, the one I was able to have repaired after the rebs smashed it. I could not leave that behind, no matter how much D. complained when we lugged it onto the train.

D. moved us away from Gettysburg without a fight from me, at least that I can recall. For close to fifty years I walked the fields and the streets of that town, the smells and sounds of it at the center of who I thought I was. He led me out of my life there, and even if I had cared, I think there was nothing I could have said that would have swayed him.

I would say that the move away was when my mind truly started to wander far off. I already had outlived so many folks in Gettysburg, and I cannot tell you why. I would have preferred to die when my Mollie passed. But here I am today, writing this, unsure of the order that all of my names go in, my mouth emptied of teeth, my hair thin as cobwebs. *Ach,* my ending is coming too late.

You could talk it all through—about the year I came to this strange house, who their names are and the faces that the names go with out there, what all was left behind in my younger life, and in two minutes I would ask you to repeat the whole business. I cannot hold a thought beyond the end of my old nose.

As far as I can recollect, the rest of my family remained Gettysburg farmers on those lush fields. Probably the children and the children's children took over working the land from my brothers. Out West in Indian country and all the way to the Pacific Ocean, gold had a long hold on people's minds, and one of George's brothers was among the adventurers who pulled up their Pennsylvania roots and moved out there to homestead or mine. Men like him chose to seek a fortune they would not find in the likes of Adams County.

They were not close, those Shriver boys. ❧

Chapter 23

As much as I desire a peaceful exit from this life, my bones plod on still. I limp through the hours of my day, dragging along with me a beautiful burden of unfinished love. The promises George and I declared on a winter's day in 1855 remain steadfast, secure, locked into my heart. I can feel the sureness of our bond as I write here. All else may have failed me, but I cling to those vows like a lifeline.

I have known too much history, that whole tangled chain of events past that we humans try to puzzle out to see where we fit into this world, who we are, who we were. People spout off their stories of bygone years as fact. But, of course, what *really* happened, what I witnessed at the same moment everyone else did, is a different thing for me than it is for you and the rest. Different views from different hilltops and opposite valleys where we find ourselves standing at a particular passage in our lives.

Who can say what is real and what is not? Such is the certain uncertainty of this world, of our town that no one knew

of until war pounded onto its streets. Our stories grow from
fancy into fact, and a plaque gets posted to commemorate the
whole business as God's truth.

Meanwhile, one day passes to the next, and suddenly, you
wake up old. I have certainly seen better times. I knew their
names: the shopkeepers, the ministers, the girls' friends, their
teachers, the people who lingered in my doorway. I knew how
supper made its way to the table and what season we were
standing in. I can no longer pull a lick of sense out of any of it.

This is a strange house in a strange town, and I wake up
most mornings with a longing to sit with Ma at her table and
to lie down for a bit on my own bed upstairs. I want to smell
the lilacs beneath her windows. I want to hear Pa's chickens
gossip while they scratch their curious circles in the garden
dirt. I am prisoner in this strange place, and I cannot figure
how it came to this.

Do you like lilacs? Ma has a dozen bushes—trees, really—a
leafy pallet from deep, deep purples and violets, to all shades
of pink and even a white one, on the south side of the house.
In May she flings open all the windows for that sweet scent to
push its way into the rooms. And when they reach full bloom,
she clips their long stalks and piles her apron with the cuttings
to fill up jugs of color for the kitchen table and the big room.

After a long winter of being cooped up, lilacs are a promise
kept, of longer days and warmer nights, of the end of hearth
fires for a season. But, you know, the lilac's bloom is brief, and

you cannot dally when those tiny blossoms begin to open.

She brought me three cuttings for the Baltimore Street gardens, and I planted them closer up to the house for their spring fragrance to someday work its way through our windows. It takes a year or two for a bush to find its footing and push out some color. I saw all three cuttings take hold and give birth to the tiniest of flowers the summer after George left. He never saw the promise those cuttings held in our back yard. The soldiers' boots trampled them flat that fated July, never to return. But Ma's? Ma's are as stalwart and beautiful as ever!

My lilacs. George's peach and apple trees. Pa and Ma. Mother Shriver and D.—everyone's story ends. No matter how careful we are with our precious lives, no matter how we dress them or clean them up, every one, every thing comes to its final stop. And George, Sadie, Mollie? Oh my sweet loves—the endings to their stories came too soon.

Even so, there will always be more to come after us—more of us to have babies and plow fields and start wars. It will all go on with or without you and me and our attempts to do what we think is right and good.

D.'s ending was sure and swift. Have I written here how he passed? I cannot remember exactly when it was. His steps had slowed down to a crawl, and he spent less and less time on his feet once we moved away from High Street.

By then, there was not much of what you would call conversation passing between us. I was the target for his regular rants, something I came to expect, like the sunrise. At any rate, it is not impossible that those blow-ups were somehow my fault. Who can know? It was not something I could figure, why he was forever angry, irritated with me in particular, as though he could find no one else to spew his venom at.

To his credit, he never lifted a hand against me. But there were times his words felt as sharp as any blow to my face would feel.

If I am not mistaken (and I do not think I have told this to a soul) the last thing he said to me was something like, "You are all played out, you old hen." I think it was the day before he woke up too sick to move.

I was used to him calling me "old hen" by then. And what a colorful picture that is, Miss Hettie Weikert, wings all dusty with patches here and there of feathers bent or missing altogether. There I am, rooting around in the yard like Ma's girls do, red comb flopping left and right while I scrabble around for bugs, scratching up the dirt with my teetering, stick-thin legs.

Anyone could see D. was failing, beet-faced and huffing, and one morning he wet his bed and could not hoist himself out of it. Anything he struggled to garble out sounded like baby's babble, as though his mouth was full of river pebbles. And there was such a veil of terror to his eyes.

I felt bad for him. Who could stand in front of someone trapped and ruined like that and not feel some *Sympathie*? The doctor who came that afternoon stood by his bedside and almost right off said there was nothing to be done. I think it was two days that he lay in that state. Maybe it was less. The room was kept darkened, and they would part open his lips to pry in spoonfuls of water. But beyond that he could not take in a morsel of anything.

I was not with him when he departed this world, but they told me that his passing was a quiet one.

When we were children, at bedtime Pa used to say to us, "*Gottes Frieden!*" God's peace. I sat beside D.'s body at his wake, and that "*Frieden*" came to mind. This I can recall! I repeated "God's peace" plenty that night. D. had been a hard man for so long, and there he was, laid out, covered in the peace of death.

Every one of his business schemes failed with nary a success to his name, and he wore his frustration like a badge of honor. For a long time after he died, I tried not to think of his face. But when I do, it is always set in a dark, stony frown. What would it hurt for me to wish that he find some "peace that passeth understanding" in the afterlife, if there is one.

What did I feel to find myself a widow again? I felt nothing.

D. left me without a penny, you know, and now I live by the good graces of the wardens out there. They feed me, and I have my bed here. But these people take it upon themselves to disagree with me on practically every subject, from when I last ate to what their names are. It is a confounding situation, and not much different from how my times were with D. before he passed. Then and now, I have little say in how the hours pass.

My life has grown as tasteless as the stuff set before me that they call supper.

They do not know me any more than I know them. I can hear them talking behind me, then they peer at me up close and my ears rattle with their shouting, as though I were a child. It wearies me to the bone. I tell you, my deepest longing is to go home.

Still, I want you to know that not all the blame should be heaped on D. I slept with him for more years than I can count. We came together such empty souls in the beginning, both of us trying to hold onto the tatters, trying to plug up the holes in our lives with anything we could find.

I never expected D. to be any sort of Moses in my shattered life, to part the sea of sorrow that stretched before me in my widow blacks. Ours was an understanding, a sort of business deal, a contract that soon dwindled into a silent agreement that we would live out our lives together, for better or for worse, without bringing up the death of the two of them. Cynthia and George. But I would say that as the years reeled out, our arrangement became more a wall of misunderstanding.

Without the sight or sound or touch of George for so very, very long, and with all the shambled years that lie between him and me, you would think I could be done with my longing for him. *Mein Gott,* these thoughts of mine can tangle into such a knot. If only I could settle all of it out and find my own portion of *Gottes Frieden.*

But, you see, I daydreamed too often of sitting with George on the back stoop at sunset on Baltimore Street. Before he left us, he and I had only that one spring and summer to talk in the quiet of the evening with our world spread out before us in the dying light.

In the long years that followed, especially in my lowest moments with D., I never gave up the fantasies, the stolen moments with my young husband, in the church pew, on the Diamond, in the morning gardens, in the quiet of our bedroom above. I kept a sure grip on George in my memory.

If you were to ask me right now how it is that I sleep, I will tell you sleep is not my friend. The vale between my dreams and my waking hours has grown thin as rotting muslin. There are times I cannot reckon which is which.

Were the girls and I trapped in a carriage a few nights ago, with cannonballs slamming down around us? Did I step into my parlor last week to find a whole bevy of soldiers lined up on the floor, missing their eyes and hands and begging me for more water? *Ach,* those horrid images of torn apart men, their pleading with me to help them, and blood coming out of the bureau drawers, dripping onto my feet until my stockings and shoes are soaked by the red puddles that rise around me like a flooded creek.

Was I really standing on Baltimore Street last night? Did I actually knead bread in the kitchen there, or did I dream that my hands were covered in flour and the scent of yeast and dough was rising up into me? Was I running across Pa's field with my brother? Oh, the wonder of a summer afternoon like that!

I dream of gathering blackberries with them, of the taste of her preserves. I dream of summer twilight from the upstairs window, the long view of the fields lit up with glowbugs as though the very stars are coming down to dance a ballet of light to pleasure Sarah and me. *Ach,* I have not seen a firefly since D. packed me away from Gettysburg.

When I wake from sleep, most of what I can bring to mind is the worst of the dreams, the gore and the suffering. The rest of it is jumbled and knotted.

What are dreams and what is real? I have dreamed often of opening the front door here and setting out on my own to walk all the way home to Baltimore Street. I have a notion to do that, you know. If I were to get an early enough start, while the household sleeps, I could slip out in the stillness and rest along the way. It is possible that I could make it home by sunset.

Was it a dream I had that night? No, I think it could not have been. I believe I was awake as you are, reading this. He surely was not an eerie specter, gossamer and hovering there before me. He was not glowing or levitating or the least bit frightening. I can tell you, no spell had been cast over me. But there he stood.

Except for that long scar that trailed down his check, (the

one he brought home that last December), on the night of his dream-visit, he looked no more than a twenty-year-old to me, more like the morning we married than when he left the final time.

George stood strong and true right there by the window, dressed in his army uniform, the tired one I fussed over that Christmas, only now the wool was clean and respectable looking. He wore his good boots, all polished to the shine he was so vain of. I have dreamed of my husband more times than I can count since 1864. But I cannot reckon how this time his visit could have been a dream.

I felt such a relief that he appeared glad to see me, not angered as I so often worried over after he died. Now I can rest knowing that George is somewhere right now, waiting for me, safe and young and whole again. I know this must make no sense to you, but the more I write of it here, the more real it becomes for me.

I have dragged regret around, nursed it and protected it for so long that all the wrongs had joined up into one tangled, heavy chain. Until that night, I could not begin to gather in the weight of it to begin sorting out all the links and bends. But when George turned to me with such a soft look of *Verstehen*—of understanding—right here in this room, right over there, it all became as clear as the windowpane behind him.

I had to listen very carefully. He spoke in a tender voice, the soft one he used even before we were married, the one that was such beauty to me. He looked young, yes, and yet somehow weighted down and bone-weary. Was it because of the long journey he had been on to find his way to me? Or was he weak from some mighty struggle, like Jacob in the Bible, wrestling all night with a distant angel before he came into my room here?

Ach! No matter. He looked so fine to me, and I could see him so clearly, even with these clouded eyes of mine. To hear him speak my name in that voice that was so dear to my young ears! I can tell you, no one calls me by my name anymore. To hear "Hettie Rose" harkened everything in me, as though I was a girl again catching the lilt of his voice across the Diamond.

He stood there silent for a spell. I thought of the afternoon he asked me to be his wife, of that same long pause as we waited by the hearthstone. And then he spoke, as clear as day, and said flat out, "I lost my way." I lost my way. I was struck dumb and could not make a reply. But I thought, yes, there must be a whole barn full of reasons why he did not come home to us. He lost his way.

I have spent so many years attending to the unknown *whys* of the bank of losses that is my life, looking for the loose threads in the fabric that was my first marriage. He lost his way.

Was my husband indispensible to his company, or was he too sick to come home during those two long years? Back then I read what everyone else was reading. I knew how illness raged through the army camps, how many of them died miserable deaths from burning fevers and bad water. I saw with my own eyes how a Minié ball could make for a slow bleedout of death, of pain and infection and madness. I knew.

I was full aware that I was not alone in what I lost. I knew the sadness Dr. Huber carried for his son. I knew the Stangler boy, and Margaret's and Susan's husbands, and that was just from church. Death came to a whole host of Gettysburg doors, not from the three days of our siege, but from all the months before and after, as North and South locked their teeth onto each other's throats in all those fields distant to us. We are the ones who did the soul-numbing work of waiting at home.

We all knew there was a whole nation of towns like ours with too many front doors draped in death crepe.

If you could have seen the rain of gunfire the morning we made our ill-fated flee from the house! It was a wonder that, save for the one girl, no townspeople died in that flurried madness.

Did I tell you about her? It was on the final day of the fighting, and young Ginnie Wade was standing in her sister's kitchen, only a stone's throw from our Baltimore Street house, when a soldier's bullet fired through the wall and slammed straight into her heart.

You can imagine the stories that sprang up around her: a pan of biscuits tumbling from her hands when she was struck; the soldier she loved dying days later a short distance away in Virginia, never to learn of his sweetheart's fate before he drew his final breath; her mother baking bread for the wounded with the dough her daughter mixed together before she was struck. Any little bit to build a tale on and fatten up the Gettysburg story. Still, Ginnie Wade was somebody's daughter who dreamed of a future, as my poor girls and their father did.

It was a time of tall tales and hearsay. Concocting a story could sometimes fill the gap left by not knowing. I wove a fair share of possibilities around my husband's absence. I kept all of that to myself, but I confess there were times I worried that George may have slipped into his Union Blues and forgot what it was to be my husband, to be a father to Sadie and Mollie. I worried that he may have married that *verdammt* war, took the army on as his new wife, as though he had changed parts on some stage, giving up one role for another.

I tried to sort out what we might have become to him—the daughters and wife waiting in the quiet of Gettysburg. Had we become symbols, decorations, part of the perfect tintype of the prosperous businessman with the best house in town? Had he taken on the role of the brave and handsome cavalryman in some patriotic drama gone wrong?

When the first Christmas came and went in Gettysburg and my husband was missing from Ma's table, I made all manner of *Ausflüchte*—hopeful excuses for him that folks like me grew weary to the bone of repeating. And those who were polite enough to receive my concocted stories must have grown wearier yet. With each letter he told me less and less, and that led me to make up more and more excuses.

I found myself stewing over what might be the worst of all his duties as a cavalryman: seeing his friends cut down, not wanting to abandon them in a crisis, fearing for his own life and feeling responsible to stay put and do his duty as a Union man? Hospital, prison, grave…I went to bed many nights lost in a forest of fears, terrors over his fate, over *our* fate, all of it fueled by the scenarios I had spent too much time worrying over in my mind.

In the dragging months that followed the hellish week holed up at my folks' during the siege, the nightmares became more and more vivid. I dreamed that it was George bleeding out on Ma's dining table, George's body rotting in the hot sun, waiting for a few more shovels of mud to be thrown over his swollen corpse, a curtain of flies descending onto his black-ened face, his lifeless eyes peering straight up into mine.

Once, awhile after the stink of battle had finally lifted from town and the girls and I walked out to the farm for a Sunday visit, my brother and I got into a tiff about something, and he blurted out that Pa said he wondered if maybe George had become a dandy, fallen in love with his life as a fine cavalry sergeant. Had he maybe chosen a new life, or someone else, over me? Tell me, sister, he said, why has he not come home in all this time?

Who knows what my father had really said, or when he said it, or why.

I knew Pa was not himself those days, full of rage one moment, tender and sad the next as he limped on, picking up the fragments of their broken farm, realizing the government was weaseling out of a payback after the armies' melee. If he was worried about me and the girls, I cannot know. Pa never uttered a word about George's whereabouts to my face, and I never confronted him with Levi's account.

But I will admit, my brother's taunt took root in me. I had a whole forest of hurt growing in my chest, stacks and rows of doubts and worry. Like that bowl of bread dough covered and set to rise, the questions slowly swelled up and grew into its own house of fear and then into bitterness that I tried to keep covered up, hidden from my girls, from my family, from the curious souls of Gettysburg. The fears swelled into anger, and there seemed nothing I could do about my own war between the light and dark rising up from deep inside me.

More than once I dreamed I was standing in a murky river, the undercurrent tugging at my ankles and sucking me down, and much as I fought and strained to stand, there was no power in me to get free of it. There was no one around to lend me a saving hand. There was no George in that dream. I would wake as drenched in sweat as though I had struggled up out of the water.

Goodness, what was I writing? Oh my wandering thoughts… Let me see…dreams…visions. Oh yes. His visit here that night.

There George stood before me, with a sorrowful countenance, saying he had lost his way, he was sorry, and could I find it in me to forgive him.

It was as though, after all, none of it mattered to him: that everything he built was lost at my hands, that I married another man and had his babies, that I let our daughters pass away, that I abandoned our life on Baltimore Street. And I thought, "*I* lost my way" should be *my* confession, *Liebling*, not yours. The dear man was standing before me, meeting my disgrace with his grace, with a mercy I did not think I merited.

How long did he stay here with me? I cannot say. A few moments? An hour? I had not felt that much tenderness, that sense of peace, that kind of wonder, in a very long time. I could not help but step over close enough to him to take in his smell, and I wanted to push over that strand of hair that fell across his forehead, as I used to when I watched him dress. I reached up to touch his scar, but the instant I did, he vanished, slipped away from me, out of my sight in a heartbeat. I called out to him, but to no avail.

Listen, I do not care to know how he made his way into this house that night, or why he left in a twinkling. I was flooded with the radiance, the pleasure of my husband's company. Those moments were a new beginning for me, as though a stone of blame had been rolled away to set him free, to set me free, as though I had received absolution. Is that the right word? I was as certain as the sun that he would return to me unannounced, and as suddenly as he vanished.

Do you know that book in the Bible about the love between a man and woman? A Song of something. I cannot remember the name. But I can still hear Pa standing at Ma's open grave the afternoon she was lowered down into the earth, his grief-sealed pronouncement in unashamed German: *Liebe ist stärker als der Tod.* Love is stronger than death.

This is what I felt to my very bones that night after George's visit. The doors of my memory were parting open, and one by one, my sins, one after the other, were being forgiven in the strength of a promised love. Not even death could nudge the anchor of his love on my heart. That night, the bonds of waiting at last began to loosen and fall away.

And then. Then began the gathering together of the scraps of me that had wandered off afar. It was as though George brought a satchel with him, packed full of the pieces of my life, the bits of who I once was. That night was when I felt myself returning to me, returning from all the corners it had slipped off to back in Gettysburg.

If I had begun these writings you hold *after* his visit that night, you would read a different slant, I am sure. What is done is done, and I am at peace with what I have recorded here. But surely, as a forgiven woman, the writings would have been otherwise. ❧

Chapter 24

I HAVE RUN DRY OF REMEMBRANCES. I know there is much more to write here, but I find myself all but finished with my story and cannot conjure any more for now.

Do you know what I think? I think the minute your ma teaches you to shape out the letters of your name, from then on every one of us should record a few words every single day— something of what you saw or did, even if the only thing that grabbed you was to spy a deer cross the meadow, or to steal your first kiss from your sweetheart, or to be stunned by the sight of a field fire in the distance that scares you to the core and at the same time is so powerful beautiful to your eye.

I wish I had written down the bits day by day from the start, when I first learned to spell out Henrietta.

A lifetime is made up of those brief, common-day happenings that get pressed down and hidden in us, heaped on by all the comings and goings that were not nearly so important as the notice we gave them, until we can no longer remember the beauty of the ordinary moments that molded us. Maybe you are young enough as you read this to begin the practice right now. If you started today, you would not regret taking up your pen. Of this I am certain.

I can tell you that of late this wearied room has somehow ceased holding me captive.

I hardly take in their voices anymore. The tumult that has so long waged inside my chest has stilled, and I have, in a way, hoisted up a white flag of surrender, my struggle finished and done. I have become a patient woman, willing to wait in the quiet, right here in this spot, until he returns.

It has taken me a lifetime to learn that the calamities—the death and dying of that bloody week and the separations that followed—all of them taken together were too great a burden for me to bear. Without my knowing, the sum of my losses took me apart, and I let what they have come to call the Great Civil War rob me of a life.

I am no longer willing to be lost to myself. I cannot see the needle's eye or a length of thread, nor can my fingers hold on to either of them with any sureness. But I have decided that I *can* become a quilter in my own manner, bit by bit reclaiming, reassembling the snippets of me that have lain scattered for far too long.

I can see myself picking up a patch and laying it alongside another, again and again, to admire the blues of love and loyalty that lay right alongside the bright, lively yellows, the greens of peace and plenty next to the bold, passionate reds. I want to stitch my life back together, to see all the good remembrances joined up in harmony. That would be beauty to me.

There is a gravestone near my Sadie's plot that I used to stand before and read almost every visit I made to Ever Green. It gave me no small comfort, and now as I write the words here, I am flooded with a most certain hope: *And God shall wipe away all tears from their eyes; and there shall be no more death, neither sorrow, nor crying, neither shall there be any more pain: for the former things are passed away.*

*Die früheren Ding*e—the former things, the questions and doubts and regrets. They may all still be sitting there in silence, lined up alongside me like a row of old women at a social. But their nagging at me that has haunted my years? That has passed away. I have made my peace with the whole lot of them, as though they, too, have become patient. Is this God's doing?

Dear reader, who can know?

But here is what I do know with great certainty: My *Schatz*—my treasure, my dearest George—has promised he will come for me, and no matter the hour, I will be ready to sweep out of this strange house, down the front steps to meet his smile with mine. All that has prevented us from making our way home to Baltimore Street will be knocked down and swept out of our way, and the roadways will beckon us to return to our beginnings.

Every last obstacle that blocked our return for these count-less years—the former things—they *are* passed away. The death, the sorrow, the pain, has all rolled off the byway, down into ditches on both sides, to be swallowed up and covered over with wildflowers and vines. With every beat of my heart I can see this in my mind's eye. I am ready to join him, ready for us to make our way home at long last.

Oh, what beauty it will be to see his father's carriage glide into view, the one with the tooled leather bench, waxed and rubbed until it gleams in the glint of the sun. I will wait here at the window for as long as it takes to be the first to see Valentine rounding the corner, slowing to a halt out front.

When George calls for me, it will be one of those fine mornings when the clouds are heaped and brushing across the sky, great tuffs of cotton weaving in and out around the sun, ready to warm us into its embrace. He will leave his waistcoat in the carriage. Back in the day, I could not resist fussing over his shirts, poor man. But when he catches my eye that morning, the one I spy when he steps out onto the street will be snow-white and pressed to my exacting standards.

I will hear the fall of his footsteps climbing the front porch stoop, and I will feel that familiar surge of love for my young husband, the rush of excitement that owned me from the beginning.

I will wear my pale blue silk and plait my hair just as he likes it. His ring at last returned to my finger will catch the sun's rays and glisten for every eye to see. My bag will be packed and waiting beside me here. Sadie and Mollie will already be out at the farm waiting for our return, and Ma will coddle and ploy them with treats until we call in the morning. What a happy surprise it will be for them to see their Papa walk through the door and for the four of us to stand in the morning glow of Ma's kitchen encircled in the family embrace so long in the coming.

He will stand before me, and he will look into my eyes with the love I have waited a lifetime to see again. He will speak of my beauty and how he has for too great a time missed the sight of me, my touch, my voice.

There will be no reason for him to speak to the people here. They will not stop us. When he rests his hand at my waist and guides me out of this house, our footsteps will be as light as our spirits. With Valentine's reins in his hand, George will help her find our way out of the confusion and noise and dust of this teeming city, out into the fields under the porcelain blue canopy above us that I have never stopped longing for. We will not for a moment look back.

The house stands ordered and polished, waiting there for this very hour, eager and ready for our return. The larder is filled with last summer's harvest, jars and pots lined up on dress parade. The wood is cut and stacked beside my blacked-clean stove, waiting at attention for its morning fire. The kitchen floor is swept and wiped to a sheen, the clock wound and ticking, the table set for supper, the carpets swept upstairs and down, our bed linens fresh-washed and smelling of the cuttings of lavender I bound together for our pillows.

We will travel in the satisfied silence of each other's company, away from all that has been strange to me. The weight, the yoke of confusion I have heaved around these many years will at last tumble away from me. This is our blessed homecoming.

You know of the wagon wheel—Gettysburg's ten roads leading to the town center. I will be grateful to finally travel down any one of those byways as the day's end begins to settle over the fields, that holy hour when all is healed and whole in the quiet glow before sunset.

The birdsong, a fine feathered choir coming at us from all directions, will already have crescendoed and by then begin its fade as the crickets strike up their dusky concert. The air will be weighted with the scent of the wild roses that grace the roadside and the new hay cut earlier that afternoon from the farmlands that skirt Gettysburg like a queen's robe.

I will slip my arm through his as he holds the reins. We will pass by the Stangler farm, and without a word, George will set up a song, as he so often did when the girls were small, and we headed out of town after marketing, returning to the farm on a summer morning. His voice is still such beauty to me, and there is nothing more I can ask than to hear it beside me at that precise moment:

O my love is like a red, red rose that's newly sprung in June;
O my love is like the melody that's sweetly played in tune.

> *So fair art thou, my bonnie lass, so deep in love am I,*
> *And I will love thee still, my dear, till all the seas go dry.*

And then—oh my heart—Valentine will round the turn onto Baltimore Street.

At long last, when the carriage comes to a halt, we will linger for a moment more beside each other in the still air of early evening, and we will gaze at the home we loved into being. The last of the sun's rays will be blazing through her from the back windows, welcoming us as though we had been gone only a fortnight.

George will get out to tie the horse to her waiting post and come around to offer me his hand, steady and assured, as I step out into the sundown stillness that settles over the fields of Gettysburg. And with a soft smile, he will look straight into my eyes as he did on our wedding night: "Mrs. Shriver?"

And I will reply, *"Danke, mein Schatz."*

Together we will climb the front steps, and he will lift the latch to swing open the door. And we will pause there as we did the morning he mustered. "It is a fine place," he will murmur, and with my arm linked through his, I will nod in agreement.

Then room by room we will be welcomed home, standing in each hallowed doorway, every corner brimming with *Frieden,* the very "peace that passeth understanding" returned to its proper places, the peace that left with George that September as he rode out of sight.

While George surveys the rooms he dreamed of when he wore a uniform and longed for comfort, I will set out a light supper of bread and apple butter and a slab of Ma's cheddar. My Mason tureen will stand heaped with cool, tender-cooked potatoes from our garden. We will sit at that dear table and eat together while he tells me of his long journey to me.

After our plates are cleared, George will take my hand to lead me past his kitchen window and out to the gardens. We will settle on the stoop to lean back and watch the stars blink into view over our heads.

He will remind me of Mollie's old shoe, how the girls and I watched him stash it into an open crossbeam in their bedroom ceiling one late autumn evening after the builders left. We will smile, remembering our promise to them of the luck it would bring us in our fine house. Their trusting eyes watched him struggle to make the thing stay put, secured and safe, jammed into its hiding place for the carpenters to nail it over with lath the next day.

It is important that I write down for you here that this will be a time of rejoicing. George and I will have found our way home. The Shriver family will be safe and whole in our nest again. I can already feel in my bones that goodness and grace have returned to our town. The curse of war, the vast ocean of tears shed by so many, the sorrow finally wiped away, the storm of pain Gettysburg and the rest of our sad country weathered those years—all of it is finally gone for good.

It is as though everything is fresh and new, that we have laid down a heavy burden and shaken our arms free at last to pick up our lives again, together, in our hearts' home. I cannot think how else to say this: Our starting over will be a time of rejoicing…

When the birds have tucked themselves away in sleep and the crickets and creepers take full stage with their chirping song, when the stars are so bright they flood the gardens and our faces with the soft blue light of evening, we will rise to go inside our house.

And as we did in the beginning, from the first night we slept there and took in the quiet and calm and clean balm of the new cut timber, we will light our candles and climb the stairs together to the proud bedroom waiting to welcome us. We will take up again the story of our lives together on Baltimore Street.

We will step into our beautiful room, and George will point to Ma's linen runner spread across our bureau top. And there, right there will be waiting my rosebud, whole and restored and as red as the autumn day he first handed it to me. It is such beauty.

He will pull the pins from my hair, one by one, and comb his fingers through the long braids to set free that soft cascade of waves he used to praise. And true to form, he will sing to me in the sweet darkness before we drift to sleep:

Her voice is low and sweet, and she's all the world to me;
And for bonnie Hettie Rosie I would lay me down and die.

My George is a man of his word, and he has promised to come fetch me soon. His hand will take hold of mine, and together we will find our way home to begin again. I believe that he is very near. I am a patient woman.

Danke, mein Schatz. ❧

MRS. HENRIETTA PITTENTURF

Mrs. Henrietta Pittenturf, a native of Adams county, died at the home of her daughter, Mrs. Lillie Hollebaugh, Washington, D. C., Friday, from infirmities of age. She was 80 years and one month old.

Deceased was a daughter of the late Jacob Weikert and was born in the old Weikert homestead near Round Top. She spent practically her entire life in Adams county. She was frist married to Lieutenant George Schriver and he was killed during the Civil war. She later married Daniel Pittenturf, for many years engaged in the stonecutting business in Gettysburg. For a number of years since his death Mrs. Pittenturf has been living with her daughter.

She is survived by three brothers and one sister, Emanuel and David Weikert, of near Gettysburg, George Weikert, Woodsboro, Md., and Mrs. Levi Plank, Gettysburg. Mrs. Hollebaugh, with whom she lived is the only child living.

Funeral and interment in Washington, Monday.

Acknowledgements

WE WERE ON OUR WAY FROM MICHIGAN to a family reunion in Virginia when my husband and I made a detour to see historic Gettysburg—our first visit and a surprisingly moving one for both of us. A sunset walk of Pickett's Charge piqued our curiosity, his with the desire to learn more about the battle, mine with a leaning toward what the town folk might have experienced when war came to their streets and fields in 1863.

Standing in Hettie Shriver's parlor the next morning, I at once knew I was at the start of a friendship with a woman about whom little is known and who died in 1916. That day led to my first attempt at writing historic fiction, the piece you are holding.

In the two years that followed, I learned enough about the Civil War to know that there is a great deal I do not know. I have learned that history is not necessarily built on fact and that the world is still filled with Hetties, all-but-forgotten women whose lives were and are upended by wars begun and carried out by men.

Sheldon Jones, a Bay Area psychiatrist who happens to be my brother, listened to me read a chapter from my manuscript one crisp fall evening in the presence of my other brother at his Oregon ranch. The good doctor's speculation was that my character suffered from post-traumatic stress disorder, a diagnosis that did not even appear in the American Psychiatric Association lexicon until 1980.

Hettie witnessed unimaginable horror at the epicenter of the Battle of Gettysburg in and around her parents' home during that bloody week. PTSD could well account for a mistaken assumption that she died in the grips of senility. No drug therapy or counseling was available to most of the women whose minds were taken apart by the world's wars. But even with her compromised state at the end of her life, for whatever the reason, Hettie's voice merits our attention.

I have enjoyed every step along the way in the creation of my Shriver family story, based very loosely on the "facts" at hand from ancestral and military records, census reports, and the writings of the few period eyewitnesses whose recollections made their way into print. In my pool of research, I have encountered more points of factual disparity than I can count. As Hettie asks, "Who can say what is real and what is not?"

What I do know for a fact is that I could not have embarked on this project without the help and support of many people who were patient with my questions, generous with their input, and endlessly tolerant of my sharing the bones of what I was creating out of where my research was leading me.

My deep gratitude to: Nancie Gudmestad and Kim Cora-detti, who generously and patiently shared their insights about the Shriver house and the family who once lived there, the forgotten four they care deeply about; Elizabeth and Gerald Hoffman who live in the Weikert farmhouse standing on the battlefield and who welcomed me in for tea and stories one sunny autumn morning; Carolyn Sautter and the staff of the Musselman Library, Gettysburg College; Lauren Roedner and the staff at the Adams County Historical Society, and Licensed Battlefield Guide Tim Smith who met me there; Susan Watson at the Adams County Library; Gettysburg Licensed Town Historians Jane Malone, Linda Seamon, and Susan Swope for their early read-through of the July 1-7 pages; Anne Nemeth for kind correspondences around her great-great-grandmother Henrietta, for whom scant family lore remains; writers Steven Polansky, Rob Stone, and David Healy for valuable editing and publishing counsel; Mike Mihelich for website design; Kathy Jones and Melody Schloss for ancestry research assistance; my brothers Del Jones and Sheldon Jones for being my first reading audience, and again to Sheldon for his editing assistance; authors Thomas Desjardin and Jocelyn Green, whose writing inspired me to begin this book; Catherine Lilly for the wisdom that always shows up on our early morning walks; Karen Oiseth for sharing her creative artistry; Patti Brennan and Parvin Keller for priceless design and publishing assistance; and (because everyone needs the support of a sister, and since no other girls were born to my parents) friends Amy Mullins, Julie Healy, Frederika Charles, and Renee Keogh for their unceasing encouragement in more areas than writing.

Then there's my family, the grown children and their partners who have tried their best to keep me "with it," the grandchildren whose eyes and ears constantly remind me that stories really do matter, and Raymond, who has supported me all along the way. Being his partner has been a long, rich journey for me, a gift Hettie and George surely would have treasured. *Danke, mein Schatz.*

Finally, I am grateful to the Shriver family, to Henrietta and George, Sadie and Mollie, for allowing me to create a tale around them, for once upon a time standing in that welcoming home on Baltimore Street, for the mark they left on humanity and history during their time on this earth. Their lives mattered.

Learn more about the Shrivers at www.shriverhouse.org.

Made in the USA
Middletown, DE
05 August 2022